Trouble in the

White House:

A Black President Novel

Trouble in the White House:

A Black President Novel

Brenda Hampton

www.urbanbooks.net

Urban Books, LLC
300 Farmingdale Road, NY-Route 109
Farmingdale, NY 11735

Trouble in the White House: A Black President
Novel Copyright © 2019 Brenda Hampton

ISBN 13: 978-1-60162-106-1
ISBN 10: 1-60162-106-X

First Mass Market Printing January 2019
First Trade Paperback Printing October 2017
Printed in the United States of America

10 9 8 7 6 5 4 3 2 1

*This is a work of fiction. Any references or similarities
to actual events, real people, living or dead, or to
real locales are intended to give the novel a sense of
reality. Any similarity in other names, characters,
places, and incidents is entirely coincidental.*

Distributed by Kensington Publishing Corp.
Submit Orders to:
Customer Service
400 Hahn Road
Westminster, MD 21157-4627
Phone: 1-800-733-3000
Fax: 1-800-659-2436

President of the United States,

Stephen C. Jefferson

With the exception of those who worked closely with me, along with past presidents, no one knew just how strenuous being the commander in chief really was. But you can be sure that many people—Republicans, Democrats, Independents, world leaders . . . even Blacks—had something to say about how I needed to do my job and how *they* preferred I conduct myself in this position. The truth was that no one's opinion really mattered, simply because no one other than me was tasked with sitting behind the *Resolute* desk in the Oval Office and dealing with what I was faced with on a daily basis. I had to acknowledge some of the perks that came along with the job, and a four-hundred-thousand-dollar-plus salary wasn't so bad. But some people . . . I just didn't get them. Some couldn't even run their own damn households, and even politicians had the audacity to gripe on social networking sites or run to the media and blab about what I needed to do. Many of them were totally responsible for the mess we were in. I could only shake my head and laugh at some of the madness I'd heard.

On a serious note, all that was transpiring in our country was no laughing matter. The middle class was vanishing. Taxes were too high, as was the cost of higher education. Poverty was at an all-time high, and so many of our children were suffering. Throw domestic terrorism into the mix, and the fact that hate crimes were on the rise, and this was a disaster. I experienced major headaches during my morning briefings. The classified information about known planned attacks against the United States was unbelievable. My number one job and highest priority was to keep our country safe. My biggest fear, however, was failing to do so. I trusted my team—there was no doubt that we had one of the most experienced intelligence agencies in the world. Still, I'd be foolish to believe that many terrorist organizations didn't have knowledgeable individuals working for them. Since I knew this was so, my fears wouldn't subside.

Doing the norm, I was up late on this day. Vice President Bass was in the Oval Office with me, pondering how she should deal with the Republican Party going forward. Many were upset with her for standing with me to pass gun control legislation. She had been dissed and called every name in the book for assisting me. And while she suspected that some would turn against her, she had never expected for things to be this bad.

"They fucking hate me," she said, pacing back and forth. "Everywhere I go, people are shouting at me, calling me names, even throwing things at me. I don't know what to do, but I can promise you this." Holding a glass of alcohol tight in her hand, she paused to look at me as I sat on the sofa. Her eyes were watering, her chubby cheeks were red, and her hair was disheveled. "I won't be going to Capitol Hill anytime soon to help you push your agenda forward. Members of the House Republican Conference are catching hell over that vote, and I'm not sure if we did the right thing."

The political environment was, simply put, fucked up. The truth was, there weren't many congressmen or congresswomen here to do what they were voted in to do. Winning elections was more about power, perks, and the almighty dollar. I guess with Congress having an 8 percent approval rating, many Americans understood

what it was about too. In my position, I had to
stay hopeful. I had to make VP Bass understand
how much I needed her, especially going forward.

"Listen," I said, trying to gather my thoughts
as I stood and walked up to her. I didn't want
to say the wrong thing to her; I could see she
was on the brink of losing it. "We all did the
right thing for this country. You may not realize
it now, but eventually, you'll see the impact
of passing that law. As for me, I don't have an
agenda. The American people do, and they're
counting on us to cease some of the madness
that is going on. We must work together to make
the lives of others much better. If we can't do
that, then there is no purpose in us being here."

VP Bass shut her eyes, causing a slow tear to
run down her face. She stepped away from me
and walked closer to the sofa. Her finger tapped
against the glass in her hand, and before taking a
seat, she tossed back another swig of the alcohol.

"If you're the president, take ownership,
because it is considered *your* agenda. I already
know what you're pursuing next, and I must
confess that I am not on board with doing anything that has to do with assisting only one race
in this country. I get that African Americans feel
let down, left behind, screwed over . . . what-

ever. But we won't and can't continue to create legislation that revolves around handouts. Too many taxpayers are already on the hook as it is, and my party will not stand for it. Implementing more and more programs will only put this country further in debt, so the question is, Mr. President, when are we going to start digging ourselves out of the ditch?"

There was a tiny button inside of me that could always be pushed. Unfortunately for VP Bass, she'd touched it. I moved closer and stood over her just so she could get a glimpse of my stern gaze.

"I made a mistake in believing that you had some courage, but apparently, you don't. Thought you were a brave woman, but your words tell me you're a coward. When things get a little rough, you proved to me that a bottle of alcohol becomes your best friend, and it can cause you to spew stupid shit that doesn't make sense. I could go on and on about what most black people in this country really want, but unfortunately, your ignorance will not allow you to comprehend. Therefore, to answer the question you posed to me earlier about what you should do, here is my suggestion. Dig your ass off that sofa and go resign. If I can't use you, I don't need you."

Apparently offended, she shot up from her seat like a rocket. Her face was scrunched up; a whiff of her alcoholic breath attacked me.

"Mr. President, I suspected that this little love affair between us wouldn't last long, and several weeks after you used me to get what you wanted, here we are. You will need me again, so you'd better think long and hard about how you intend to approach me going forward. I won't subject myself to your continuous disrespect, nor will I follow your lead on legislation that isn't beneficial to all Americans. Like it or leave it, asshole. It's as simple as that."

I shrugged; she could definitely come better than that. "First of all, don't insult me. I would never have a love affair with a woman of your caliber. Sorry, but you're not my type. And you're the one who'd better think long and extremely hard about how you approach me. You will need me, especially after the GOP gets finished dragging you through the mud, hanging you out to dry. Now I'm done with this conversation. And before I say anything else, I ask that you leave now or leave later with regrets."

The one thing VP Bass knew was not to challenge me. She stomped toward the door, bumping into Raynetta, who was on her way in.

"You must be out of your freaking mind, staying married to a jerk like him. What a waste of a beautiful woman. I applaud you, my dear. May God bless you," VP Bass said.

Raynetta's eyes grew wide. She had a smirk on her face as well. Obviously, she didn't trip off the VP's name-calling as much as I did. All she did was shut the door behind VP Bass, and then she headed toward me.

"I guess you pissed her off pretty good, huh?"

"Real good. But she pissed me off too."

"What a shame. I figured something was going on, especially since you haven't made your way upstairs to the bedroom yet. I got kind of lonely up there, and you promised me earlier that you would find a little time in your schedule to, uh, *play* with me tonight."

I nodded and snapped my fingers. "I did promise, but by now, you do know how things go around here, don't you?"

Raynetta sat on top of the desk and crossed one leg over the other. I was still standing by the sofa; my eyes scanned her pretty, smooth legs, which peeked through the pink silk robe she wore. We had been indulging in sex like there was no tomorrow. It felt good to know that at least my marriage was back on track.

"I do know how it is, sweetheart. That's why I came down here to relieve you from the daily stress. It's written all over your face, but if I have my way, that frown can easily turn into a smile."

Raynetta untied the belt at her waist and dropped it on the floor. She rubbed the tips of her fingers between her cleavage and then opened the robe just a little to allow her firm breasts to peek through. Giving me a clear view of something even more enticing, she opened her legs wide. As my eyes focused in, she spoke with seduction in her voice.

"I'm not sure if there has ever been this much action on this desk or inside the Oval Office, but I can't resist these spontaneous opportunities. And since you had your way the last time in this office, I figured it was my time next."

I strutted over to where Raynetta was, displaying a smile that was a result of what I had just witnessed between her thighs. Once my arms were secure around her waist, I searched her sparkling eyes, which exemplified how happy my wife was. All of this felt good. It saddened me to think I had almost given up hope that we could ever feel this way about each other again.

"Indisputably confirmed by what I do know to be facts," I said. "There have been numerous heated moments in this office. But, with that being said, there has never been the kind of action in here that only you and I can create. It is time for you to have your way. So please, Mrs. Jefferson, do as you wish."

Raynetta took her time unbuttoning my white shirt, then peeling it away from my chest. She then removed my leather belt and tossed it to the side. She lowered the zipper over the sizable hump rising in my slacks, and after dropping to her knees, she had her way with me. The feel of her warm, deep throat made my legs weaken, my toes curl, and my eyes shut tight. I was locked in a trance. My breathing became heavy, and before I knew it, I had to reach for the desk to help me maintain my balance.

I struggled to speak. "If . . . if this is what giving you your way means, I . . . I must surrender to you more often."

Raynetta backed away from my goods and looked up at me for a few seconds before responding.

"Yes, you should surrender to me more often, because for as long as I can remember, allowing me to take charge never hurt you one bit."

She resumed. So did I, and I was soon in deep thought about how skilled Raynetta really was. In the bedroom, in addition to outside of it.

President's Mother,

Teresa Jefferson

It had been three long weeks since I left the *little* White House to go see my grandson in St. Louis. I was having the time of my life. Ina, my real daughter-in-law, was so sweet, and like always, she made me feel as if I was right at home. That was, of course, after I had to clean up the whole house and disinfect it. Her ass was downright lazy, but every woman was entitled to have a flaw, maybe two. Two was my limit. I guess I couldn't hold her laziness against her, but when it came to my son, I most certainly would. He was better off without her being his wife. Friend, fuck buddy, side ho . . . that was fine.

As for my grandson, every time I saw him, he had got even more handsome and taller. He played basketball at one of the most prestigious high schools in St. Louis, where he maintained a 4.0 GPA. He was smart as a whip, just like Stephen was, but Joshua also had a wild and

sneaky side to him. He had no idea that his
father was president of the United States. Years
ago, Ina had told Joshua that his father, my son,
was in jail for murder. I hated to lie, but for now,
it had to be this way. Soon, though, things would
change. I was prepared to come clean, and
whatever happened, so be it. Of course, Stephen
would be upset with me for keeping this secret,
but it wouldn't be the first time he'd been upset
with me. He would get over it, and like always,
he would call to apologize, just as he'd done a
few days ago for speaking ill to me. I'd forgiven
him and told him we would chat when I returned
to Washington. He'd inquired about where I was,
but I'd reminded him that he was my son, and I
was his mother. Where I was and who I was with
were none of his business. He'd agreed.

My bags were packed; I was ready to head
back to Washington. Joshua and Ina hated to
see me go. They both walked me to my car, with
sad looks on their faces.

"When will you be coming back?" Joshua
asked, with a basketball tucked underneath his
arm. "You keep saying that I can come visit you,
and as a reminder, school will be out in less than
a month."

I rubbed his wavy hair, with a smile on my
face. "I know, baby, and you can come visit me
as soon as I get finished renovating. Meanwhile,
think of another place you would like to go on

your summer vacation. Maybe we can go on a trip to Paris. Or what about Dubai? You mentioned something about going there before, didn't you?"

"I did, but some of my friends who have been there before said it's boring. They also complained about the air quality, but Paris sounds nice."

"Okay. Let's put that on our to-do list and go from there. Meanwhile, keep those grades up, and stop spending so much time on that Internet. That cell phone is attached to your hand. I don't know how in the world you get anything done. Do you even part with it while you're doing your homework?"

Joshua laughed. Ina shook her head.

"I tell him that all the time," Ina said, rolling her eyes. "He sleeps with that thing right next to him. I can only wonder how he's able to keep up his grades, especially when he's on that phone twenty-four-seven."

"I'm bright like that, and it's called multitasking," Joshua said with a wide smile. "It's also a kid thing, and you two beautiful ladies would never understand."

I pursed my lips. "Save all that sweet talk for those little chicken-headed girls you've been talking to. And be sure to keep your penis in your pants, because we—"

"Yes, I know, Grandma. Trust me, I already know."

I looked at Ina, just to confirm that she had been doing her duties as a mother and had already discussed the birds and the bees, as well as the cornbread and sweet-potato *thighs*, with her son.

"He's good, so don't worry," she said. "Now, you'd better get on the road before it gets too late. And don't forget to call me as soon as you get home."

I gave both of them hugs, told them I loved them, and with worry in my eyes, I watched Joshua go back inside. I worried about him a lot. Not having a father figure wasn't a good thing, and Ina didn't seem to have much time for him. Maybe it was just me. I complained about everything.

"I'll be in touch about his trip to Paris," I said. "And if I can't make it, perhaps he can go with some of his friends."

"I'm sure he would like that, but I hope you can make it too. He's been talking about traveling to more places, and a trip to Paris will do him good. I thank you so much for continuing to look out for us. Your generosity will never be forgotten."

"No problem at all. Just . . . just do me a favor and keep your eyes on him. Also, keep your house a little cleaner. I paid too much money for it, and you know they say that a woman who doesn't keep her house clean doesn't keep her ass clean, either. A pretty woman like you wouldn't want that kind of reputation, would you?"

Ina swallowed hard; she was used to how blunt I could be.

"I assure you that I keep myself very clean. It's just that I have a lot on my plate with Joshua and with my new business venture. While I appreciate all that you've done for us, I do need to figure out a way to increase my income."

"I won't argue with you on that, and good luck on your new business venture, whatever it may be. I should be back in Washington no later than ten or eleven tonight, but I want you to consider doing something for me. Raynetta is having an LGBT gala at the White House next week. I would love for you to be my guest, and I'm sure Stephen would love to see you."

Ina knew how I felt about Raynetta; it was no secret. She could also sense that I was up to something, so she appeared reluctant to accept my offer.

"I'm not sure if I should be in Stephen's presence, Teresa. It's been years since I've seen him, and it may seem awkward if I just all of a sudden showed up. Besides, I still have very strong feelings for him. And while I am more than satisfied with my current boyfriend, you know that Stephen will always have my heart."

"He may feel the same way. It's just that he's been so unhappy lately. He and Raynetta haven't been getting along, and I thought it might take a woman like you to perk him up. I'm not recommending that you have sex with him or anything like that. By all means, he is a married man. But just show up. Be there for him. Talk to him, and let him know that you support him and still care. He needs that right now, and unfortunately, the love I have for him doesn't seem like it's enough."

Ina sighed, knowing that she couldn't resist. "Let me think about it. I'm hesitating because seeing Stephen may also make me want to tell him about Joshua. I figure that's the last thing you want, so that's why it may be best for me to keep my distance."

"What I want doesn't matter anymore. Think about what you want, and if this is the perfect opportunity for you to go get it, don't hesitate to jump on it."

On that note, I left it right there. We hugged again, and then I watched Ina slowly walk toward the door, as if she was deep in thought. Raynetta thought that she was the only woman who had a figure that was out of this world, but she didn't have anything on Ina. Her curvy hips had gotten wider over the years, but her tiny waistline was perfect. Her P-shaped ass could snap a man's head to the side in a second, and as a longtime beautician, she kept her short pixie-cut style always on point. She was a winner for sure, and with her being Stephen's first love, there wasn't a chance in hell that I would come out on the losing end of my battle finally to rid my son of his lying, cutthroat, and vindictive trophy wife.

First Lady,

Raynetta Jefferson

I hadn't felt this amazing and free in a long time. Stephen and I had finally got our act together. There was plenty of lost time to make up for. I loved my husband with every fiber of my being, and it hadn't dawned on me how much I had been putting his needs aside. I had become so bitter and angry about so many things. That included his mother, whom I hadn't seen in weeks. It had been very peaceful around the White House lately, no denying that. Stephen had said she was alive, and that was good enough for me. He'd also mentioned a little spat they'd had. I was so proud of him for taking up for me, and for finally putting Teresa in her place. I was sure she didn't appreciate what he'd told her, but maybe she would learn to stay out of our business and get some of her own.

My assistant, Claire, and I had been in my office for hours, putting the final touches on the LGBT gala, which would be held in a few days. I was overly excited about it, and planning events like this was my specialty. Claire was excellent at event planning too, and every single thing that went on at the White House had her name written all over it. People raved about our parties, especially the media, which praised us for seeming to have it all together.

"The only thing left for us to do," Claire said, sitting across from me, with her legs crossed, "is to go over the guest list again, confirm names, addresses, Social Security numbers, and then give a final copy to the Secret Service. Other than that, the menu is done, and so is the itinerary for the night."

"Then that about takes care of everything. You did get in contact with the musician, Mr. Cook, didn't you?"

"Yes. He, along with all his band members, has already been cleared."

"Great. I'm looking forward to the gala. Stephen is too. I'm also glad that your sister and her wife will be joining us. I hope that your parents change their minds and decide to come."

"Not a chance in hell. They don't approve of my sister being married to a woman, but who

cares? My sister is happier than she has ever
been, and she's married to an amazing woman.
They're planning to adopt soon, and I couldn't
be happier for them."

"Awww, that's so sweet. I'm sure that adding a
child to their union will enrich their lives in ways
they never thought possible."

"No doubt. And since we're on the subject, and
you and the president have been shaking things
up quite a bit lately, when can we expect to have
a little one around here? I hope I'm not being
too nosy, but I'm pleased that the two of you
have reconciled your differences."

I coughed, then reached for the bottled water
on my desk. After taking a sip, I screwed the
cap back on. "What makes you think we've been
shaking things up around here, and who says
that we've reconciled our differences?"

Claire uncrossed her legs, then moved closer
to me. She swooped her long hair behind her
ears, then pointed to me as she whispered,
"Because, my dear, there is only one thing that
can cause a woman to glow like you've been
glowing. Your entire demeanor has changed,
and I haven't seen you smiling like . . . like a
Cheshire cat in a very long time. Not to mention
all the lip smacking and body rubbing I've seen
going on between you and the president these

past few weeks. Plus, there has been no gossip about the president's middle-of-the-night runs, so it's pretty obvious that the two of you have patched up things."

I rolled my eyes and shook my head at the same time. "You all are so nosy around here. With all the work that needs to be done, how does anyone find time to keep tabs on me and my husband? And as for the baby thing, don't get your hopes up. That's not going to happen anytime soon."

Claire cleared her throat, then sat back in the chair, with her arms crossed. "Like it or not, you guys have an interesting life, one that is so intriguing to many people, including me. I'll wear my nosy badge with great pride simply because I get a thrill out of working with you and knowing your every little move. Sounds horrible? Yes. And maybe I need to get a life, get a man, whatever. Until then, you are stuck with me, and there is nothing you can do about it," she teased.

"Yes, I can. I could fire you, but then the next assistant would come in and do the same thing. You're so lucky that I like you, because if I didn't, your nosy tail would be out of here."

We laughed. Then, as Claire handed me the long guest list, she inquired again about me having a baby.

"I know you've been waiting to have a child, but I figured you would soon change your mind."

Normally, this subject was off-limits, but since I trusted Claire not to run her mouth about something so personal to me, I revealed how I truly felt.

"I've given it much thought, but I'm still not there yet. And even though things have been going well between me and Stephen, I just can't ever see myself having a child. I know how he feels about it, but this is my body. I can do whatever I decide to do with it."

"You're absolutely right, but have you told him that you're adamant about not having a child? And what about your birth control pills? Wouldn't he know if you're still taking them?"

I bit my nail, thinking about a conversation I had with Stephen just last week. Out of the blue, he'd asked about my birth control pills. Trying not to spoil the mood, I'd said what I had to.

"I told him that I stopped taking my pills. In actuality, I haven't stopped, probably never will, or at least not until I'm a very old-ass woman with gray hair. I will let him know my final decision about not wanting a child. I hope that he understands why. If not, there's not much that I can do. There is no compromise that I'm willing to make, and it's not like he's going to divorce me over a decision that is mine to make."

"Well, it seems as if your mind is made up, so what else needs to be said, other than I think the two of you would have a beautiful baby? It would be a bless—"

I quickly cut Claire off, feeling as if I had already shared too much information. "I'm done, Claire. Let's direct our attention to the list."

We started going over the list, double-checking the spelling of names and everything else. We also examined the preferred seating arrangements. I paused when I saw Teresa's name, along with that of one guest, Ina Monai Chatman.

"Did my mother-in-law request that her name and one guest be added to the list? I don't recall adding her," I said.

"Yes, she put in the request a few days ago. I didn't think it would be a problem."

"No problem, but did she mention anything about her guest? More importantly, has her guest been cleared yet?"

"I assume so, because I haven't heard anything back yet from Homeland Security or the Secret Service. Teresa said Ms. Chatman was one of her friends who supported the LGBT community."

Trying not to be so ugly, I brushed it off. Ina was probably one of Teresa's old uppity friends who sat around with her all night, gossiping and judging people.

Claire and I wrapped up everything around noon. At three o'clock, I was scheduled to join four other first ladies at a new library in Washington, D.C. The library was named after one of the first ladies who had focused her time while in the White House on reading, writing, and higher education. I was delighted to attend the event and offer my support. It definitely made me think more about my own legacy. Stephen had suggested that I create my own legacy as well, but I just wasn't sure what cause I wanted to dedicate my time to and totally get behind. This was still his first year in office, so I felt as if I had plenty of time to decide what I wanted to do.

After glancing at my watch, I made my way to the second level of the White House. I had only a few minutes to chill before I had to get ready and go to the library. My mind was all over the place. Wondering where Stephen was, I reached for my cell phone in my pocket. I was about to send him a text message, but as I stood in the Center Hall, right in front of the Yellow Oval Room, I heard someone clear their throat. I looked up, and to my surprise, I saw Teresa sitting in a chair next to the fireplace. A fake smile covered her face, and as usual, she was dolled up, as if there was a party going on. Pearls were draped around her neck, her salt-and-pepper hair was styled in a layered cut, her makeup was flawless, and the white linen pantsuit she wore would look better on someone like me. I refused to pay her a compliment; the least I could do was speak.

"Hello back," she said from a distance. "And why are you still standing in the hallway? I'm not contagious, and I promise you that I don't bite."

I wasn't sure why she was being so friendly, and in no way did her fake kindness move me. I did, however, want to know why she was here. I walked into the room to address her.

"I never said you were contagious, but I do have somewhere to be soon. I'm surprised that you're here, especially after the unfortunate, brutal argument I heard you had with Stephen."

She threw her hand back, as if it were nothing. "Yeah, well, we do have our differences at times, as do the two of you. But like always, he respects his mother more than he does anyone. He apologized to me, and I accepted. I told him that I was still concerned about my safety, and that I thought it would be wise for me to stay here for at least another month, maybe two. He encouraged me to stay for as long as I wanted to, so here I am. I thought it may be a good opportunity for you and me to kind of squash our little beef, especially since you and Stephen seem to be getting along a little better these days."

I wanted to throw up. Stephen hadn't mentioned any of this to me. And why would he want her to stay here, knowing what a pain in the ass she was? This seemed like a no-win situation for me. For him to apologize to her was ridiculous. She should have been the one apologizing to us. I just didn't get it, and I hated for her to see how much she had gotten underneath my skin. The frown on my face said it all. The smirk on hers implied mission accomplished.

"Yes, we are getting along a lot better, and this time, no one will be permitted to interfere. So stay as long as you want. Just stay out of my way, and please stop being so fake." Having nothing else to say to her, I turned to walk away.

She released a cackling laugh. She always had to have the final word, so I wasn't surprised when she spoke. "Being a bitter bitch suits you well. And when you get back this evening, meet me in the Queens' Bedroom. That's where I will be, because I'm the number one lady in this house. We have so much to talk about, and trust me when I say the news I want to share with you is going to knock your socks—well, your dirty panties—off. Until then, have fun and tell the other first ladies I said hello."

Ignoring her silliness, I kept it moving. But the second I entered the Master Bedroom, I reached for my cell phone to call Stephen. Thankfully, he answered.

"Make it quick, baby. I just arrived at the Pentagon for a meeting," he said.

"I'll try to make it quick, but why is your mother here? She's already causing trouble, and I think it would be best if she stayed at her own house. The Secret Service can certainly watch over her there."

"They can, but I kind of feel as if it is my duty to make sure she's protected, considering all that has happened. I'm still concerned about her drinking as well, and I know that she hasn't fully recovered. She told me how she feels about being alone. Having family around, especially me, may help to put her at ease."

All I could do was shake my head with disgust. That manipulative heifer had Stephen wrapped around her finger.

"No matter where she lives, she's going to drink what she wishes. You don't have time to babysit her, Stephen, and I don't know why you don't—"

"When all is said and done, she's my mother. That will never change. I know how you feel, but please do not spend your time worrying about her. Focus on us, like you've been doing, and everything will be fine. Now I have to go. I'll be home real late, so enjoy the rest of your day and get some rest."

Like I said, this was a no-win situation. He just didn't get it, but what the hell ever. I sighed before telling him I loved him.

"Love you too."

The call ended, and several hours later, I found myself in the presence of some of the most remarkable women, all of whom I had so much respect for. We laughed, talked, and also gossiped about unforgettable things that had occurred in the White House. I could only smile when one of the oldest first ladies reached for my hand and held it in hers as she offered me some sound advice.

"Stay strong. Always smile for the cameras and let no one see you perspire. Behind closed doors, fight for what is rightfully yours, and make sure your husband knows that you are the real commander in chief, not him. Now let's go take these beautiful pictures for the history books yet to be written."

With great pride, I stood before the photographers as I held hands with the two other first ladies at my side. The cameras flashed for several minutes, and no matter how I felt inside, you'd better believe I was smiling.

President's Mother,

Teresa Jefferson

Unfortunately, Raynetta never did come to the Queens' Bedroom to chat with me that evening. I had planned to show her the photo album I had been keeping of my grandson for years. I wanted her to know about him first simply because I knew she wouldn't have the guts to tell Stephen about Joshua. She would keep it a secret, and it would just be one more thing for him to be upset with her about, in addition to her flat-out refusal to have his child and her secret meetings with his enemies.

What Raynetta didn't realize was the walls in this place talked. So did that bigmouthed assistant of hers, and it didn't surprise me when the head chef, Frank, mentioned what Claire had said to one of his staff members. Since I had been whipping up some of my own dishes in the kitchen, Frank and I had gotten real close. He

didn't move me with his cooking, but for a fif-
ty-eight-year-old man, his sex was pretty good.
I needed some sweet loving from time to time,
and I could never resist a man who was tall,
midnight dark, buffed, and handsome. He was
extremely polite, and his kindness reminded
me of those house Negros back in the day who
happily served their masters. He had a thick
Southern accent too. I had nothing against him,
but there were men who were what I considered
too damn nice.

"Ah," he said, relieved, as he got off me and
moved next to me in bed. "Is there anything . . .
anything else I can get you, other than another
orgasm?"

Since I had faked the last one, there really
was nothing else he could get me. "No, but what
you can do is give me some space. You know you
can't sleep here, so go ahead and retreat to your
sleeping quarters and rest well. You have a big
evening ahead of you, and I can guarantee you
that the first lady is going to keep you and your
staff very busy at the gala later tonight."

"I reckon that she will. And, hopefully, you and
I can finish up soon."

Frank kissed my cheek before yanking the
covers aside. As he sat on the edge of the bed, my
eyes examined the muscles in his back and his

broad shoulders. Even the back of his thick neck was sexy, and his strong hands worked wonders on my body. I had finally found a big, south-ern, pork chop–eating man who could satisfy my every need.

As he took his time getting off the bed, I kneeled behind him. With my slightly sagging breasts pressed against him, I rubbed his back and massaged his shoulders.

"You feel tense," I said. "Maybe you need a warm bath and a relaxing body rub before you go."

Frank turned his head in slow circles, making his neck crack. As I began to plant soft kisses against his neck, he closed his eyes.

"I . . . I think you may be on to something with that bath. Care to join me?" he said.

I hesitated to answer, but before I knew it, Frank swooped me up in his strong arms and carried me to the sitting room that was just outside the bathroom. At my request, earlier, he had brought me a bottle of red wine and also a bottle of vodka. I hadn't touched either yet, but the moment seemed appropriate.

"Let me get that for you," Frank said, and then he began filling our glasses with wine.

"Please do. And let me get the tub ready for you."

I sauntered off to the bathroom to fill the tub with water. While inside the bathroom, I reached for a fluffy white towel and covered myself with it. When I returned to the sitting room, Frank extended a flute glass to me.

"Thank you," I said. "No time for toasting, but please do enjoy your bath."

"I thought you were going to join me?"

"Not really, and no offense, but I just don't like the griminess from someone else's body in the same tub as me. I would make an exception, but the more I think about it . . ."

Frank lifted my hand, kissed the back of it. "No need to explain. Enjoy your bath, and I'll take one when I get to my room. Sleep well. I'll see you at the gala."

I thanked Frank again, then watched as he put on his clothes and quietly exited my room. My bath awaited me. I was in heaven as I sank deep inside the tub. I couldn't help but to think about Raynetta's reaction when she saw Ina and discovered who she was. I appreciated Ina for agreeing to come, but there wasn't a chance in hell I would have accepted her telling me no.

Later that evening, the East Room and the State Dining Room on the State Floor were packed wall to wall with people. Maine lobster, roasted lamb, broccoli au gratin, and so much more were available at the buffet tables, and people were certainly indulging themselves. Music thumped loudly in the background. After seeing so many happy couples together, I couldn't help but to smile and enjoy my surroundings. I halted my steps after being snatched by a gay white man whose partner stood next to him.

"You look stunning tonight," he said. "Oh my God, what are you wearing? Is that Valentino? I can spot one of those dresses ten miles away. Not everyone can do off-white vintage with a tail like you, baby doll. And when I say *tail*, I'm referring to the train on your dress, not your backside."

I had a good sense of humor, so I laughed right along with them. I was flattered as well. "You would be correct, and I totally agree that not too many women can pull this off. I was skeptical about the train, but I went with it because it's not one of those trains that flow all over the place."

"I agree. It's perfect, and your figure is . . ." He paused to bite his knuckles playfully. "It's to die for. You and the first lady are true fashion queens. I'm so eager to see what she's wearing tonight."

On that note, I thanked the young man and his partner for the compliments, then walked away. I was sure Raynetta had gone out of her way to look nice as well, and I was counting on Ina to show up looking out of this world. About an hour ago, she had called to let me know the limo driver had just picked her up from the hotel and she was on her way. Meanwhile, I continued to mingle. I even whispered a few words to Frank, letting him know what a great time I'd had.

When the announcement was made that the president and the first lady would soon join us, many exited the room and stood by the Grand Staircase to greet them. Minutes later, Stephen and Raynetta appeared at the top of the stairs, looking as happy as ever. Gasps could be heard, in addition to many whispers. As usual, my son was on point. Black tuxedo fit his cut frame perfectly. Haircut was razor sharp. Leather shoes had one hell of a shine. And his shaved, smooth face had my stamp of approval on it. As for Raynetta, Lord knows I didn't want to hate, so I didn't. Her sheer rainbow dress flowed like a Cinderella gown and had everyone gazing at it in awe. She had taken a big risk with those colors, but from what I could see, it was a winner. A dip in the front showed a hint of her cleavage.

Her long hair was parted down the middle and fell several inches past her shoulders. The competition would be steep for Ina tonight, but I was banking on the love Stephen had once had for her showing up and causing a little damage.

"Good evening," Stephen said, standing on the staircase, with his arm locked with Raynetta's. "Thank you all for being here, and let's all have a wonderful time tonight. My wife and her staff prepared an amazing evening for all of you. We just want to say thanks for your patience, and for having so much faith in my administration. We are committed to making even more changes that will help to better your futures, in addition to the futures of your lovely families. So enjoy, and feel free to stop and briefly chat with me when we assemble the greeting line in the East Room."

The guests cheered and applauded Stephen and Raynetta as they proceeded down the red carpeted stairs to make their way to the East Room. I was eager to greet them, so I bullied my way through the crowd until I was face-to-face with my son.

"Hello, sweetheart," I said, air-kissing his cheeks. "I knew you were looking for me this morning, but I was rather busy. Did you need something?"

"I did, but it's not important right now. Enjoy yourself tonight, but not too much, if you know what I mean."

"I do, and just so you know, I haven't had a drink in almost three weeks. Being here has relaxed me. Thank you again for agreeing to let me stay here."

From the corner of my eye, I saw the irritated look on Raynetta's face. She quickly spoke up.

"Honey," she said to Stephen, "I think I see someone over there I know. I'll catch up with you in a few." Not waiting for him to respond, she walked off.

Stephen grabbed my hand, lightly squeezed it, and spoke in a whisper. "What I wanted to tell you earlier was to be nice tonight. Don't stir up any trouble with her, Mama, and if you don't have anything nice to say—I'm saying this nicely—keep your mouth shut."

"There is no way to put it nicely, because in other words, you're telling me to shut the fuck up. I intend to keep my distance from Raynetta, but do me a favor and tell her not to move around so much in that dress. Her titties are bound to pop out of it, and I'm sure you wouldn't want any man to see what you've been sucking on during the night. More importantly, what has your mind so twisted lately that you feel compelled to tell your own mother what she shall and shall not do?"

Stephen released my hand; then he gave me a look that felt like a punch. "You heard what I said, Mama. Enjoy yourself, or return to your bedroom, where there appears to be much more action going on."

My mouth dropped open as he walked away. Nothing in this house was a secret. I assumed his comment was about me and Frank. I didn't bother to ask him. Instead, I did what I was ordered to do and enjoyed myself. I also kept my distance from Raynetta, and when Ina showed up, I wanted to throw my hands in the air and shout hallelujah. The money-green off-the-shoulder dress she wore was fabulous. It was tailored to fit her perfect waistline and voluptuous hips. Her diamond-studded silk shoes and silver accessories made her look like a million bucks. I had handpicked everything she wore, but I had no idea she would look like a perfect ten.

Her hazel eyes grew wide when she saw me, and a smile followed thereafter. I wasn't sure if Stephen had seen her yet or not, but as crowded as the State Floor was, I predicted that he hadn't.

"Girl," I said, stepping back to take a closer look at her. "Black is sho'nuff beautiful, isn't it?"

"Yes, it is. And look at you too, Miss Lady. You did an awesome job picking this out for me. It's been a *long* time since I got all dressed up like this."

"Well, you did good. And thank you again for deciding to come. You have no idea how much this means to me."

"I'm here, but I am so nervous. Butterflies are all in my stomach. I keep telling myself to just breathe," she said.

"Breathe, mingle, and have some fun. Everybody in here is so nice, and you are going to meet so many good people. Just stay away from the people with those media badges on. If they start asking questions, just tell them to go fuck themselves."

We laughed, then proceeded to the State Dining Room, where there was seating and a buffet line. Before we even got there, we had to stop and have our pictures taken. Many questioned who Ina was, and all I said was that she was a close friend of the family. Stephen's adviser, Andrew, nodded when I told him, and then he shook Ina's hand.

"Glad you could make it," he said with suspicion in his eyes. "And any friend of the president's mother is a friend of mine."

"Thank you," Ina said, presenting much class. Given the way she looked, no one would ever predict how filthy her house was. I cleared my mind, putting that bit of information on the back burner for tonight.

"If you don't mind me asking," Andrew said, refusing to let us walk away, "what do you do—"

I quickly intervened. "She's already been cleared by the Secret Service, and don't you think this is the wrong time to query someone about their occupation? I don't know if you're trying to hit on her or not, but isn't your boring wife around here somewhere tonight? If so, please go find her before she leaves with one of these women in here tonight."

Andrew was used to my behavior. Ina was too, but she appeared stunned by my words.

"Teresa," she whispered after Andrew had walked away, "you need to calm down. I'm already nervous, and stuff like that doesn't help me one bit."

"Well, lighten up, because here comes the bride. Her dress may knock you over. I'm just warning you."

Raynetta pranced our way. She glanced at me, then quickly turned her attention to Ina. Raynetta extended her hand and waited for Ina to reciprocate. She did.

"I take it that your name is Ina. I saw it on the guest list, but I hadn't a clue who you were. My mother-in-law knows so many people, I can barely keep up with all her friends."

"She does have a lot of them. Anyway, yes, I am Ina Chatman. I've heard nothing but great things about you, the president's wife. It's a pleasure to finally meet you."

"No, the pleasure is mine. Have a great time tonight, and be sure to try the shrimp rolls. They are out of this world," Raynetta said.

"I will, and thanks for the recommendation."

Raynetta smiled at Ina, then shifted her eyes toward me. Her smile vanished, she winced, and then she walked away. I wasn't sure if she knew who Ina was or not.

Ina and I moseyed over to the buffet tables, where there was an array of food. Almost immediately, I noticed that the greeting line had started to assemble. I wanted to see Stephen's reaction when he saw Ina. I suggested that we wait a few more minutes to eat, and Ina didn't seem to have a problem with my suggestion.

"I'm too tense to eat anything right now, especially after seeing Raynetta. She's gorgeous and very polite," she said.

"Don't allow your eyes to deceive you. She is fake as ever. And please don't turn your back on her, because she will jab you with a knife. Trust me, I know. Unfortunately, my son is too pussy whipped to see her for what she is."

"Maybe so, but do you think she knows about me and Stephen? I mean, he probably told her about me before, don't you think?"

"I doubt it. He's always been very private. It wouldn't be like him to share his past feelings for another woman with Raynetta. She's the jealous type, and she would feel threatened by what the two of you shared in the past. Not to mention Joshua."

We stood in the long line, chatting some more while waiting to greet Stephen. The closer we got, the more Ina fidgeted. She was starting to work my nerves.

"By the way, Joshua told me to tell you hello," she said. "He's at a friend's house, and he is very much looking forward to that trip to Paris. I've been thinking a lot these past few days, and the truth is, I honestly do not know if I can hold on to this secret much longer. But telling Joshua and Stephen the truth isn't going to be easy. I'm having so many regrets. When you have some free time on your hands, I would love for you to give me some advice on how you think I should handle this whole thing."

"I will, but first, let's get through the night. It's been a long time since you've seen Stephen, and I can't wait to see the look on his face when he sees you."

The line stalled because everybody kept rambling on and on, taking pictures, and sharing their own. Raynetta had joined the line too, and with five people in front of us, I noticed her peeking at us from the corner of her eye.

"You're doing an incredible job, Mr. President," one man said to Stephen. "But you need more people like us in your administration. When you revamp your administration in a few years, don't forget about us, okay?"

"I won't," Stephen said, gripping the man's shoulder. "And be sure to give me your résumé before you leave."

They laughed, took a photo together, and it was on to the next person. Stephen was so focused on the person in front of him that he didn't even notice us coming. That was until I stepped in front of him, and right next to me, Ina stood in front of Raynetta.

"So, we meet again," Raynetta said to Ina.

"Yes. I haven't tried the shrimp rolls yet, but I promise you that I will."

"Please do."

Raynetta shifted her eyes to the next person in line, while Stephen stood looking at Ina as if cement had been poured over him. He didn't blink, didn't breathe. I saw him take a hard swallow, and then he released a breath into the air, as if his life had just been saved.

"Ina," he said with furrowed brows. "Ina Chatman?"

"Yes, that would be me," she said.

With narrowed eyes, I stood to the side, watching every single move.

Stephen appeared stunned. "I can't believe it's you. What are you doing here?"

Ina was silent, unsure of what to say. I quickly intervened.

"I invited her to come. I saw her while I was on vacation. Asked her if she would come, and she said yes."

By now, Raynetta had tuned in. The line wasn't even moving. Like me, she watched Stephen's every move. He didn't bother to look my way as I spoke. His eyes were still on Ina.

I would have paid a fortune to know exactly what he was thinking.

"I'm pleased that my mother invited you." He finally extended his hand, but I hoped Ina rejected it. It was a relief when she did, because it was very important for him to feel her more up close and personal.

"You can keep that handshake," she said, opening her arms. "May I have a hug?"

Without hesitation, Stephen opened his arms. They hugged tightly. I could see Raynetta peering past them to evil eye me.

"We'd better go get some food," I said to Ina. "Let that man go, and catch up with him later."

Ina didn't want to let go. She held on for as long as she could, and was definitely lured in even more by the smell of Stephen's masculine cologne, which breezed through the air.

"I won't continue to hold up the line," she said to him. "But I just wanted to say how proud I am of you. Never, ever in my wildest dream did I think you would be here, but then again, I always knew you would position yourself to have an impact on the world. Good seeing you, Stephen. Take care."

"Likewise," he said with a nod. Then his eyes shifted to the next people in line, two newlyweds, who were just as giddy to be in his presence.

Ina walked off, nervously holding her stomach. I followed behind her, but instead of returning to the buffet tables, she busted into the restroom.

"I . . . I can't believe I did that," she said, gasping, as if she was having a panic attack. "Teresa, why . . . why did you make me come here? I have to get out of here now, please."

I touched her back as she stood in front of the mirror and almost lost it. "Calm down. It's not that serious, is it? Stephen is still the same—"

"No, no, no, he isn't. He's not the same. He's so much more mature, so well put together, and, and . . . oh my God, Teresa. Why did you make me do this?"

I wanted to slap her face and yell at her to get it together. "Do what? What did I do?"

"You made me face him. For so many years, I told myself to forget about him. When I walked away, I just knew it was the right thing to do. He hadn't a clue what had happened to me, and I know I hurt him by not responding to him. This is so messed up. He's married now, and I . . . I need to get the hell out of here."

"That would be very wise to do," Raynetta said as she came through the door. "At first, I didn't know who you were, but it's pretty obvious now, since my mother-in-law invited you to come here. All she's looking for is someone who can cause harm to my marriage. If that's the plan, you two can forget it. Don't waste your time, because Stephen is a man who is focused on his future, not his past."

A toilet flushed, and as our heads snapped to the side, a reporter came out of one of the stalls with a grin on her face.

"If you ladies would excuse me," she said, waving her hands in front of her. "All I want to do is wash my hands. I'll be out of the way, so you ladies can continue the discussion."

We remained silent as she washed her hands. After she finished, she rushed out of the restroom. Probably couldn't wait to share what she'd heard. As a precaution, I checked the other stalls. When I opened the door to the last one, another reporter was squatting on top of the toilet seat, a camera in her hand. She looked shocked to see me.

"I was, uh, just—"

"Just leaving. Get your nosy, tacky ass out of here, and don't bother to wash your hands. Don't you know when to stay out of grown folks' business?"

Without saying a word, she rushed out of the restroom as well. I stood by the door so no one else would come in.

"Stephen may or may not have interest in the past," I said, continuing the conversation. "We'll let him decide. But just so you know, Raynetta, I didn't invite Ina here to cause any trouble. We have been friends for a long time. Mainly because she has something, or someone, I should say, who is very close and dear to me. I'll tell you all about him later, but for now, please go back out there and entertain your guests. After all, I don't want that slick mouth of yours to get you in trouble. Ina may clean up well, but from what I know, women from the Midwest, particularly St. Louis, they don't hesitate to beat ass when necessary."

Ina quickly spoke up. "It's been a long time since I had to resort to anything like that, but just do me one favor, Raynetta. Don't speak to me with that tone. I'm not here to take Stephen away from you, and the past is the past. I'll be leaving here tonight, and you will never have to see my face again."

Raynetta sucked her teeth while rolling her eyes at both of us. "That's good news, and in closing, no woman, not one, will ever take Stephen away from me. That's just a little something I thought you both should know."

I started to trip her as she left the restroom, displaying much attitude. But knowing that Stephen's mind was probably traveling to the past was good enough for me.

"She's a piece of work," Ina said. "I see why the two of you stay into it. Now I understand. But please, please avoid her for the rest of the evening. I don't want Stephen to think I came here to cause trouble. I didn't, and you already know that I really did this for you."

"Okay. I'll be good, as long as you stay, like you promised. Afterward, you can go back to the hotel, check on Joshua, and wait for Stephen to come."

Ina threw her hand back at me. I was glad to see that she had calmed down and was now ready to eat.

After our plates were filled, we sat at a round table to eat. Two other couples joined us, as well as a reporter and three people from Stephen's administration. There was a flowing conversation going on, but my attention was focused on Stephen. Surely he was engrossed in plenty of conversations, but his eyes shifted to where we sat way too many times. Ina hadn't noticed like I had. And one other person who'd noticed was Raynetta. She laughed and pretended as if everything was dandy, but I knew my daughter-in-law all too well. Stephen was going to get an earful tonight.

As the sneak-a-peek game continued, I excused myself from the table. I headed Stephen's way to chat with him, but from a distance, I saw Andrew whisper something in Stephen's ear. All of a sudden, the Secret Service started making moves. Stephen rushed out of the room, as did several people from his staff. No one knew what was going on, but within a few minutes, word had spread that there was another mass shooting. This was the first one that had occurred since Stephen had signed the gun control legislation. I was sure that he viewed this as a setback.

"Everyone, please settle down," the VP said. "The president will not be able to join us for the rest of the evening, but he wants everyone to continue to have a good time."

That was difficult to do, especially when news started to flow throughout the room. The killer was a teenager who had gone into a gymnasium during a high school basketball game and had started blasting people. No one knew how many casualties there were, but one reporter said there were seventeen, and another reporter said the number was more than thirty. No matter what the number was, this was a sad situation. I said a silent prayer for the families and for my son.

President of the United States,

Stephen C. Jefferson

I had been briefed about the mass shooting and felt numb as hell. It wasn't that I had expected the new gun control law to have an immediate impact, but I had surely hoped that things would calm down after the law was passed. According to the information I received, the teenage shooter was a loner who had been bullied and treated as an outcast. His parents were gun owners, and over seventy guns had been found in the home.

For there to be no limitations set forth for gun owners was a big mistake. Because of the new law, that would change, but it was too late for all those students who had lost their lives today. That included two coaches, who had attempted to intervene and stop the student. Ultimately, the shooter had turned the gun on himself. Bullying had become a major issue.

Much of it was done over the Internet, and not only were kids attacking each other, but so, too, were adults. I was just downright disgusted, especially when VP Bass marched into the Oval Office and told me what a waste of time it had been for her to assist in passing the law. I looked at Andrew with fury in my eyes.

"I can't recall if I have ever put my hands on a woman, and I don't want to start now. Please escort her ass out of here. I do not have time to listen to dumb shit!"

"Mr. President!" she shouted, then boldly stepped around Andrew to approach my desk. "That is my opinion, and for the last time, you will not use that kind of language when speaking to me! I don't know who you think you are, but you can't continue to throw me out of here because I disagree with you. Your temperament, sir, does not make you fit to be president!"

"What doesn't fit is your dress. I can do what the fuck I want to, and who in the hell is going to stop me? Definitely not you. And if you come any closer, you will get a taste of more than just my words."

Her eyelids batted fast; her face was as red as fire. "Are you threatening me? For the sake of God, please tell me you are not threatening to put your hands on me."

"One more step or one more word, and God won't be able to save you."

The way my face was twisted, she didn't dare say another word. Nor did she step closer to me. Andrew reached for her arm, then attempted to move her toward the door. Sam, my press secretary, watched with a smirk on his face.

"It . . . it's been a long day," he said, stuttering. "Why don't you come this way and let the president, Sam, and me come up with our next move? Get some rest, and . . . and we'll talk more after things have calmed down a little."

When Levi, my only trusted secret service agent, entered the room, I guessed VP Bass thought he was coming in to handle me. This emboldened her to speak, but the second her mouth opened, I quickly warned her by slamming my hand on my desk to get her attention.

"Not one word, not even a vowel," I growled.

Levi could see that I was near my breaking point. He hurried to get the vice president out of my office. After she left, I dropped back in my chair.

"That was painful," Sam said, standing with his arms crossed. "I know that you really weren't going to hurt her, Mr. President, but you sure did have me fooled."

"Then don't be a fool all your life, because she was about to catch hell. Moving on, please prepare a statement tonight, and stop repeating the same ole bullshit. I'm too disgusted to say what I really feel, so I'm counting on you to prepare a statement on my behalf that is different and very sincere."

"Will do, sir. After I'm done, I'll send the statement to you for approval. Is there anything else?"

"No. Nothing else."

I thought Sam was getting ready to leave, but he didn't budge. He just glared at me as I sat with a mean mug on my face, sweat beads dotting my forehead. My wrinkled shirttails were outside of my slacks, my bowtie was off, and my jacket was on the chair.

"What else do you want?" I snapped.

"I just want you to know that we all feel your pain. Every last one of us does, and we know that there is a possibility that one day the same thing could happen to any of our children. No matter what the vice president says, you pushed to do the right thing. And one day, hopefully soon, people will fully understand why that law had to be implemented."

"You're damn right it did," I responded, appreciating his words. "Because with seventy fucking guns in the house, someone was looking for trouble. Those people knew their son had issues. Somebody knew what he was up to, and not one single person said a word. I can't express how disappointed and disgusted I am. And to hear my VP speak that way angers me even more."

I looked at Andrew as he stood close to Sam. "I know some of my limitations with executive orders, and I also know that Congress can't reverse anything that I do. They can defund some of the programs that I set forth, but you know I'll veto any legislation that comes to my desk that does so. I need to make some major moves, because it's apparent that I won't be getting any damn help around here. Let me know what you suggest, and do so soon."

"For starters, I suggest that you do what you must, but don't go overboard," Sam replied. "The American people wants a president who uses his bully pulpit to work with Congress, not one who decides to take all matters into his own hands and does as he wishes. I'll get more information for you, but the last thing we want is to be faced with legal battles that ultimately have to be decided upon by the Supreme Court. From experience, we all know how that goes."

"Don't remind me. I thank you both, and if you all don't mind, I'd like to be alone right now to gather my thoughts."

They both headed toward the door, but I called for Sam just as he was getting ready to walk out.

"In the statement," I said, "please let the families know that I intend to pay them a personal visit."

"Will do, Mr. President. I should have the statement prepared and delivered to you within the hour."

I nodded, then slumped in my chair after he closed the door. My mind was on overload. I assumed there were times when every single president probably questioned why they had fought so hard to be here. The stress was unbelievable, and it was very difficult for me because I didn't even have a vice president who had my back. That was discouraging, and every time my thoughts switched to her and her reckless words, all I could think about was snapping her fucking neck. I was just that mad, and I couldn't control my ill feelings. And when my thoughts turned to my mother and Ina, that didn't help much, either.

While I'd been surprised to see Ina, I figured she was here for a purpose. What that purpose was, I didn't know. The only person who could tell me was my mother, so after I chilled for about thirty more minutes or so, I sent Levi a text, telling him to go get my mother and bring her to the Oval Office. Fifteen minutes later, she entered the Oval Office, with Ina following closely behind her. I sat up straight in the chair, not even bothering to stand.

"Sweetheart," my mother said, standing next to me, as if she was concerned. "Are you okay?"

"Don't sweetheart me, and stop talking to me like I'm a child. Tell me what this is all about, and do not lie to me, because I'm not in the mood for it."

My mother looked at Ina; Ina looked at her.

"You don't have to be so nasty, Stephen, especially not in front of Ina. You and I can exchange blows later, and I don't care how old you are. You can still get slapped in the mouth."

I glared at my mother like she was crazy, but instead of getting into an argument with her, I lowered my tone and questioned the purpose of Ina being here.

"There is no purpose," Ina said. "Your mother saw me at a mall while she was in St. Louis, and she invited me to come here and join her. I honestly didn't think it would be a problem, but you're making it sound like it is. *Why* is the question I have for you, and when did you become so disrespectful toward your mother?"

My mother quickly weighed in. "I've been wondering the same thing, but a part of me already knows *who* is responsible."

I wasted no time firing back. "I guess you didn't hear what I said. I'm not in the mood, and if all you want to do is come in here and insult Raynetta, then you know where the door is."

My mother winced before tucking her purse underneath her arm. "Ugh. Don't you get tired of throwing me out of here? You can't even hold a pleasant conversation with people anymore, and being so ugly all the time doesn't suit you. I'm leaving, but the least you can do is treat Ina with kindness and speak to her like you have some sense. It's been a long time since you've seen her, and you don't want her to think that being the president has caused your head to swell, do you?"

Without responding, I stood and walked to the door. When I opened it, a Secret Service agent was standing on the other side, close by.

"Escort my mother to her room and make sure she stays out of trouble. Also, I don't want any more visitors. That includes my wife. If she happens to come by, please tell her that I'm in a meeting and I'll see her shortly," I instructed the agent.

My mother happily left my office, and when I turned around, Ina was standing there, with glee in her hazel eyes, which I used to think about day in and day out. I also used to think about how she'd broken my heart. That had left me feeling slightly bitter.

"I don't mean to stare at you like this," she said. "But it feels so awkward being here, in this office, and knowing that you're the president. Make no mistake about it, I voted for you and everything, but I didn't think you would win."

"That's because you always viewed me as a loser."

"No I didn't, Stephen. Stop your lies. You know better."

I headed over to the sofa and took a seat. "Please," I said, tilting my head in the direction of the sofa across from me. "Have a seat."

She sat down on the sofa, with a smile locked on her face. My expression, however, was flat. That was because some women didn't understand how men felt when they were dissed. They also didn't recognize that we held grudges for a long time. Seeing a first love wasn't always a good thing, no matter how sexy she or he still was. There was silence as we looked at each other. I didn't know about Ina, but I was thinking about choosing my next words very carefully.

"I predict that your mind over there is traveling back down memory lane," she said, breaking the silence. "If so, what exactly are you thinking about?"

"I'm thinking about all my phone calls never being returned, and about how much I begged and pleaded with you to just simply reach out to me. More importantly, I'm thinking about those parents who lost their children tonight."

"I know. It's sad, isn't it? And if you'd like, we can get on our knees, hold hands, and pray, like we did while in college. Do you remember how we used to pray for better grades, for money, and even for our professors not to show up for class?"

I nodded, thinking back to the good old days. "Yes, I do remember. Very well. I also remember praying for you to return my phone calls. And now that I've been given the opportunity to ask, what was up with you? Why did you do that? What made you just disappear like that?"

"It was complicated, Stephen. Very complicated. And at the time, you wouldn't have understood."

"Maybe not, but now I will, so tell me."

Ina appeared to be fishing for an answer. "Why does it matter?"

I shrugged. "It doesn't, but since you're here, I just want to know."

"If it doesn't matter, then why?"

"Because it mattered then, but it doesn't matter now. I'm not going to play this game with you, Ina. All I want is a simple answer."

This time, she shrugged. "What about what I want? Are you prepared to give me what I want?"

"Not really, but it depends on what that may be. But before you tell me, please answer my question."

Ina's eyes shifted from one side of the room to the other. She licked her bottom lip, then fixed her eyes on me again. "I stopped calling, didn't return your calls, and ran away because I was seeing someone else. He told me to choose, and I chose him. Eventually, I dropped out of college and returned to St. Louis. After he and I broke up, I was too embarrassed to tell you I'd made a big mistake, so I never reached out to you again."

In no way was I moved by her fabricated story; I knew Ina all too well. She'd been in love with me too, and there wasn't a chance in hell that she'd been involved with someone else.

"Seeing someone else, huh? I'm not sold on that lie, but if you're sticking to it, fine. I am, however, going to give you one more opportunity to come clean. If you refuse to do so, it will be your loss, not mine."

She didn't hesitate to respond. "I just told you the truth. What more do you want? And what makes you so sure that there was no one else?"

I turned my wrist to look at my watch. It was several minutes after midnight. I stood, stretched, and then made my way toward the door.

"Stephen," Ina said. "Where are you going? I'm not done talking to you yet, and you never did hear me tell you what I wanted to tell you."

"You don't have to tell me. I already know. You want to play these little games, lie to me, have sex with me, attempt to ruin my marriage, and then tell my wife how good I was to you. I'm not going down that path, so don't allow me to waste any more of your time."

I opened the door, gestured for Ina to exit. She appeared stunned by my actions, and she slowly rose from the sofa, took a few steps, then halted before going out the door.

"My, have *you* changed," she said. "I still have much love for you, though, and that is, and will always be, the truth."

"It mattered then. Doesn't now," I told her. "Good seeing you, Ina. All the best."

Her smile vanished, and she left without saying another word. I felt good about leaving things as is with Ina, and after I got to my bedroom and saw Raynetta lying in bed, I felt even better. That was until she sat up in bed and pouted about how late it was.

"Really, Stephen? It's almost one o'clock. What's going on with that shooting, and where have you been?"

Raynetta knew the routine, so I didn't quite understand the big damn deal. I was calm but irritated, nonetheless. "What do you mean by where have I been?" I removed my shirt, tossed it on a chair. "You know where I've been. It's called working."

She didn't say anything else until I took off the rest of my clothes and got in bed. I scooted my naked body close to hers. And when I wrapped my arm around her waist, she removed it.

"Tell me this," she said, facing me. "Do you still have feelings for her?"

I figured I was going to have to explain Ina's appearance at the gala, but I was too tired to do it tonight. Even so, I quickly did my best to put Raynetta at ease. I wrapped my arm around her waist again and this time held her real tight so she wouldn't pull away. I then moved her head to my shoulder and locked her legs with mine.

"Now you won't be able to run away when I tell you this." I felt her body get tense. "I no longer have feelings for Ina, and what we shared happened a long, long time ago. It is my wish that you stop being so insecure. I don't care how beautiful or intelligent a woman is, how perfect her ass may be, how luscious her lips may look, or how addictive her eyes may appear, she still has nothing on you."

Raynetta playfully punched my stomach and then lifted her head off my shoulder to look at me. "So, you think she was all that, huh?"

"She was, but you're so much better. Besides, I'm not interested in traveling back down memory lane, and I'll choose you any day of the week."

"You'd better. And what man in his right mind wouldn't?"

"Exactly," I said with my eyes closed. "Lucky me. I'm so lucky that I get to lie here tonight with my beautiful wife in my arms, while so many others are in anguish, crying over the loss of their children, and knowing that their kids will never be coming home again. So, yeah, lucky me."

"I know, baby. It's heartbreaking, isn't it? Try to get some rest, and . . ."

I was out. The last thing I remembered was Raynetta telling me she loved me.

President's Mother,

Teresa Jefferson

The very next day, things turned from bad to worse. Stephen was notified that two white cops had killed an unarmed African American preacher, leaving behind four kids and a wife. The incident had been caught on camera, but the police chief stated on television that he wasn't going to relieve the officers of their duties until a thorough investigation had been completed. Just as the news hit Stephen, I was on my way to the Oval Office to chat with him about his ill treatment of Ina. I stopped dead in my tracks when I realized he was not alone in the Oval Office. As I stood near the door, I eavesdropped on his conversation with the head of the Department of Justice about making sure that those officers were fired and that the FBI investigated. He also made preparations to meet with the preacher's wife and kids.

After hearing that, I decided to cut Stephen some slack and save our conversation about Ina for another day. There was too much going on, and all day long, people had been tiptoeing around the White House, as if they were on pins and needles. When Stephen was under pressure, it was best to stay far away from him. I hoped things would settle down soon. He seemed excited about attending the Millennials Summit next week, and the atmosphere there would do him some good, because he was all about empowering our youth.

I got a quick bite to eat before returning to the Queens' Bedroom. I was so tired from last night. After Stephen had booted me out of his office, I had messed around with Frank until four in the morning. When Ina had called after leaving Stephen's office last night, our conversation was brief. She hadn't sounded too happy about how things turned out last night, and all she'd kept stressing was that Stephen had really changed. After entering my bedroom now, I lay across the bed and reached for my cell phone to call her back.

"Good afternoon," I said after she answered the phone. "Are you still at the hotel?"

"Yes, but I'm leaving tonight."

Her response was flat. I could sense that she was upset about something, but it wasn't my fault that things hadn't gone according to plan. She should've stepped up her game. What a waste it was, asking her to come here.

"I'm sorry that I didn't have more time to talk when you called last night, but I had to take care of a little itch that needed to be scratched. What exactly did Stephen say, and why are you leaving so soon?"

"Because it was a big mistake for me to come here. During my conversation with Stephen, I got the impression that he thought I was here to break up his marriage and use him for sex. I was seconds away from telling him about Joshua, but he was so mean and bitter about what had happened in the past that I never got to it. I told him that I had chosen someone else over him. In no way did he believe that, because he knows how much I was in love with him. This weekend has been a complete disaster for me. I just want to go home, find out where Joshua is, and get back to my *regular* life."

"I regret that you're throwing in the towel already, but that's your choice," I said. "And as for Joshua, I thought he was at a friend's house?"

"He is, but he's not answering his cell phone. I've left him several messages, but he hasn't responded. It could be that his phone needs to be charged. That's happened before. I'm sure he's okay."

"You can never be too sure, especially when it comes to kids. Don't you have his friend's parents' number?"

"I do, but I don't have it with me. And even if I did have it, I don't want Joshua to feel as if I'm calling there to check up on him," she replied.

"Well, good luck with that, okay? When Stephen spent the night anywhere, I always knew numbers, addresses, backgrounds . . . everything about the people he was with," I informed her. "You younger mothers, as well as fathers, are too lenient for me. That's why so many kids are getting into trouble, and it's a damn shame what that boy did at that basketball game."

"I agree. It's terrible. I've been watching the news all morning, and what happened is so sad. I also saw the video that shows what those cops did to that preacher. I can't believe people are out here defending those cops' actions. Something needs to be done, because this has been going on for a long time."

"Yes, it has, but I'm confident that the people in power who continue to turn a blind eye to these incidents will be forced to pay more attention and take action real soon. It's not a good day for Stephen. Neither was last night. Whenever you get a chance, and when things calm down, you should reach out to him again. The timing may have been off. Deep down, I know he still cares for you. I can see it in his eyes."

"Maybe so, but I'm not going to push," Ina said. "I haven't had much sleep, so I'm going to return Joshua's call. He just beeped in on my phone. And then I'll get a nap before I head back to St. Louis. Thanks again, Teresa. Joshua and I love you, and we hope to see you soon."

"You will, very soon. When you get home, give my love a squeezing hug."

"Will do."

After we hung up, I turned on my back and gazed at the high ceiling. My thoughts turned to Raynetta; I wondered where she was. We needed to finish up the conversation we had begun in the restroom last night. Ina might be out of the picture now, but there was still so much unfinished business between Raynetta and me. I got off the bed, grabbed my photo album, and went to find her.

As soon as I strolled by the Lincoln Bedroom, I asked the Secret Service agent who monitored the stairs if he had seen Raynetta.

"Yes, but it was about thirty or so minutes ago. She was on her way to the gym, but I can buzz Alex, the agent who has been covering her, to see exactly where she's at. Give me a minute."

"Thank you," I said, then waited patiently as he reached out to Alex.

"Okay. I'll let the president's mother know. Thanks." The agent looked at me, then pointed up. "She's on the third floor, in the Solarium."

"Is she alone?"

"I'm not sure. Alex didn't say, but I can reach out to him again, if you wish."

"No, that's fine. I'll go see for myself," I said.

The agent told me to have a good day. I intended to do just that, especially when I stood at the entrance of the Solarium with my photo album close to my chest. Raynetta was sitting on a white lounging sofa, with a spiral notebook and a pen in her hands. The huge windows surrounding the Solarium brightened up the place, as did the numerous beautiful plants that almost touched the high ceilings. The Solarium was a very peaceful place to be. I assumed Raynetta wanted to get away from all the chaos on the lower levels.

"Are you busy?" I asked, causing her head to snap up.

"I'm always busy. May I help you with something?"

I moseyed into the room, still holding the photo album close to my chest. "I'd like to think that we can help each other."

I sat on the other end of the long sofa and placed the album on my lap. I pointed to the spiral notebook in Raynetta's hand and asked her what she was doing.

"Not that it's any of your business, but I'm working on a list of things I want to accomplish during Stephen's term in the White House. I'm also reading some information regarding upcoming events. So, if you don't mind, whatever you came to say to me, make it quick, because I'm really busy," she said.

Her attitude sucked. Raynetta hadn't a clue how much I despised her. Her funky little attitude, which she'd exhibited ever since the day I met her, had a lot to do with it.

"Yes, you are busy, so I will do my best to make this quick. Meanwhile, you don't have to be so nasty toward me. Is it possible for us to have a pleasant conversation every now and then?"

She was straightforward. "No, and let's face it, Teresa. You don't like me, and I don't care much for you, either. I don't know what your motive was for inviting Ina to come here last night, but whatever it was, it doesn't seem that it paid off for you. I won't be distracted by your ongoing shenanigans. And if you continue on, you're going to live a long, lonely life without your son."

Her words made me grin. "Since when did you become a psychic and think that you could predict the future? See, that's just one more thing that I have never liked about you, Ne-ne. You're always talking about Stephen distancing himself from me, and for as long as I can remember, you've been trying to create a wedge between us. You never accepted how close we were, and less than a month into your relationship with him, you tried to convince him what a hateful person I was. You didn't even know me, yet you passed judgment on me, as if you had known me all your life."

I went on. "You even threatened to leave Stephen if he didn't cut his ties with me, and to this day, you're still making predictions, hoping and praying that my relationship with my son diminishes. That only spells out part of the reason why we can't get along. And what kind of mother wants a daughter-in-law who constantly lies to her son, keeps secrets from him, takes his money, in addition to money from others, to set up her own bank account, just in case things don't work out?"

From the weary expression on her face, I could tell I had her attention. "I don't know—"

I held up my hand to cut her off. "Wait a minute, please. I'm not done yet, and before you respond, I am well aware of the money that was given to you by Stephen's number one enemy, Mr. Christopher J. McNeil to assist in bringing my son down. I know all about your meetings with him. And the last time I checked, the account you set up has over two million dollars in it, doesn't it? Then again, there could be more, since you've been adding Stephen's money to that account too."

Raynetta pretended as if she wasn't nervous, but no question about it, she was. She sucked in a deep breath, then did her best to explain her actions.

"If you were made aware of my meetings with Mr. McNeil, then I assume you know that I told him to go to hell. I made it clear that I would never betray Stephen, and in the process, I kept the money he gave me for Stephen and me to have. As his wife, there is no reason for me to steal Stephen's money. What's his is mine. We share everything, and he has access to my savings account as well. I don't know where you're getting your information from, but I promise you that there aren't any secrets between us. I have no reason to lie to him about anything. And no matter what I say or do, you will always hate me, because you are a crazy bitch who has nothing else to do with her life, so you keep interfering in mine."

"Yes, I'm a crazy bitch who loves her son and will do whatever to protect him," I assured her. "You can say what you wish, but Stephen has no knowledge about that bank account. He doesn't know about your secret meetings, and even though you decided to renege on Mr. McNeil's offer, you still took the money. Stephen wouldn't approve of that, and you know it. He also wouldn't approve of you lying about your birth control pills, so you can stop pretending that you're such an amazing, innocent wife who does no wrong. I know better, and I have known better for quite some time."

Raynetta closed the spiral notebook and placed it on the table. I definitely had her attention; all she could do was cross her arms and continue with her lies.

"If you think I'm such a horrible person, why haven't you said anything to Stephen?" she asked. "You haven't, because you know how much I love your son. You know that he loves me too, and if your main concern is to see him happy, it would be wise for you to cease this vendetta against me and to do it now."

"*Love?* Girl, please. You haven't a clue what that means. I'm the only person who truly loves my son. I haven't said anything to Stephen, because I needed to let many more cards stack against you. I also wanted to give you a few choices, so let's start talking about the real reason I'm here."

I scooted close to Raynetta, then opened the photo album to a page with a picture of Joshua when he was first born. I pointed to it, with a wide smile on my face. "See, that's my real baby right there. His name is Joshua, and from the day he was born, I knew he was going to be something special." I flipped the page to show Raynetta Joshua's pictures from when he was age one and two. "Isn't he adorable? Look at those cute little cheeks and to-die-for dimples. His eyes are more telling than anything, and when I tell you this child look just like his father, I mean it. He really does."

Raynetta jumped up from her seat and snatched the photo album from my hands. She flipped through the pages, and when she came across a few photos of Ina, she looked at me with fury in her eyes, gritting her teeth.

"Are you telling me that this is Stephen's son?" she hissed. "That bitch Ina has his son!"

"Calm down. That face you're making right now is an ugly one. I know this is upsetting to you, but yes, the *bitch* has his son. Stephen doesn't know about Joshua, and he never has to know, as long as you wake the hell up and give him the family he wants. I would be thrilled too, and all this hatred I have inside of me for you just may very well go away. Your fix to these little problems you have is very simple, and lying on your back a little more often isn't such a bad thing, is it?"

Raynetta ignored me and continued to look at the pictures. Tears welled in her eyes as she flipped the pages. Her hands trembled and her eyes narrowed when she glared at me.

"I don't know how you think this is going to damage my relationship with Stephen, especially when you're the one who hasn't told him about his son. I plan to tell him right now, and if you think you're going to use this against me, you're crazier than I thought."

"Maybe so, but do me a favor. Reach above your head and click the lightbulb switch on. Let me know when the bulb becomes brighter. Hopefully soon. You're not going to tell Stephen anything, because if you do, he and Ina are going to spend a lifetime together raising their son. I'll tell him about your lack of enthusiasm for having a child. And this thing with Mr. McNeil, of all people, is going to send Stephen over the edge. We don't want that, Raynetta. He already has enough on his plate."

I continued. "If you love him as you say you clearly do, what is so wrong with you having his child? I already have a grandson. Now all I need is a granddaughter. Can you imagine how beautiful she would be? Girl, Stephen would spoil her to death. Jus-just sit on this for a while. Give it some thought and let me know how you're feeling tomorrow. Better yet, after all of this sinks in."

I got off the sofa, knowing that this was a win-win situation for me. When I held my hand out for the photo album, Raynetta slapped it in my hand. Neither of us said another word. After all, there was nothing left to be said.

First Lady,

Raynetta Jefferson

This whole situation was horrible. The news about Joshua had knocked the wind out of me. I didn't know if I should scream, cry, or beat the hell out of Teresa for trying so desperately to ruin my life. Much of what she'd said was true, but the bigger piece to all of this was that I loved Stephen. I would never do anything intentionally to cause him harm.

When Mr. McNeil reached out to me, it was a month after we had moved into the White House. Stephen and I had been having problems. Anyone in their right mind could have sensed that we had issues, and Mr. McNeil had thought that I despised my husband. He'd wanted inside information that could damage Stephen. He'd also wanted me to do whatever I could do to make Stephen step down and thus allow Mr. McNeil's grandson, Tyler, to become president.

The money he'd offered me couldn't be ignored, and even though I had never planned to follow through with anything, I'd felt as if the money would be a big help to me, just in case I decided to leave Stephen. Basically, I wanted to have a safety net. I put the money into an account; then I told Mr. McNeil to fuck off. He was angry, and he even threatened to retaliate if I didn't return the money. I told him that I wouldn't return one dime, and that if he continued to bother me, I would tell everyone about his plans to destroy the president. After that, he backed off and pursued other options, which ultimately led to Tyler's demise.

Should I have told Stephen? Yes. Did he need to know that I didn't want any children? Absolutely. In due time I had planned to tell him both things, but our marriage was so broken, I could deal only with repairing it one day at a time. Unfortunately, Teresa had beat me to the punch. She knew it all, and this wasn't looking good for me. My so-called fix might seem simple to her, but it wasn't to me. Only because, baby or no baby, Teresa would always hold this over my head. She would treat me like her little puppet, and I couldn't let her do that.

It was time to let the chips fall where they may, and after I gave Claire a piece of my mind for spreading my business, I intended to go to Stephen and tell him my secrets. That included what I knew about his son. If Joshua brought Stephen and Ina closer together, what could I do? I had faith, though, that the news about Joshua wouldn't affect our marriage at all. More importantly, I held on to the love that I knew for a fact he had for me too.

Claire was a few minutes late. She rushed through the door to my office, apologizing for her tardiness.

"I'm sorry for being late," she said, almost out of breath. "But it's a madhouse out there. Since yesterday, I don't know how much you've heard from the president, but he has everyone around here, like, going crazy. He got the DOJ involved in that situation with those officers, and they were fired immediately. The chief of police was fired too, and the police union is livid. They view it as a war against them, and many cops are speaking up on every media outlet about the president intervening."

She paused to catch her breath. "So are other people, especially African Americans, who are damn happy about it. From out of nowhere, more video footage is being released, and the networks are flooding every channel with videos of officers throughout the country doing horribly bad things. Everyone is predicting that the president is behind the release of those videos, because he wants the American people to see what is really going on. I must say that I'm surprised. I didn't know it was that bad, and even though there are many good cops, those videos paint a very ugly picture. There are a lot of bad cops too."

"We've been saying that for a long time, and if Stephen is doing something to wake people up, good for all of us," I said. "I'm proud of him, but this makes me very nervous. I don't have to tell you why."

Claire nodded. "I know. Plenty of threats are being made against him, and the Secret Service is all over the place."

I was worried. Didn't even want to discuss this anymore, so I changed the subject. "Is there anything else that I should know before we get started on my schedule for next week?"

Claire plopped down in the chair in front of me. "Yes. One more thing. Your anniversary is next week, but just so you know, the president won't be here. He has to meet with world leaders at the UN, and he's going to the funerals of the students killed in the gymnasium. He's also meeting with the preacher's wife, and he recently agreed to attend a conference next week with the founders of the Black Lives Matter movement. I haven't even included the Millennials Summit, *and* that he's planning a surprise visit to the troops in Iraq. Even though many of them have moved on to other missions, he still thinks it's important to support the ones who have been deployed there for many years."

Finally, Claire took a deep breath and waited for me to respond.

"If I didn't know any better, I'd think you were working for the president, instead of for me. How is it that you know so much about what Stephen is doing? And please tell me who is sharing so much information with you."

Claire hesitated for a few seconds before speaking. "I don't want to get him into any trouble, but Andrew and I have to work closely together to examine what goes on with your and the president's schedules. You already know that we have to make sure there are no conflicts, and we also talk about numerous things that go on around here. I don't tell him everything, and he doesn't share everything with me. I try to share with you the information that he relays to me, especially if I believe it may be helpful."

"I get that, but did you just happen to tell him about what we discussed the other day? If so, that was none of his business. You know he's going to share information like that with Stephen."

Claire moved her head from side to side. "No, I didn't tell him anything about our conversation. I would never share anything like that with him, and I have set limitations on what I speak to him about. Personal things like that are never discussed."

"Well, you told someone, and they told my mother-in-law. I want you to tell me who else you've spoken to, because I need to put an end to that person feeding Teresa information about me. Not to mention what I need to do about you."

Fear rose in Claire's eyes. I was sure that she meant no harm, but the gossiping needed to stop. As she gathered her thoughts, I waited.

"The . . . the only person I probably mentioned it to is Holly. She works in the kitchen, and we kind of whisper back and forth about some of the things that go on around here. While we were having lunch the other day, I mentioned what you told me. I didn't think that she would say anything to anyone. I trusted her because we've known each other for almost five years." Claire spoke with tears in her eyes. "I'm so sorry. Please forgive me. I didn't mean to—"

"I know you didn't, but please do not share anything else that I tell you with anyone. I should've kept my mouth shut, because the truth is, no one around here can be trusted. I'm not sure how I'm going to handle Holly, but whenever you see her, please let her know that I do not approve of her actions. I'm done talking about this. Let's move on, because I need to get to my luncheon."

"Okay. Thank you for understanding. Let me go get your schedule. I'll be right back."

Claire left the room, and even though I was still a little upset with her, all I could concentrate on was telling Stephen about my fuckups.

It was almost three o'clock when I returned to the White House. I had been at a luncheon where I met many military wives. It had turned out to be a fabulous event. Being there had taken my mind off of things for a while, but the second I stepped into the White House, a horrible feeling came over me. Alex, one of my Secret Service agents, rushed up to me and asked me to follow him. I responded with an attitude.

"If you don't mind, I would like to go upstairs, bathe, and then spend some time with my husband. Where do you—"

"This way," he said, directing me down the corridor leading to the East Room. He stopped right at the door to the East Room.

"The president wants to see you inside," he informed me.

Immediately, my heart fell to my stomach. Apparently, Teresa had gotten to Stephen before I did. I almost didn't want to face him. Knowing that I had to, I released a deep breath and put my big girl panties on. I could very well explain all of this, and like I said before, I was prepared to let the chips fall where they may. With that in mind, I opened the tall cherrywood door to the same room where the gala had been held the other night.

This time, however, the room did not feature numerous tables and chairs. No music was playing, and no people were dancing. The gold curtains covering the windows were closed. The Steinway grand piano sat close to the wall, a portrait of Washington behind it. The chandeliers hanging above were all dim, as were the wall sconces, which were shaped like candles. The lighting set a certain mood. In the center of the room was one round table, draped with a white tablecloth. A vase with several red roses stood on top of it, and to the left, the fireplace had a blazing fire. With his shirt off, slacks on, Stephen stood at the far end of the room, near a window. One of his hands was in his pocket as he leaned against the wall. *Handsome* wasn't the word to describe him—he was so much more than that. I wanted to rush into his arms, but I waited. Waited to see what this was all about. When he headed my way, I proceeded to move forward as well.

"Glad you finally made it back," he said, strutting with so much sexiness that I wanted to fall to my knees. "I've been waiting for you."

Finally, we stood face-to-face in the dimly lit room.

"If I had known you were waiting for me, I would have come sooner," I replied.

He eased his arms around my waist and pulled me closer, leaving no breathing room in between us. His smell, the feel of his package pressing against me, and his strong arms lured me in.

"I have a full plate next week, so I won't be around for our anniversary. I thought we could have a little dinner, make a lot of love, and celebrate this wonderful life we have together."

Lord knows I wanted to cry. I hated myself right now, only because I would have to put off what I wanted to tell Stephen for another day, possibly another week. There was no way I was going to spoil the mood, no way in hell, especially when he inched me back to the table, lifted me up on it, and started to plant sensual kisses against my neck.

"Say something," he whispered between his pecks. "Anything to let me know if you prefer dinner or me first."

"You," I rushed to say. "Without a doubt, you first." I dropped my purse on the floor, happily hiked up my skirt, then wrapped my legs around him while leaning back on the table. He leaned over me, kissing my lips and touching me in all the right places.

"Somehow, I knew you would say that."

Stephen unlatched his belt, then dropped his slacks to the floor. His long muscle stretched far in my direction. With my skirt already up and my legs wide open, he stretched the crotch section of my wet panties and pulled it to the side, then drove his thick meat right in. He was parked there for a few seconds, but just as he started to shift inside of me, and our kisses became more and more intense, there was a loud knock at the door. The knock echoed loudly in the almost empty room. We couldn't ignore it.

"Damn," Stephen said with furrowed brows. His frustrations showed as he eased his goodness out of me, releasing my juices, which had already started to rain on him. I was pretty pissed too, and I watched as he hurried into his slacks, then walked fast to see who was at the door. I removed myself from the table and lowered my skirt over my hips. Stephen yanked the door open, and on the other side stood Andrew.

"What is it?" Stephen said, sounding irritated.

"I'm sorry to bother you, sir, but I need to speak to you about something very important."

"It can't wait? Please tell me it can wait thirty or forty more minutes, so I can spend just a little more time with my wife."

"In my opinion, it can't wait. Not even five minutes. I think this is something you should know right away."

My heart dropped to my stomach again. Maybe Andrew was planning to tell Stephen about what I'd said to Claire. I had to find out if that was what it was, and if it wasn't that, what else was so important. I hurried toward the door, hoping for answers.

"Wha . . . what's so important, Andrew?" I asked. "We were kind of in the middle of something. Is it possible for us to have just a little peace for one day?"

"Yes, it is, and I'm truly sorry about this. But it is imperative that I speak to the President. If he wants you to know what it pertains to, I'm sure he will tell you."

Stephen shook his head, then turned to me. "Stay here. I'll ask Joe to go ahead and serve you dinner, and I'll be back as soon as I can.

Your anniversary present is underneath the table. I don't want you to open it, but if you must, I understand."

I reached for his hand, starting to panic. "D-don't go right now. I want to share some things with you too, and I had hoped to do so tonight."

Andrew spoke up again. "Now, Mr. President, it involves safety concerns pertaining to the American people. We need to act soon."

Well, since he mentioned that this was about the American people, it obviously didn't have much to do with me.

"Go," I said to Stephen. "But hurry back, please. I'll be waiting right here."

Without saying another word, Stephen and Andrew left. I shut the door, tearfully hoping and praying that when Stephen returned, everything would be okay.

President of the United States,

Stephen C. Jefferson

The second Andrew and I entered the Oval Office, I hurried to close the door behind us.

"This better be good," I said, still on edge about being interrupted.

"Actually, it's pretty bad, and it's not exactly about safety concerns. I think you may want to have a seat. If not, I need to."

Andrew removed an envelope from his suit jacket, and then he took a seat on the sofa. I sat on the other sofa, and with my shirt still off, I leaned back and put my hands behind my head.

"Nothing surprises me in this position anymore," I said, ready for whatever. "I'm already preparing myself for what may come."

"I think even this is going to surprise you, and even though the director of National Intelligence wanted to speak to you about it, I told Rick to let me speak to you first. As you know, our intelligence agency, along with the FBI, has been focusing more and more on individuals in our homeland who are becoming radicalized by terrorist organizations around the world. There are many programs designed to catch these people in the act, and you already know that through cell phone data spying, the NSA is privy to a substantial amount of information. Through domestic surveillance, well, we can tap into anything."

He went on. "Many of the individuals we are focusing on are, surprisingly, young people. Some are not as serious as others, but we are well aware of the ones who are readying themselves to cause major damage to the United States. Those people are being closely watched, and through surveillance, this is what the agency discovered."

Andrew reached out and handed me the envelope. I pulled the flap back, then extracted several photos. The first photo featured my mother, Ina, and a young man standing by my mother's car. For the first time in a long time, I was confused.

"I don't know what this—"

"Your mother visited St. Louis several weeks ago. Those pictures were taken because the agency has been watching a fourteen-year-old, tech-savvy teenager who lives in that house. Surveillance has also been on several of his highly skilled and very educated classmates. We have many reasons to believe that all of them became radicalized. They'd been planning something big, but a few hours ago things took a drastic turn. One of the bombs they put together exploded, killing three of the teenagers, badly injuring one of them. There are young people all over our country being led in the wrong direction and getting involved in messes like this.

"I had to bring this case in particular to your immediate attention because your mother . . . There is a connection with the people who live in that house. The woman in the picture, Ina, was here the other night. Her past relationship with you is well known." Andrew shifted in his seat before hitting me with the next part of his statement. "The agency also believes that the fourteen-year-old teenager who was killed earlier was, indeed, your son."

A jolt went through my body, causing me to sit up straight. It also felt as if someone had punched me in the gut, so I leaned forward, tightened my stomach, as if another blow was coming. A lump had risen in my throat; I swallowed it so I could speak. This had to be a bad joke, and the one word that came to mind was . . . *bullshit*.

"C–come again. What did you just say? My son? Radicalized? Dead? I don't know what kind of game you're playing, but, muthafucka, I don't have a son. If this is an attempt to distract me and—" I stopped speaking suddenly and tried to wrap this shit around my head. Slowly but surely, the pieces started to come together.

Andrew continued. "I . . . we do believe that Joshua Chatman was your son. His birth certificate has your first and middle name on it, with a made-up last name. Apparently, your mother has known about Joshua for quite some time. Her name is on the property deed to the house Ms. Chatman lives in, as well as on her cars. There seems to be several conversations—"

Numb all over and in a complete daze, I lifted my hand. "Please, say no more. Leave me, Andrew. Please leave me and pray hard for me tonight. Do not speak about this to anyone, and tell Rick that I want to speak to him before eight o'clock in the morning."

Andrew slowly stood, looking at me as I sat there, distraught. "I will pray for all of us. I'm sorry about your son, and let me know if I can assist you further in any way. I'll be in my office."

I stared straight ahead, thinking, thinking, thinking. Now it all made sense. Years ago, Ina had been pregnant. My mother had intervened,

and now my son was *dead*? I couldn't wish what
I felt inside on my worst enemy, and as I started
to look at all the photos in my hand, I just wanted to hurt somebody. Bad. Joshua looked so
much like me. I was in pain—for him and for me.
Tears welled in my eyes; I closed them tight to
bring about darkness. I stayed there for a while,
thinking some more. And the more I thought
about everything, the more my heart raced. A
sheen of sweat formed on my forehead; the thick
wrinkles there deepened. I crumbled the photos in my hand, and when I opened my eyes, I
ripped the photos to shreds. The only person on
my mind was my goddamned mother.

I rushed out of the Oval Office and stormed
down the West Colonnade to make my way to
the Executive Residence. Then I ran up the
Grand Staircase to the second floor. Levi and
another agent followed after me, but I was
moving so fast that I left them in the dust. When
I reached the Queens' Bedroom, I damn sure
didn't bother to knock. I could hear music coming from inside the room, and when I turned the
knob, the door opened. Inside were my mother
and Frank, looking like two deer in headlights,
caught in action. They both were naked, and
Frank was handcuffed to the bedpost, while my
mother had a black whip in her hand. Funky

music played in the background and made me even more disgusted.

"What in the hell is going on?" my mother shouted, rushing to cover herself with a sheet. With one hand loose, Frank eased the sheet toward him, attempting to cover himself too. Shame covered his face as he pointed to the key on the bed and told her to uncuff him.

I walked farther into the room, displaying much rage, until I stood by the bed. "You have to ask what is going on? Don't you already know? You know everything, Mama, and to keep my son away from me was pretty damn low."

She shrugged, acting as if it was no big deal. "I see that Raynetta decided to finally spill the beans. Her big mouth doesn't surprise me one bit." She used the key to uncuff Frank, and in a matter of seconds, he wrapped himself with the sheet, then jetted past Levi and another agent, who stood outside the door with stunned expressions on their faces. I tried to process what my mother had just said about Raynetta. *She knows about this too?*

"This isn't about Raynetta," I shouted. "It's about you, your goddamned lies, and your secrets that have hurt me time and time again! If you knew I had a son, why didn't you tell me!"

She threw her hands in the air and shook her head. "Because, at the time, you just didn't need to know. You were on your way to doing great things, and Ina was a loser. Her whole family consisted of losers, and I couldn't let her or her crackhead-ass mother bring you down. Meanwhile, I took good care of your son, and I made sure that he never, ever wanted for anything. I wanted to tell you about him, but Ina begged me not to say a word to you. I was caught in the middle. I didn't know what to do, and she said that if I told you about Joshua, I would never be able to see him. All I wanted to do was keep a close relationship with him. He's a bright kid, makes good grades, and he's a star on the basketball team. Wait until you meet him—"

"It's too late for that! I . . . I will never be able to meet him."

The thought and those words pained me. I had to pause for a moment just to blink away my tears and gather myself. I was losing it for sure. Didn't quite know how I was going to recover from this.

"You can and you will meet him. Don't be upset. And . . . and wait until he finds out who his father really is. I can't wait to see the look on his face, and on yours, when you see him. You're going to be so happy. We can go to St. Louis right now if you want to."

My mother grabbed my hand, but I yanked it away from her. "Y-you have lost your fucking mind. My son, Mother, was radicalized by terrorists. He'd been on the NSA's radar, and while you and Ina were busy keeping secrets, he and his friends were busy making fucking bombs to kill Americans! He . . . he's dead! Thanks to you!" I pounded my fist on the bedpost. "He is dead!"

"Hell no!" she shouted back. "Who told you that bullshit? You believed them? Joshua is too smart to do anything dumb like that, and I . . ." She paused and frantically searched for her phone. "I'm calling Ina right now. Just wait. You can speak to her and him! Someone is lying to you, and when all is said and done, I want an apology from you!"

She hurried off the bed and covered herself with a silk robe that had been thrown over the chair. With her cell phone up to her ear, she pouted and gazed at me with fury in her eyes. I snatched the phone from her hand and threw it across the room. It shattered into pieces after hitting the wall.

"Do you think I give a fuck about what that lying bitch says? She has already lied to me enough, and so have you!"

I stormed into her walk-in closet and started yanking her clothes from the hangers. She followed, yelling for me to calm down and trying to convince me that Joshua wasn't dead.

"Please, baby, just listen to me. There has been a huge mistake, and I don't want you to listen to these idiots around here. It's a game. It's all a game. Please, you have to trust me on this. Yes, I have lied, but others are lying to you too. Ina has, Raynetta has, and she . . . she doesn't even want to have your child. She's still taking her birth control pills. And ask her about her meetings with Christopher McNeil. He—"

I reached out and grabbed my mother by her throat so she couldn't speak. Her back was pinned against the wall, and her tongue was hanging out of her mouth like that of a thirsty dog. "That's right! Throw everybody under the bus to save yourself. I'll deal with Raynetta, but definitely with you first. You're always hollering and hooting about me throwing you out of my office, but you haven't seen anything yet. I'll show you how to throw somebody out! This, my dear mother, is how you do it!"

I released her throat, then shoved her away from me. She doubled over, trying to soothe her neck and breathe.

Levi touched my shoulder and asked me to calm down. He spoke softly. "My brotha, let me gather her things while you go somewhere—"

Without turning around to face him, I continued to yank my mother's clothes from the hangers. "Don't touch me, man," I said. "Please back up and let me handle this."

Levi knew how I was, so he didn't push. He just kept my mother away from me, especially when she swung out her arms, trying to stop me from stuffing her belongings into her luggage.

"See, Mama? This is how you do it." I filled her luggage to capacity. Also swiped my arm across all her expensive jewelry and accessories that were on the island in her closet and made sure that those items went into her bags too. I removed her shoes from the racks. Everything, every single thing, was packed, and that was when I dragged her five bags to the top of the Grand Staircase.

"Stop this!" she yelled after me. She got loose from Levi and tugged on my arm as I tossed the first bag down the stairs. Since the bag wasn't zipped, her clothes, shoes, and jewelry were strewn all over the place. I pulled away from her grip, swiped my hands together.

"Yes, this is how it's done! This is what throwing somebody out of your fucking house looks like."

As she looked at her things decorating the stairs, tears welled in her eyes. "Don't you dare throw another one of my Louis Vuitton bags like that. If you do—"

She looked over my shoulder, and when I turned around, I saw Frank peeking from another room. She lashed out at him.

"Can't you see I need some help? Nigga, don't stand your scary ass in that room and not come out to help me! Don't you see what he's doing?" she shouted.

"Th-that matter is between you and your son. I don't have anything to do with it," Frank answered.

Right answer. I tossed another piece of her luggage down the stairs and then another one. That was when she reached out and slapped the shit out of me with enough force to turn my head to the side.

"Oh, shit," I heard Levi say. He rushed forward, as did the other agent and the one who had been monitoring the main level. All three of them looked as if they were about to gang up on me, but with a tight grip on my mother's arm, I dared them.

"Stand down!" I yelled. "That is an order!"

They all froze. I pulled my mother down the stairs, using much force. She tried to keep her balance, but on the sixth step, she lost her balance and collapsed. I kept on dragging her, ignoring every word that spilled from her mouth.

"Let go of my arm and legs, Stephen! Is this how you treat your own mother? We're family, and you . . . you gon' make me break something! My ankle is twisted . . . my leg. God help me. Jesus, please don't let this fool kill me! Owww! I done bumped my head!"

I was beyond mad, didn't even recognize her as my mother. I didn't release her until we had reached the next level, where I shoved her away from me again. While on the floor, she made threats and cried. I looked down at her pathetic self, darting my finger at her.

"That, Mother, is how you do it. If you can't walk, crawl the fuck out of here, and never come back again."

I walked away and headed for the East Room to see Raynetta. Levi ran after me, holding some of my mother's belongings in his hands.

"What . . . Do you want me to take her home tonight?" he asked.

"No. Take her to a mental institution. Tell them to strap her up, put her in a cell, and throw away the goddamned key."

"You don't mean that, do you?"

I looked at Levi with a straight face. "Does it look like I'm joking to you?"

"No, but—"

In a hurry to get to Raynetta, I stormed away. Minutes later, I entered the East Room, where Raynetta was sitting at the table, eating with Joe, another White House chef. They appeared to be engaged in a pleasant conversation, but when they noticed the rage in my eyes, the conversation ceased. Raynetta stood up, with her fearful eyes fixed on me. My eyes shifted to Joe, who stood up as well.

"Mr. President, if you're ready for me to serve you, I'll be happy to go get your food too. The first lady and I were just speaking—"

"That won't be necessary, Joe. Thank you. Please exit. I need to speak to my wife."

Joe encouraged me to have a good evening, then hastily left the room. That was when Raynetta stepped closer and threw her arms around my neck.

"The ring is beautiful," she said, referring to the anniversary gift I'd gotten her. "Thank you, Stephen. I love you so much."

With a blank expression on my face, I peeled her arms from around my neck, then stepped a few inches back.

"Three questions." My chest heaved in, then out. "Did you know about my son, where are your birth control pills, and have you ever met privately with Christopher McNeil?"

She swallowed hard and was now barely able to look at me. Trying her best to distract me again, she reached for her purse and started rummaging around inside of it.

"My pills are somewhere in here, but as you can see, my purse is junky as ever."

I snatched her purse and shook it upside down so the contents would fall on the floor. They did, scattering all over the place.

"Why did you do that?" she said. "I told you my pills were in there and . . ."

As she rambled on, my eyes searched for her birth control pill package. And just my luck, there it was. I snatched it off the floor, and as I looked at the last pill taken, it showed that it was today.

"Now that you answered that question, how about my other questions?" I snapped.

She slowly nodded. "Yes, I recently learned about your son, and I also met with Mr. McNeil. But please let me explain."

I swear, this was it. I was done. She jumped when I snatched the black suede ring box from the table and pitched it into the blazing fireplace. It was a replacement for the one she'd already had on her finger, and I was tempted to break her finger and take that one off too. But in an effort not to put my hands on Raynetta, I just . . . just turned and walked away.

"Stephen!" she yelled after me. "Please listen! You don't understand, baby. It's not what you think! W-where are you going?"

I pivoted to respond before exiting. "The question is, where are *you* going? Think fast. You don't have much time."

Raynetta fell to her knees, crying out to me. "I'm sorry. You have to listen. . . ."

I had no sympathy for her, and in an effort to run the White House like I was voted in to do, and to keep my sanity, I had to get rid of some people. I knew exactly who the troublemakers were—some were the same ones who had kept me from my son. All I could think about was him. I hadn't even got a chance to hold him in my arms. It couldn't get any worse than this, but then again, this was the White House, where good news ran rampant through the halls and bad news made it to the media. They had already begun to spread vicious lies, which had many Americans in shock and hating me even more.

President of the United States,

Stephen C. Jefferson

As president of the United States, I couldn't even think straight. My heart was broken. Mind wasn't right. Temper was at a level I couldn't control. Focused, I was not. Consuming my mind was my son. His funeral was on the day of my anniversary, the same day I was supposed to be on my way to Iraq to visit the troops. I pushed that visit ahead to the next week, along with my visit to the United Nations to meet with world leaders. My conference with the Black Lives Matter organization had been rescheduled, and the only things left on my agenda was attending the funerals of those kids killed in the gymnasium, participating in the Millennials Summit, and meeting with the wife of the preacher who had been killed by cops. I hated to reschedule anything, but I had to. After attending those funerals and meeting with the preacher's wife, I was exhausted. I now knew how those parents felt inside, and when the preacher's wife and kids cried on my shoulder, I was angry, yet sympathetic at the same time.

No doubt, I was at a point where I wanted to do some major damage and then pack up my shit and go. But because of the oath of office I had taken, and my pride, I had to suck it up and hold it all in. Showing strength was a must, even at a time when I was broken. Somehow, I had to pick up all the pieces and go to St. Louis just to be there for my son. I only wished that I could've been there for him when he was alive. Things would've definitely turned out much differently. No words could express what I felt inside about a secret that had taken a huge chunk out of me.

I couldn't wait to look Ina in the eyes, just so she could witness how much I despised her. She was responsible for this. There was no way in hell I would ever forgive her for not telling me about Joshua. And what kind of mother was she to deny her own son a chance to be with his father? I just didn't get it. I also wasn't done with my mother yet. With her being ordered to a mental institution, she wouldn't be able to shed crocodile tears and say her final good-bye to her grandson. I had made sure that she was out of the way, and, hopefully, she had time to think about the magnitude of the bullshit she'd done. That went for Raynetta as well. I didn't know where she was, and quite frankly, I didn't care.

I hadn't been spending much time at the White House, but I sat in the Oval Office today with Andrew, watching the news and listening to everyone rip me apart.

"If the president can't handle his job and has to cancel appointments, maybe he needs to step down," a commentator said to a group of contributors who were chilling at a table with him. "World issues can't wait, and I think it was a big mistake for him to reschedule his visit to the UN, considering all that is going on. Some of our allies have turned their backs on us. This was the president's opportunity to strengthen those relationships, but now many leaders feel snubbed. They don't respect this president, and the reputation of the United States has been clearly damaged."

"I agree," one of the contributors said. "He should be able to handle a full plate. His speeches at those funerals were very touching, but I have no sympathy for what happened to the young man who was allegedly his son. Seems like that kid was troubled, and judging by his appearance alone, he was a thug. I'm sure he belonged to a vicious gang. I'm still trying to gather more information about his ties to terrorist organizations. In my opinion, it would be a slap in the American people's faces if our president attends the funeral of a terrorist."

"You're darn right it would be, and you can be sure that his poll numbers will drop tremendously," another contributor asserted. "What I'm upset about is his lack of support for African Americans. How can he make a decision to attend the Millennials Summit yet cancel with the Black Lives Matter organization? That speaks volumes about where his priorities are."

Finally, a male contributor with sense spoke up. "I'm embarrassed to sit at this table with all of you. World issues must wait, especially when we are dealing with matters affecting our own country. The president had to attend those funerals, and it was important for him to visit with the preacher's wife and kids. To say he's not supportive of African Americans is ridiculous, and if he had canceled his event with the Black Lives Matter organization, instead of merely rescheduling, then you may have a leg to stand on. We don't know all the details surrounding his son yet, but if the young man is, indeed, his son, the president should be at his funeral. I would lose respect for him if he wasn't. As a parent of a deeply troubled teenager with many issues, I would never walk away from my child. Not in life or death." This contributor was so upset that he got up from the table and left everyone speechless as he walked off.

Andrew took a deep breath, then turned to me as I sat at my desk. "It's a cruel world out there," he said. "And as your senior adviser, I don't think you should go. Are you sure you want to—"

"Yes, I'm going, and no one will change my mind. I'll deal with the repercussions later, but in the meantime, I need you to do something very important for me."

"Anything, Mr. President. How can I help you?"

"I want to meet with General Atkins again, to stress the importance of finding and/or killing the leaders of several terrorist organizations that are putting forth every effort to destroy us. Going after their leaders is the only way to cripple them, and I don't have to remind you how personal this is. Shit has gotten out of hand. I can't believe how much homegrown terrorism has increased over the years. We must get it under control. You are well aware of the leader my son and his classmates pledged their allegiance to. I want him alive and brought to me. Sooner rather than later."

Andrew cleared his throat. "Unfortunately, Mr. President, I know I said I'd do anything, but that won't be an easy task. We can't catch these leaders at the snap of our fingers. It takes time, strategic planning, and preparations to cripple these organizations. These individuals are highly intelligent, and they are constantly on the move. I'll set up a meeting so that you and the general can discuss a new strategy. But I'm sure he'll remind you how difficult it is, and has been so for years, to completely shut these organizations down."

"I won't dispute much of what you just said, but I will say this. Greed got us into this mess, but there is a way out. Those leaders may be intelligent, but if one sharp-minded president and his team could bring down Osama bin Laden, can you imagine what my team and I can do? Don't underestimate me, Andrew, and do not underestimate yourself. More importantly, never underestimate the brave men and women who fight for this country. When the right president occupies the Oval Office and makes smart decisions, the United States is unstoppable."

"How can I argue with that? You're right, and I'll set up a meeting for after your son's funeral. I plan to attend it with you, and afterward, Sam would like for you to speak to the American people. You often say that you don't care how anyone feels, but you wouldn't be occupying this office if you didn't care."

Andrew had a point. I did care about some of the things being said, and as painful as it was, I had to brace myself for the next few days.

Andrew left my office, allowing me time to go through a file he had given me in reference to Joshua. From a very young age, he seemed to have been a bright kid. He was handsome, and many of his pictures looked identical to mine, especially when I was younger. He made straight As, was very athletic, loved computers, and had numerous friends from different ethnic groups. The schools he attended were some of the best, but things had started to take a turn about a year and a half ago. He'd gravitated toward the wrong crowd. Started hanging with kids who felt as if the world was against them.

In some of the letters he had written, he expressed his anger with America. As a black kid, he felt as if our country had no respect for people of color or for those who were affiliated with certain religions. Like his friends, he was determined to cause damage. None of them were afraid to die. They viewed what they were doing as God's work—payback for decades of mistreatment. And when all was said and done, they all felt as if they would be rewarded for their deeds whenever they transitioned to the other side. Sadly, in no way did I believe the other side was what Joshua envisioned it to be. There would be no rewards. Only consequences for his hateful ways, thoughts, and actions.

In deep thought, I slowly closed the file. A lump was stuck in my throat. No matter how many times I swallowed, it wouldn't go away. I got up to get some water, and after several swallows, my throat cleared. I put Joshua's file in my desk, and seeing that it was almost midnight, I decided to go to my bedroom and get some much-needed rest. Thankfully, when I opened the door, the bed was still made. Raynetta wasn't there, but her clothes were still in the closet. Many of her belongings remained in the bathroom too, but they wouldn't be there for long.

Trying not to think about my fucked-up marriage, I removed my clothes to take a shower. I wished I could wash away thoughts of my son, but all I could see was his smile in those pictures. I envisioned him running into my arms, calling me Dad, playing sports with me, showing me his good grades. . . . I even thought about the explosion that had taken his life. I kept telling myself how things would have been different if I had been in his life. And with each second that passed, my hatred for Ina grew.

Feeling disgusted, I stepped out of the shower, dried myself off with a towel, and then put on my Turkish terry robe. The second I stepped into the bedroom, I saw Raynetta sitting on the edge of the bed. Her hair was brushed back into a ponytail. Eyes were narrow and swollen. Skin looked pale; clothes were wrinkled.

"I know you don't want me here, but I'm still your wife, and you will listen to me."

While I stood in the doorway to the bathroom, my eyes shifted to a black briefcase on the bed. I didn't have much to say, so I remained quiet. She continued.

"I was wrong, and I know that sorry doesn't cut it. I never wanted to lose you, and I was so afraid of telling you that I didn't want a child. Call me selfish or whatever, but I doubt that I will ever want one. Being a mother scares me, and with me being an adopted child who was abandoned by my real mother, I don't know if you will ever understand my concerns. As for your son, I didn't know about him until several days ago. Your mother told me, and she had so much hanging over my head that I had to think about when and how to break the news to you."

She took a deep breath and went on. "That goes for this thing with Mr. McNeil too. In no way would I ever do anything to harm you. You know that, Stephen. I took the money because I wasn't sure where our marriage was headed.

If you had divorced me, I wouldn't have had a safety net at all. That's why when he presented the money to me, I couldn't walk away. I pretended to be on his side only to get what I needed at the time. I took a big risk, without even knowing or understanding how deep his hatred was for you."

She paused, waiting for me to respond. I didn't. All I did was step farther into the room, but I halted my steps when she jumped in front of me, blocking my path. I looked into her eyes and immediately saw her frustration with my coldness toward her.

"I wish you wouldn't be so stubborn at times," she said. "I really need to get through to you. You can have every single dime of that money. It's in that briefcase. I don't even want it. All I want is for the love that we have for each other to prevail through all of this. I have your back, and I am here for you every step of the way."

With tears in her eyes, she reached up, held my face with her hands. "I . . . I know you're hurt. I can see it in your eyes. But let me help you get through all of this. I can help you, and we can claim victory together. We can win against your mother, against people like Mr. McNeil, and against Americans who just don't understand you. I am here, and no matter what you say or do, I'm not going anywhere. Nowhere, Stephen, unless you pick me up, carry me to the door, and toss me out on my ass. Is that what you want to do? If so, do it."

Raynetta didn't want to tempt me right now. I removed her hands from my face, then stepped around her. Still having nothing to say, I exited the room, thinking about one person—my son.

The day of Joshua's funeral had arrived. Air Force One landed at Lambert Airport in St. Louis, where the presidential motorcade awaited me. It had already been transported to St. Louis by a C-17 Globemaster III aircraft. The only people who joined me were several members of my Secret Service detail, Andrew, and Sam. Vice President Bass had offered her condolences at the White House, but we all felt that it was best for her not to attend the funeral.

Many people were upset about my decision to pay my respects to my son, and the second I exited the plane, the welcome I got from some of the politicians who greeted me was ice cold. They barely wanted to shake my hand, but today I just didn't give a damn. My expression backed up my thoughts. Dressed in a tailored black suit that was cut perfectly to my frame, I strutted to the motorcade. From a distance, I saw many members of the media.

There were protestors at the airport as well. Signs calling for me to be impeached were visible, and there were plenty of signs referring to me as a traitor. Some even said that my being here was an act of treason. I couldn't help but to wonder what drove these people to make themselves look like fools. I wanted to laugh at some of the ridiculous signs I saw, but unfortunately, I couldn't laugh. Not today. Possibly tomorrow. I just climbed in one of the vehicles, sat back, and relaxed, and as the motorcade rolled on, I shut my eyes. Darkness was before me, and for the next several minutes, I found a sliver of peace inside of me.

"Mr. President," Andrew said, interrupting me. I opened my eyes and saw him texting. "The vice president has been trying to reach you. Is your phone available?"

"Mine isn't, but yours is. What does she want?"

"She just received an urgent message from the Pentagon. Seven soldiers were killed earlier today, when their plane went down in Syria. We don't know yet if it was a result of terrorism or not."

Just when I thought things couldn't get any worse, they did. We awaited more information, but by the time we reached the church where Joshua's service was being held, nothing had been confirmed by the Pentagon. On the streets and the steps to the church, however, were more protestors. Many were in support of me being there; many were not. I was advised not to stop or respond to anyone when I made my way inside the church.

"I know how you are," Levi said. "Just keep it moving and ignore what you hear."

I assumed that would be easy for me to do. That was until I exited the motorcade and proceeded toward the doors of the church. The Secret Service covered me, but that didn't silence the noise. I was surrounded by many concered people who were there to exercise their First Amendment rights. It was a real circus, and with the media rushing in to get as close as they could to me, they got an earful.

"Mr. President, why are you here?" one man shouted. "Do you support terrorism?"

"How did your son learn to make bombs?" another said. "Did you teach him? Do you also hate America?"

"We can't trust you!" a lady shouted. "You're a liar, and you need to step down and let someone who is not related to a terrorist take over!"

"March on, my brotha. Keep your head up! We got you!"

"Yes, we do! 'Cause you are finer than a mutha! Dang, Mr. President. Allow me to bow down!"

People were pushing and shoving each other. The police had the area surrounded, but that didn't appear to strike fear into anyone, especially a man who lashed out at me with his fist lifted in the air.

"You created a monster that needed to die! May he rot in hell, like you will when someone has the courage to assassinate you!" the man shouted.

In a flash, I snapped. And before I knew it, I reached out, grabbed the man by his collar, and pulled him toward me until he was face-to-face with me. Thick wrinkles were visible on my forehead, and my brows were arched inward. The cameras flashed; I gave everyone a pretty picture of me.

"Why don't your tough ass do it!" I yelled while spraying spit in his face. "If you're brave enough to stand out here, talking shit, then show me your gun!"

Fear was trapped in the man's eyes. He was speechless. His whole body trembled. No one could believe what I had done. Not even those in my Secret Service detail, who were saying words I couldn't hear. I was too occupied with the cowardly fool before me. I shook him hard, and before shoving him backward, I head butted him, trying to knock some sense into him. He hit the ground hard.

"I . . . I will sue you for every dime you have! How dare you put your fucking hands on me, nigga!" he yelled.

"What did he say?" one lady shouted. "Oh, no, he didn't!"

"Yes, he did! Nigga, who, what, and where is he?"

"Did he just call the president a nigga?"

The boisterous crowd of people went after each other. The Secret Service rushed me inside the church, then ordered that the doors be locked. Outside, the police had their hands full. Sam and Andrew were still out there, and in no way did I want them to get hurt. As I reached for the doorknob to open the door and let them in, Levi put his big hand on my chest to stop me.

"I'll go see what's up. Follow Rich down the hallway now."

I ignored him and turned the knob.

"Now, Mr. President!" Levi roared. "Listen to me for once and let us handle this!"

At that moment, shots rang out. People already inside the church started to run for cover, and not only was Levi yelling for me to get away from the door, but so were my other agents.

"Please, Mr. President! Go now!" Levi urged.

This was a mess. Maybe I shouldn't have come here. Maybe I shouldn't have touched that man for saying what he did, but I hadn't been able to control myself. Not today.

I was escorted to a room where I couldn't hear much of what was transpiring outside. Minutes later, Andrew rushed in, with a small gash on the side of his cheek. Sam followed. His jacket was ripped, and a scratch was visible on his chin. They both were out of breath.

"Th-those people are out of control." Andrew dropped into a chair, trying to catch his breath. He was given a handkerchief to wipe his cheek. "It's a madhouse out there. Jesus Christ."

I took a deep breath, feeling awful, because this was on me. "Are you hurt? Do you need a doctor . . . anything?"

With disgust on his face, Andrew threw his hand back at me. I sensed that he was upset with me, but he didn't want to say it. "I'm fine. Some woman hit me with a stick. She got me on my leg too. Crazy broad."

"Her and the guy she was with almost got me," Sam said, looking at his ripped jacket. "Luckily, I got away from them."

Levi rushed in and closed the door behind him. He also took a deep breath. "More police officers are here, so everything should be under control soon. Thankfully, no one was shot, but a man with a gun was arrested. I don't know what to say about you, Ma . . . I mean, Mr. President. You have to cool out. I know you're under a lot of pressure, but this really doesn't help."

No, it didn't, but the damage was done. I swung around, closed my eyes, and asked silently for God to forgive me. After all, I was in His house. There was a very ugly side to me, and whenever I was pushed, I couldn't control that side.

There was a hard knock on the door, which caused everyone to pivot. Levi opened it, and Ina walked in. A visible frown was on her face. The black-and-white dress she wore hugged her curvy figure, and the black floppy hat on her head was slightly tilted. Dark shades covered her eyes, but she removed them to look at me. Sadness was clearly visible in her eyes; the bags underneath showed she was under a lot of stress.

"Can . . . will you all please leave the room so that I can have a moment with Stephen?" she said.

The Secret Service agents received a nod from me, and after they all left the room, Ina looked at me with tears on the rims of her eyes.

"I know you have plenty of questions, but I can't answer them for you today." Her lips trembled as she spoke. "I don't know when I'll be able to answer them, but today is about Joshua, nothing else. I don't know what happened outside, but I wish you wouldn't have come here. This spectacle is too much, and the things that are being said about my son hurt like hell. He . . ." She paused to suck in her quivering lips. Tears rolled down her face as she struggled to speak. "He was the best son—a good kid. A very good kid who was ju-just confused and . . ." She paused again to gather herself. Appearing weak, she reached for the chair in front of her, then grabbed her stomach. "Help me understand why. Why did this happen to my child, and how did I not know what he was going through?"

I couldn't answer those questions for Ina, and upset as I was with her, I couldn't even say some of the harsh things I wanted to say to her. Especially when she dropped to her knees, crying and blaming herself for what had happened.

"I failed him, Stephen. I lied to him about his father and denied him an upbringing with a decent man." She wiped the dripping snot from her nose while gazing at me. "Y-you would have been a great father. You would've taught him right from wrong. He needed that. That's all he needed, and his life wouldn't have ended like this. I so hate myself right now. If I could trade places with my baby, Lord knows I would. In a heartbeat. Just bring him back to me."

Ina was a mess. Then again, so was I. Everything she said was true—she had definitely denied Joshua and me the opportunity to have a healthy relationship. Nonetheless, it pained me to see her like this. I walked up to her, then reached out my hand.

"What's done is done. I don't want any answers to my questions. It doesn't matter anymore. Let's stand together for Joshua today. We know he wasn't the kind of kid people are making him out to be, and I ask that you hold on to the good memories that you have of him. I'm sure there are plenty, so think about those memories to make it through this day and the days ahead. I know you may not have wanted me to come here, but after finding out that he was my son, there was no way in hell I wouldn't be here, regardless of my status."

Ina slowly stood, looking at me through the slits of her very narrow eyes. "Thank you," was all she could say before wrapping her arms around me and breaking down in my arms. I held her up, even when we entered the sanctuary and saw Joshua's gold casket before us. Seeing a huge picture of him beside it caused my legs to weaken. I straightened my back, trying my best to stand tall and not break down in front of everyone. Whispers could be heard, but Ina's cries drowned out everyone.

I helped her to a seat and felt a substantial amount of relief when I was able to take one right next to her. My eyes shifted to Joshua's picture again—he looked like he was a happy child. A huge part of me wanted to open the casket, just to see him, touch him . . . whatever. But I had seen plenty of dead bodies, the bodies of people who had been killed by bombs. I could only imagine what he looked like inside of the casket, and opening it would do me no good. Pictures were all I had. No memories like Ina had, no nothing.

The service got under way, and after several songs, people came forth to say nice things about Joshua. One friend spoke about how Joshua had been there for him when he was being bullied. Another talked about a time when he had tried to teach Joshua how to play the trumpet and how horrible it had sounded. Joshua's uncle, Ina's brother, talked about how much fun they used to have playing sports. He admitted that the competition was always steep. Even one of his teachers spoke. She joked about his love for Twizzlers.

"Every single day Joshua brought Twizzlers to class. I could always hear the bag rattling, and I would tell him to open the bag quietly and not to interrupt the class. Then one day, he came to class without them. I said, 'Joshua, where are your Twizzlers today?' He said he didn't have any money to buy them. I missed the sound of that rattling bag so much that I went to the vending machine to buy him some. He thanked me, and the next day, instead of an apple on my desk, there were two bags of Twizzlers and a note, thanking me for being such an amazing teacher. It truly is the little things that count, and I am really going to miss him."

Everyone laughed, but sniffles could also be heard throughout the sanctuary.

Ina cracked a tiny smile and nodded her head. "Yes, he did," she whispered. "He loved Twizzlers and ate them every day."

I smiled myself, but deep down, I wanted to cry. I was holding it all in, and right when a lady got up to sing "Amazing Grace," my stomach started to tighten into knots. A sheen of sweat started building on my forehead. My heart rate increased, and one of my legs shook. Ina's loud cries, along with those of many others, echoed throughout the sanctuary. I couldn't console her when I was trying my best to hold in all that I was feeling. I kept wiping my forehead, shifting in my seat, and taking deep breaths. Ina finally let it all out, and she rushed from her seat to Joshua's casket and latched on to it. She held it as if she was holding him. Her mother joined her. It was devastating to watch the two of them suffer from a loss that shouldn't have ever happened.

"Sweetheart, no," Ina hollered. "Mommy loves you! I love you, and I am so sorry for all of this. You didn't have to die! God, why would you take my child from me?"

I slowly stood to go and console her, but my legs were too weak. I fell back on the pew and twisted my tense neck from side to side. Secret Service agents approached me, but I lifted my hand as a signal for them to back away. My leg shook faster; I couldn't control it. All I did was rub it, and when I felt someone's hands touch my shoulders, massaging them, I turned my head slightly to the side.

"It's okay," Raynetta said in a whisper. "I got you, baby. You'll be fine. Joshua will be too, and Ina."

Seeing her and hearing her voice calmed me. So did her touch. My leg stopped shaking. When she came around to the front of the pew, she sat next to me. She took my hand with hers and didn't let go until the funeral was finally over.

First Lady,

Raynetta Jefferson

I felt horrible for Stephen. Even for Ina. I wasn't about to let him go through that alone, and it was such a relief to have the funeral behind us. Stephen's attitude, however, hadn't improved much. He was back at the White House, trying to run a country that needed some serious direction. The incident with the soldiers had nothing to do with terrorism. It was an accident, but the loss was felt all over the country. Emotions ran high, and after the fiasco that happened in front of the church, all kinds of hurtful things were being said about Stephen. If they didn't say he belonged to a gang, he was now referred to as the new thug in chief in the Oval Office.

Today he was scheduled to respond to the American people about all that had happened. In an effort to stay out of his way, I sat with Claire in my office, waiting for him to speak. I had no clue what he was going to say. But I was sure that he'd been thinking long and hard about it.

"Why am I so nervous?" Claire said, pacing the room in a tight black skirt and a silver blouse. "This is really a big moment, because the president has lost a lot of support from the American people. Why aren't you as nervous as I am?"

"I am—a little. But I know my husband. He is a bright man, and he knows how to change things around quickly. People have a connection with him. They are drawn to him, and when he speaks, even if you don't agree with his words, he makes you think and listen."

"His connection may have a lot to do with how handsome he is too," Claire noted. "Take that as a compliment. I'm just telling you what I hear from other people."

I playfully rolled my eyes at Claire. She finally sat down, and then she started to gossip about what Stephen had done to Teresa.

"I don't know if you're aware of all the details, but from what I heard, it was brutal. Have you spoken to your mother-in-law?" she said.

"No, I haven't. I've barely spoken to my husband. What exactly have you heard?"

Claire started to tell me everything she knew. I almost couldn't believe it, but it had to be the truth, because all of Teresa's belongings were gone.

"I can believe that he made her get out of here, but I'm having a hard time believing that he dragged her down the steps like a rag doll. Sounds like some people may be exaggerating," I said.

"No, they're not. I spoke to someone who saw everything. The president was livid, and she's in a mental institution until he gives the word to release her. You know the president much better than I do, but I think she's going to be there for a long time."

"I hope so. And when you get a chance, let me know where she is. I may need to make some phone calls, or better yet, I just may go see her. I'm sure she'll love to see me. I can't help but to think how God was so right when He said He'll make your enemies a footstool."

Claire nodded. "A footstool she will be, and for the first time, I think she'll be happy to see you. I could be wrong, but I'll be sure to get that information for you. Now hush. The president is about to speak."

We laughed, then silenced ourselves as we tuned in to the TV. As always, Stephen started with a stern look on his face.

"Good evening. First and foremost, my condolences go out to the family members of the seven soldiers killed in the plane crash. It is very unfortunate that this happened, and it is always a tragic loss for this country when we lose great men and women who continuously take risks and who are committed to keeping our country safe. I'm looking forward to visiting with some of our troops soon, and I want each and every one of them to know that I am a president who cares deeply about their needs, concerns, and well-being.

"I will listen to the advice of generals on the ground, because it is important for us to strengthen our armed forces and pursue a mission that can and will destroy any terrorist organization created to do us harm. In an effort to cripple them, we will hunt and kill their leaders. Our strategy will be bold, swift, and fierce. We will not back away from any threats, and if ever given the opportunity, I will, as your president, use my bare hands to bring any of these leaders to their knees.

"Many of you have heard about the events leading up to my son's death. Not many people know the specificities of what actually occurred or what led him to become radicalized. I know, and I will make no excuses for anyone who threatens to do harm to America. We must, however, be unified in our efforts to speak up when we see or hear things that revolve around terrorism. And when it comes to our children, all our children, we have to create a country where they, along with everyone else, feel as if they are treated equally and fairly. We've ignored what is happening in our country for far too long, and the utter silence should not be.

"As president, it is time for me to act. That is why I will expand on a previous executive order to confiscate military surplus equipment from police departments across the country. The new order will result in the immediate termination of any officer who kills a man, woman, or child, of any race, who did not have a weapon on the scene. A thorough investigation will be done by the Department of Justice, and within thirty days—not one or two years later—they will determine if the officer should face a grand jury with special prosecutors leading the case.

"In addition to that, and in a separate order, we will proceed once again to release numerous individuals from prisons who have been incarcerated for years due to minor drug charge violations. The initial order lost traction, and it is time for many of these men and women to be united with their families, who need them. There are too many broken households in America, and for years, an unjust judicial system has contributed to the mess we now have on our hands. I'm well aware that many of you won't agree with my decisions, but get used to it, because real change has come.

"Lastly, I owe all of you a deep and sincere apology for what occurred at my son's funeral. I should have conducted myself better, but when you're under so much pressure and someone attacks your child, it hurts you to the core. I don't care who they are or who they become. They are still your child, and some things are better off left unsaid, especially words like *nigger*, which continue to cut real deep. Nonetheless, please accept my apology. I won't be taking any questions tonight, because I may be forced to say something harsh to the reporters who refer to me as the new thug in chief. To those, I say, 'Kiss my ass,' and that is putting it nicely. May God bless America, and may you all have a peaceful evening."

Claire released a deep breath; so did I. She looked at me with wide eyes. "Oh my God. I can't believe he said that. L-let the spin begin. I don't know how people will feel about those executive orders, but I can assure you that the police union will fight back. I've also never heard the president apologize to anyone, and he actually used the *N* word. He also said he would kill someone with his bare hands. I don't know how people are going to respond. My feelings are all over the place."

"After Stephen has made up his mind, he really doesn't care how anyone feels," I said. "I suspect that after the Millennials Summit, he'll be overseas for several days. I'm so worried about him, and my only wish is for him to succeed in every way possible."

"I wish the same. And I don't mean to bring this up, but are you also worried about him reverting to his old ways? You said he wants you to leave the White House, but does he really feel that way?"

I shrugged. "I don't know, because he hasn't said much to me. He's been sleeping in another room, avoiding me. And to answer your question, yes, I do worry. I worry because women will always be women, and when Stephen is like this, he is vulnerable. He'll never admit it, but I know my husband, sometimes better than he knows himself."

Saying those words caused me to exit my office and go find Stephen. There were a lot of snakes in the press briefing room, and I was sure that Michelle Peoples had taken her seat

up front. She was a reporter who had her eyes
set on my husband. I sensed that he had taken a
liking to her as well, and sure enough, as I made
my way down the corridor, I saw her speaking
to Stephen. In no way could I hear what she was
saying, and as others surrounded them, I stood
on the tips of my toes to see if I could read their
lips. Unfortunately, I couldn't. When Stephen
turned to walk away, I slipped into another
hallway so he wouldn't see me.

I hated being so insecure like this, but with
the recent mistakes I'd made, I wasn't so sure if
Stephen would forgive me. I think the money I
had taken from Mr. McNeil hurt Stephen more
than anything. Maybe it was time to return it.
Then again, telling him that I didn't want to
have a child was probably gut-wrenching too.
Of course he wanted a child, even more so after
what had happened to Joshua. I thought about
compromising, but if he wasn't willing to talk to
me, how would we be able to set ourselves back
on the right track? Maybe space was what he
needed. I intended to give him that, but I also
intended to keep my eyes and ears open.

President's Mother,

Teresa Jefferson

I hadn't a clue what day or time it was. But I did know that I had been brought to this place against my will. No matter how much I put up a fuss, my chances of getting out of this hellhole were slim. Every time I opened my mouth about leaving, they would rush into this room, shoot me with a needle, then leave. I learned quickly to contain my yelling; after all, I was not the crazy bitch that everyone had made me out to be. I was upset about my grandson. If what Stephen had said was true, I needed to know. This was killing me, and no one was willing to discuss anything with me.

The room I was in was frigid. I wrapped a blanket around me before getting off the bed. It was a twin bed and was surprisingly comfortable. A rocking chair was in the room, along with two long bookshelves full of books. There was no TV, no window. A fluffy yellow rug covered most of the floor, and the walls were painted a bright green. Inspirational quotes were scripted on the walls; I assumed they were there to inspire people like me who supposedly needed help. Well, I didn't need help. What I needed was a doctor. My back had been hurting ever since Stephen dragged me down those steps. I couldn't believe what he had done. I was his mother, and I couldn't wait to tear into his ass whenever I got out of here.

With the blanket still around me, I walked to the door to push a button next to it. It was there to buzz the nurses for assistance, and shortly after I pushed it, a nurse came into my room. I'd had a few altercations with her already, only because I didn't appreciate the way she spoke to me. She was sloppy and fat. Cheeks were always red, and her white uniform was too tight. Her ankles looked like they had been baking in an oven, and her blond hair was in a messy bun on her head.

"What do you want?" she said with a snippy tone.

"What I want is to call my son. I haven't been able to speak to anyone, and I'm sure that's against the rules around here."

"Your son's name is not on your call list. I told you that before, but you refuse to listen."

"Aren't I the one responsible for creating my own call list? I should know who I want to speak to, shouldn't I?"

"Look, lady. I'm just following orders around here. There is no one on your call list, so you can't use the phones. Now, is there anything else?"

"Yes. I'm starving, and I would like a juicy steak, a potato, and some buttery Texas toast. A glass of wine would be nice too. I'm sure with the money my son is paying to keep me in this place, that kind of meal should be possible."

She laughed and shook her head. "No, it's not. But dinner will be served in about ten minutes. If you would like to join the others in the lounging area, feel free. It's better than being cooped up in here, talking to yourself all day."

"I haven't been talking to myself, and there is nothing that you can say or do to label me as crazy. I will join the others for dinner, but before I return to this room, can you please raise the temperature? It's cold in here."

"It feels just fine to me."

"That's because you have a mass of fat on you keeping you warm. And spray something refreshing in here too. A real bad odor came in with you, and it's going to take something strong to get that awful smell out of here."

The nurse stood with a smirk on her face, pretending not to be moved by my harsh words.

"Go have dinner, sweetie. When you come back, this room will be to your satisfaction."

"It better be."

I left the room. Unlike some of the other *patients* in here, I didn't have to be escorted around. I walked around freely, but there was no door through which I could exit the building. All the doors were locked. The windows were bolted. Security could be seen everywhere, and the busiest place in here was the lounging area, where many of the patients ate, played games, and talked. I hadn't spent much time in that area, only because I had been trying to stay to myself. But the truth was, it was getting pretty lonely in that room. I needed to converse with someone, and maybe someone knew something about what was happening at the White House.

Right before I entered the lounging area, I saw a man standing next to the double doors, facing the wall. I wasn't sure what he was doing, until I got close enough and heard him counting.

"One thousand and six, one thousand and seven, one thousand and eight . . ."

"Mr. Jenkins," a male nurse said, heading toward us. "It's time to go back to your room. Stop counting bumps on the walls, because there are no more."

Mr. Jenkins ignored the nurse and kept counting. The nurse didn't appreciate being ignored, so he yanked Mr. Jenkins's arm and pulled him in another direction. I started to intervene, but Mr. Jenkins laughed loudly and kept on counting. The only thing that silenced him was the nurse clamping his hand over Mr. Jenkins's mouth. He bit the nurse's hand, and that caused me to laugh and mosey on into the lounging area to mind my business.

A food buffet was to the right in the room, and servers were there to dish out food to the individuals waiting in line. There were numerous round tables in the center of the room, and several huge windows allowed bright light to come in. A few security guards were here and there, so were several nurses and doctors, who were tending to patients. The room was rather noisy, and when I said there was a bunch of crazy-looking folks lurking around, I wasn't lying. Stephen was going to pay for this.

But until I could get out of here, I had to eat. I waited in line to get my food, and after being served honey ham, a few pieces of chicken, mashed potatoes, and corn bread, I found the nearest table and took a seat. Two other people were sitting there. They smiled and watched me as I started to eat. I guess they knew I would frown. The chicken was cold, the ham had too many pieces of fat, and the corn bread tasted like cake with no sugar. I pushed the plate away from me, causing the frail white woman across from me to laugh.

"You shouldn't come here to eat. The only reason you should come here is to play bingo," she said.

The other lady at the table waved her hands wildly in the air. "Yay, bingo. Let's play bingo."

The bingo cards were placed on the table. I told them I didn't feel like playing, but a card was still placed in front of me. Red chips were spread on the table, and before I knew it, the lady across from me started calling out numbers.

"B-five, B-thirteen," she said, looking at the numbers on her card. She was cheating, so I pushed my card away from me. She opened her mouth wide, looking offended. "You don't want to play?" she asked.

"Not with cheaters. No thank you."

She pouted, then crossed her arms in front of her. "I . . . I'm not cheating."

"Yes you are. You're calling off numbers from your own card. Of course you're going to win."

"No I'm not. Why are you lying on me?" she replied.

I didn't have time to argue with this bitch over a stupid bingo game. It wasn't that serious, but for her, I guess it was, because she started crying and pointing at me.

"She . . . she's lying on me, and she won't play with me. Why won't you play with me?"

The other lady reached over to console the crying woman. Both of them mean mugged me, as if I had really done something wrong.

"She doesn't want to play with us, because she's a mean woman, just like her grandson was. You are not better than us, lady, and I . . . I know who you are," said the lady who was doing the consoling.

This woman, who appeared to have the most sense, now had my attention. The other one kept crying about my refusal to play bingo.

"What do you know about my grandson? More to the point, what do you know about me?"

The stupid heifer stuck her tongue out at me. My blood was boiling. The crying woman started to throw a fit about the stupid bingo game, causing many people in the room to look in our direction.

"She won't play!" she shouted and pounded her fist on the table. She was hollering as if I had just stabbed her with a knife. Tears poured down her face; she was so mad that she started throwing the red chips and cards at me.

"Macy!" one of the nurses shouted. "Stop that now! She doesn't have to play bingo with you! Find someone who wants to play."

Macy had lost it. She was on the floor now, kicking and screaming over a doggone bingo game. The only way they could get her to settle down was by injecting her with a needle. She foamed at the mouth, and while several people stood over her, she gazed at the ceiling without blinking. She was carried out of the room by people who didn't seem to have her best interests at heart. This was horrible. *Maybe I should have just played the damn game. There was no way for me to stand another day of this.*

"Look at what you did," the other woman growled at me. I was still trying to find out what she knew. "You're a mean, vicious woman. Just like your whole family. Ugly, hateful people who all deserve what your grandson got."

Her words stung, but I remained calm, just to see if she would tell me more. "We're not that bad, but we do have problems. As for my grandson, he's okay. I'm positive that he is, but if you know something that I don't, please tell me."

She started to laugh. And while cackling loudly, she slapped her leg. Within seconds, she calmed down, then leaned in closer to whisper, "What I know is, he's in hell. In hell, where he belongs." She sat back and started laughing again. This time, she clamped her hand over her mouth, as if she couldn't control her laughter.

I wanted to jump across the table and beat her ass. My heart was racing. I refused to accept what Stephen had said and what this woman was now telling me. I needed to go back to my room to think this through and come up with a quick plan to get out of here. With that in mind, I rushed out of the lounging area and hurried back to my room. The second I opened the door, I realized that the room had turned even colder. Raynetta was sitting on my bed, paging through a magazine. A smile was on her face, but my expression was flat.

"Hey, Mama," she said, closing the magazine. "How are you doing? You don't look so good. Maybe you should come over here and lie down."

While I was in dire need to speak to and see someone from the outside, I damn sure didn't appreciate seeing Raynetta. I hated for her to see me like this, and I pretended as if this place wasn't as bad as it really was.

"I don't look well because I'm tired and I want to see my son. Where is he? And please tell me what really happened to my grandson."

Raynetta got off the bed. She walked up to me with something in her eyes I had never seen before. Maybe it was the look of victory.

"You did your best to destroy my marriage, but I came to tell you that you failed. I can't believe that I stand here feeling so sorry for you today, and the last thing I wanted to do was tell you that your grandson is no longer alive. Because of your actions, you missed the funeral. You have no idea how much hurt you caused Stephen, and I hope that you take the next week, months, or years that you'll be in here to reflect on the damage you've caused. I'll be the only one visiting you, and I will determine when I feel as if you've learned your lesson. So think before you speak. And never, my dear mammy-in-law, never bite the hand that will feed you, going forward."

After I heard about Joshua from Raynetta, things started to sink in slowly. But no matter what, she wasn't going to control me.

"The only things you'll be feeding around here are the birds. Stephen is not going to leave me in here much longer, and I—"

She cut me off by wagging her finger from side to side in front of my face. "Please don't fool yourself. You know how stubborn Stephen can be, and trust me when I say he is not thinking about you. Not after what you did, and this time, you blew it. His focus is on everything else but you. He does have an entire country to run, so I think you'd better figure out how you're going to

adjust to this cozy little room you'll soon be calling home. It's quite a change from your beautiful
house, but I'm sure you'll manage."

I stepped closer to Raynetta, and as I reached
up to slap her face, she grabbed my hand. I
snatched it away from her and spoke through
gritted teeth.

"I will manage, because that's what strong
women do. No matter what situation we're in,
we always find a way. Now, get your trashy ass
out of here, and don't worry about coming back.
Stephen will come for me soon enough. That, my
dear, I am sure of."

Raynetta chuckled as she walked to the door.
This time, I snatched her up by the hair on the
back of her head and pulled on it.

"We'll see who has the last laugh! Good-bye,
bitch. I'll see you soon," I told her.

Without a doubt, Raynetta was stronger than
I was. She loosened my grip on her hair, then
shoved me on the bed. "Maybe you will see
me, and maybe you won't. I'll make that decision, and just so you know, the people around
here will do whatever I tell them to do. You are
in for a big surprise."

Not saying another word, she left the room.
And with Raynetta in control of things, I figured
that I'd better think of something fast to get out
of here.

Later that day, I moseyed around, looking for an out. Security was posted at every door, and the entire place was heavily monitored. The only choice I had was to hurt somebody to get out of here. And right before the new shift came on at three o'clock in the morning, I buzzed the nurses' station and asked one of them to come into my room. She came in and turned on the recessed lighting so that it was dim. I pretended as if my back had been bothering me, and considering that I'd been complaining about it all along, the nurse wasn't surprised.

"I'll bring you some pain medicine," she said. "Try to get some rest."

"I'm trying, but it feels like something is stuck in my back. Can you come over here to take a look at it?"

The nurse walked closer to the bed to observe my back. She pressed my spine and asked if she was touching the right spot.

"Not right there. Farther up. I feel a lump or something. Is anything there?"

"I don't see anything. Let me brighten the lights."

As soon as she turned around, I clocked her across the head with a glass shoe that was supposed to keep my books locked in place on the bookshelf. The blow knocked her out and caused her to crash to the floor. The thud was loud, so I had to hurry up, strip her clothes off, and put them on me. I also needed her badge. Her glasses helped me disguise myself even more. Wasting no time, I eased out of the room, hoping that the hallway was clear. It was. There were a few nurses behind a workstation at the far end of the hall. I had to go that way in order to exit the building.

Slightly nervous, I turned my head and didn't dare look in their direction. Down the hall I went, and from a distance, I could see several staff members changing shifts. Some were coming in, while others were going out. A security guard was there, saying hello as well as good-bye. And as I approached him, thankfully, his head was turned in the other direction. We never even made eye contact, and before I knew it, I was able to suck in a heap of the fresh air outside.

President of the United States,

Stephen C. Jefferson

The Millennials Summit truly lifted my spirits. It was a joy to sit among so many intelligent young adults from all backgrounds who seemed eager and ready for the future. I enjoyed hearing some of their ideas, and I provided the best advice that I could to them. I hadn't laughed in quite some time, and each and every seminar was full of excitement. Everyone was tuned in, even the media, who followed me everywhere I went. I conducted plenty of interviews, and at the end of the first day, it was refreshing finally to hear some positive words being spoken about me on the news.

"The president has these young people fired up," one reporter said. "The energy in every room was sky high. It has been a long time since I've attended a summit like this one. I interviewed a young lady earlier who was beaming about being here. She referred to it as a life-changing experience, and this is what she had to say about the president."

The TV screen switched to the interview.

"On a scale from one to ten, how would you rate the president's performance today and his overall performance as the president?" the reporter asked.

"On a scale from one to ten, I give his performance today a twenty. He was so down to earth, and his corny jokes made all of us laugh. The advice he gave us was helpful in so many ways, and I was totally shocked because he seemed so different. He seems much more aggressive and non-approachable when you see him on TV. But in person, he's the real deal. As for his overall performance as president, I'll give him a seven or eight. I have some issues with the new executive orders he put in place, and I wish he would reach across the aisle more to work with Congress. If he did that, I would probably give him a nine or ten."

"I'm sure he appreciates your input," said the reporter. "I'm also glad that you're having a good time. What other plans do you and some of the other attendees have?"

The young lady went on to speak about her plans for tonight and tomorrow. I did appreciate her comments, even though not many people knew that some of our congressional leaders had flat-out refused to work with me. Standing by and doing nothing didn't work for me. That was why I would probably go down in history as the president who signed the most executive orders ever. According to the statistics compiled by American Presidency Project, Franklin Roosevelt issued 3,522 executive orders during his presidency. Obama issued the fewest, between 147 and 151. Many had accused him of issuing more executive orders than any other president, but I would own that title and would do so with great pride.

Surely, lawsuits would be filed, because the truth was, there were limitations to what I could actually do as president. I had overstepped, but I didn't care. I had to send a message to America, and that message was, "Enough is enough." I expected the Supreme Court to get involved and make some crucial decisions. But I was in a very good position. I would have to appoint the next Supreme Court justice, and as I'd said before, some shit was about to change.

Things had settled down for the day, and after tomorrow, I was heading to Syria, Iraq, and then Afghanistan. There was a substantial number of troops on the ground, simply because many terrorist organizations had been brewing there for years. I was looking forward to going there, especially since I knew that our efforts to go after some of the leaders had picked up. I was being briefed on a regular basis about a very sticky situation in Syria. If things went according to plan, I would soon have my wish.

Michelle's news organization had come to cover the summit one day before my arrival. I was glad to see her well and working again. After my speech the other day, she'd come after me to find out how I'd been doing. She'd also asked if I would call her so we could catch up. Knowing that she would be here, I'd invited her to dinner with me. Nothing too private, but I was sure that the Secret Service would keep the people around us to a minimum.

With a soft blue Ralph Lauren oxford shirt tucked neatly in my dark stonewashed Levi's, I sat on the bed to put on my brown leather shoes. My face was already shaved cleanly, and I was proud about the silky glow of my brown skin. My cologne was on point, my mood was at the right level, and my wedding ring was still on my finger. I twirled it around my finger, thinking about Raynetta. In no way would she approve of me having dinner with Michelle, and I was almost 100 percent positive that my outing would get back to her. I couldn't say that I wouldn't care, because deep down, I knew I would. I just didn't want to think about Raynetta right now. She had taken me to a level that had left me speechless, and I still wasn't sure how to deal with her lies. I pushed our issues to the back of my mind. Since I was already late, I headed to the dining room, where I assumed Michelle awaited me.

Sure enough, when I arrived at the dining room, Michelle was already there. She was way more dressed up than I was, and the tan, silky dress she wore showed a nice portion of her flawless chocolate skin. Her dress was strapless. I could see the way it had melted on her perfect curves as she sat in the chair. Her head was full of natural curls that barely touched the top of her shoulders. With her perfectly arched brows and her light makeup on, there was no denying that she was simply beautiful. I knew that I was putting myself in a bad situation this evening. I could've just stayed in my room and gotten some work done. Also could've joined some of the young adults I'd met earlier who tried to convince me to have pizza with them. Instead, there I was with Michelle, visualizing in my mind what would ultimately happen tonight. She already had me to a point where there was no turning back.

The dimly lit dining room was pretty quiet. There were only three other groups occupying tables. A couple of people were at the bar, and Secret Service agents were nearby. Michelle didn't see me coming. Her head was down; she appeared to be occupied with a notepad. When her pen rolled away from the pad, that was when she looked up and saw me. Her hazel eyes were tranquilizing. The same could be said for her smile. She searched me from head to mid-section to toe. I didn't have to inquire about what was on her mind.

"You are ten minutes late, Mr. President. How dare you keep me waiting?" she teased.

"Forgive me," I said, bending over to kiss her cheek. "I was in the process of wrapping up an important phone call."

"All is forgiven. I'm glad you're here, and I'm delighted that you asked me to join you."

"You're welcome. I just couldn't think of a better way to end this amazing day."

I took a seat, and without any hesitation, Michelle and I jumped right into a spirited conversation.

"I'm having so much fun here," she said. "I miss my kids, but they're at home with the sitter. I noticed that you're having a good time as well. The people around here can't stop talking about you."

I blushed, feeling good about that. "Well, what can I say? I tend to have that effect on people once they get to know me."

Michelle laughed. "You got that right. I won't dispute that, because you've certainly had an effect on me. You helped me get through some tough times, and when I look back on my long relationship with my husband, I can't help but to think how stupid I was for staying with that man."

"I'm glad you're better, but you weren't stupid. Like most people, you just wanted your marriage to work."

"Yes, I did, but this is a new day. What about you, though? How's your marriage these days? Are you still trying to get it to work?"

Before I answered, the waiter came to the table. Our food had already been prepared, as well as inspected.

"Dinner will be served soon, Mr. President. Would either of you like something to drink, such as an alcoholic beverage?"

"No, thank you," I said. "I don't drink, but the lady may want something."

The waiter turned to Michelle.

"I'll have a glass of white chardonnay. And if you don't mind, can you please put my salad dressing on the side, instead of on top of my salad?" she said.

"No problem. Let me know if you need any-thing else."

The room was so dim that the waiter took a minute to light a candle that was in the center of the table. Then he walked off, and we resumed our conversation.

"To answer your question, my marriage is in the same condition that it has always been in. I can't say anything other than that, and to be honest, I prefer not to discuss that right now," I told Michelle.

"I prefer not to, either, so let me change the subject. I was saddened to hear about your son. How have you been able to cope with that whole issue?"

I shrugged. Didn't want to go there, either. "That's another subject I prefer not to discuss."

"Okay. Then tell me what we should talk about. I'll follow your lead, and just so you know, I'm happy to do that."

I looked at Michelle through the flame at the top of the candle. My mind traveled to the last time I'd had sex with her—it was, indeed, a perfect ten. Her lips worked wonders, and just the mere thought of her riding me made my steel react. I wiped down my face, then sat up straight.

"I think we should talk about us," I said.

"What about us?"

"About why I keep finding myself in your presence, even when this is not where I need to be."

She quickly fired back. "I beg to differ. I think that we keep finding ourselves in the presence of each other because this is exactly where we should be."

The waiter came back with Michelle's wine. He also had our salads. Mine was drizzled with a vinaigrette dressing, and Michelle's dressing was on the side, just as she had asked. After the waiter poured her wine, she took a sip, thanked the waiter, and then waited for me to respond. I did after the waiter walked away.

"No. I would have to disagree with you. In no way are we exactly where we should be. I can think of a place that is much better than this."

She looked inquisitively at me while sipping more wine. "Like I said before, I'm willing to follow your lead wherever it takes us. I trust your judgment."

"Never trust a married man or his judgment. That can get you in trouble. But following my lead is perfectly fine with me, because I suggest that we push these salads aside and save dinner for another time."

She glanced at her salad, then shifted her eyes back to me. "So, you're not hungry anymore? Is that what you're saying?"

"I'm real hungry. Starving, to be exact. But in no way will food satisfy me."

"Not only am I with you on that, but I'm also so far ahead of you. Give me two minutes to go to the restroom, and then meet me by the elevator so we can go upstairs to my room."

"You go ahead and handle your business. I'll meet you upstairs in about ten or fifteen minutes. I need to check in with the Secret Service, and then I assure you that we will both eat."

Michelle finished off her glass of wine before standing to leave. The dress looked even better when she stood. Even the men sitting far away from us had to turn their heads to take a double look. Sexy as ever, she walked off in her strappy high heels. Her walk alone made my muscle react. Why did she have to be so damn sexy?

Not wanting to waste time, I lifted my hand, gesturing for Levi to come to the table. He stood next to me.

"Has anybody important been trying to reach me?" I asked him.

"Nope. Believe it or not, things are pretty quiet."

"I can't believe that, and what you're saying is, I'm good to disappear for a few hours, right?"

"You're good, but never too good, if you know what I mean."

"I assume you're referring to Raynetta."

"Exactly. But you're the boss, and the boss can do what he wishes, whether I'm okay with it or not."

"So, what are you implying? That you're not okay with some of the things I do or have done?" I quizzed.

Levi didn't hold back. "No, I'm not okay with everything you do, only because situations like this can set you back. You don't need setbacks. You're a much better president when your eyes are on the prize, you're focused, and you're with the woman you love. Temptation is a mutha, and I'll be the first man to admit that in no way would I ever walk away from a woman like Michelle. But you're not me. You're *better* than me. That's why you're the president and I'm not."

I stood, then reached out my hand to shake Levi's. "I appreciate the kind words, but here's the deal. The woman I love is a liar, temptation feels good, and setbacks can be setups for good things to come. And even though I am better than you, I still can't see myself walking away from this opportunity tonight. Follow me upstairs. If you need me, you know where I'll be."

Levi walked with me to the elevator, and when it opened, several young women were inside.

"Oh my God!" one of the women shouted. "It's the president! Would you mind taking a picture with us? *Please*."

Giddy as ever, they all seemed thrilled to see me. I had no problem taking pictures with them, even if it stalled me for ten more minutes.

"Thank you, Mr. President. You are freaking awesome. Have a good night, okay?" said the same woman when the photo session was over.

"You all do the same. And no more drinking. I smell it, and I don't want you all out there drinking and driving."

They all looked at each other, laughing and giggling. Some appeared embarrassed too.

"Oh, no, sir," one of the women said. "We wouldn't do that. We plan to walk to wherever we go tonight. Thanks again for the pictures."

They laughed and walked off. I got on the elevator with Levi, and as soon as the doors closed, he looked at me.

"When is the last time you spoke to Raynetta or your mother?" he asked.

I shook my head, well aware of what he was doing. "I know you're trying to make me think about Raynetta, but it's not going to work. Bringing up my mother won't work, either, but when you get a chance, be sure to check on her for me. I want to make sure she hasn't attempted to burn the institution down."

Levi laughed, and when the elevator came to a stop and opened, we got off. He stood by the door to Michelle's room while I lightly tapped on it. She opened the door, wearing a beige silk and lace bra and matching hipster panties. I didn't even bother to look at Levi before I entered the room and shut the door behind me. Within a matter of seconds, she was wrapped in my arms and our lips were locked together.

"How did I ever get so lucky?" she said between severely wet and juicy kisses. She backed her head away from mine, then gazed into my eyes. There was no breathing room between us, and as she continued to speak, my hands squeezed her soft body and roamed. "You have no idea what you do to me, Stephen. I can't pretend anymore. I am so in love with you, and it is my wish that we can one day be together. Tell me there is hope. Please tell me. It is something I am dying to hear from you."

In the moment, I couldn't say anything. My steel had grown to great lengths, her body against mine felt perfect, and as I had already begun to touch the super-wet crotch section of her panties, my brain was focused on the feel of her insides. I didn't want to discuss love. Wasn't trying to be hopeful, but I did care about Michelle's feelings. I knew they were strong, but

I hadn't thought we were at a point where she wanted more than . . . this.

"I can't," I said. "I can't tell you what you want to hear, because—"

She placed her finger on my lips. "Fine. It's okay. You don't have to say anything right now. Just hold me. Make love to me, dip your tongue inside of me, and kiss me all over like you do so well."

I damn sure wanted to, but I paused for a moment to speak. "I don't want you to feel as if I'm using you. I'm not, but I just can't—"

She silenced my words, this time with another juicy kiss. "Use me. I don't care. This moment in time with you is good enough. Take me . . . take all of me to the bedroom. Have your way with me. I'm all yours."

Michelle started to remove my clothes. She could see how reluctant I was to help, and that prompted her to speed things along. She removed her bra and panties, and as she stood naked, she extended her hand to mine. My shirt was off; my jeans were unbuttoned and were barely hanging on my ass. I followed her into the bedroom, and as she lay back on the comfortable-looking king bed, I removed my jeans, then got on top of her. With her soft legs wrapped around my back, I gazed into her eyes, which weakened me by the second. Unable to stare at her and say what I wanted to, I turned my head to the side.

"You deserve so much better than this," I said truthfully. "I do want to make love to you so badly, but we can never have more than this."

She turned my head to make me look at her. "I don't care. This will have to be enough for now. Maybe one day you'll change your mind, and then you'll understand why we keep finding ourselves in situations like this."

I knew why, but I didn't tell her. I knew that I had love for only one woman, but Raynetta was a woman I didn't trust. I didn't feel as if she really had my back, like she said she did, but regardless, when all was said and done, Michelle would be the one who was severely hurt. With that in the forefront of my mind, I removed her legs from around me and lay next to her in bed. For the first time ever, she shot me a look that said she was pissed.

"What are you doing?" she said. "I said I could handle this, didn't I? I regret telling you how I felt. I should have kept my mouth shut. Did my words scare you?"

"No, but they woke me up. J-just lie back and let me hold you. I want to hold you, if that's okay with you."

Michelle didn't hold back; she was very upset with me. She got off the bed and stood next to me. "No, it's not okay. I was so hyped about seeing you again, and I don't want to hear about what I deserve. I know what I deserve, and that's you. Even if it's not all that I . . ."

As she rambled on, I pulled her back on the bed and held her in my arms like I wanted to. She attempted to move, but my hold on her was tight. I kissed her forehead, then wrapped her legs together with mine.

"One day you're going to thank me for this, because if we proceed, I'm going to hurt you in ways that you never thought were possible. I don't want to do that, Michelle, and having the greatest sex in the world won't spare us the headaches of tomorrow. I said you deserve better, and I meant it. I apologize for getting your juices flowing, and believe me when I say that this is not easy."

She pouted. "My juices are doing more than flowing. You need to go down there and see for yourself what's really going on."

"I'll take your word for it, because if I go down there, I may have to scrap everything I said and shoot for being a better man on another day."

It pleased me to hear Michelle laugh. She relaxed in my arms while laying her head on my chest and softly rubbing it.

"Raynetta is a lucky woman. I still think I am too, simply because it must take a special kind of woman to be lying here with you. I enjoy our conversations, and if we have to resort solely to that, I guess I can live with it."

"First of all, I'm the one who is lucky. Lucky to have you as a friend, and so lucky that you didn't just throw me out of here," I said.

"The only person I'm going to throw out of here is myself. I need to go take a long cold shower. There is no way in hell I'm going to lie naked with you all night and not attempt to get me some. You may be strong, Mr. President, but my flesh, all of it, is very weak when I'm around you."

Michelle moved away from me and got out of bed. Seeing moistness between her thighs aroused me again; she wasn't the only one who needed a cold shower.

"Will you still be here when I get out of the shower?" she asked.

"I hate to say it, but no. I need a cold shower too, and don't even think about asking me to join you."

She started to tease me by massaging her breasts together and touching her shaved, succulent-looking pussy, which was already leaking. "I was going to ask you, after all. You did enjoy our bath the last time we were together, didn't you? We weren't even completely intimate, but you did have fun, right?"

I did, but I didn't answer her. I got off the bed, turned to look away from her. "I'm not looking at you, and I'm not listening to you, either. The only things I'm looking for are my clothes."

Michelle rushed in front of the bed and snatched up my clothes. She held them in her hands and threatened to open the sliding door to the balcony and throw my clothes over it if I wouldn't watch her tease show.

"Not my clothes. Please don't do that. Besides, my wallet is inside of my jeans. In no way do I want to lose that."

"That would be so cruel of me, but you know I wouldn't toss your wallet. As for your clothes, well, unless you watch me or change your mind about the shower, over the rail they go."

I seriously thought Michelle was playing. But right after she tossed my wallet to me and I bent over to get it, she slid the door to the balcony open, then threw my clothes over the rail. Afterward, she swiped her hands together. A smile was on her face, but I stood there pretty damn stunned.

"That's what you get for getting me all stirred up tonight. I forgive you, and now we're even."

"Even? I wouldn't exactly call what you just did even."

I charged at her and quickly threw her over my shoulder. She playfully kicked her legs around, and when we entered the bathroom, I turned the water in the shower on cold. I placed her inside the shower stall and held her at a distance as the cold water drenched her.

"Now we're even," I said, watching her attempt to move away from the water. She couldn't; all she could do was laugh.

"Okay, okay, you got me. But you still have to leave this room with no clothes on. Good luck with that."

I released her arms, then snatched two long towels from the towel rack. I tossed one to Michelle, and the other I wrapped around my waist. As she wiped herself off, I kissed her cheek.

"Good night," I said. "I need to go. Thanks for the good time, as usual."

"You're welcome. And be safe on your trip overseas. I'll be praying for you."

I told Michelle I would do the same, and as soon as I exited her room, I came face-to-face with Levi. He cocked his head back while looking at me with the towel around my waist.

"I'll explain later. Cover me and get me to my room as quickly as possible."

With no questions asked, Levi did just that. I was so thankful to him. He was the only person in the entire world that I trusted.

President's Mother,

Teresa Jefferson

I was so glad to get the hell out of that place. It would be a cold day in hell before I would ever go back there. I wanted to go straight to the White House and let Stephen have it, but going there would probably lead to him putting me somewhere that I couldn't escape from. As for Raynetta, the nerve of her coming to where I was, thinking that she had some kind of control over me. That was laughable. I hated that woman so much, and I figured she and Stephen had worked things out. In no way did she seem like they hadn't.

Either way, I had to get to St. Louis and find out what was going on with my grandson. I had already called Ina, but she hadn't answered her phone. I didn't bother to search newspapers or listen to the media—they were known for lying about shit. Instead, I caught a bus that got me close enough to my house where I could walk the rest of the way. My feet were tired, but Lord knows I felt so relieved when I walked through the door and saw . . . saw that most of my furniture was gone. My house was damn near empty. Clothes were missing too, and the only person who could have been responsible for this was Stephen. His intentions must've been to put me away for good.

Damn him, I thought. I couldn't wait to let his ass have it. Yes, I had done wrong, but this was ridiculous. He knew that my actions were out of love. Love that was about to turn into a whole lot of hate.

I went downstairs, where I had packed away some bags of old clothing. At least those were still there. I found a baggy pair of jeans and a sweater that would keep me warm, since it was chilly outside. After taking a shower, I changed clothes, then slicked my salt-and-pepper hair back with gel. I didn't have time to jazz myself up—looking good was the last thing on my mind. I headed to my garage and was happy to see that my cars were still there. My Mercedes had more gas, so I hopped into it and hit the road.

During the long drive back to St. Louis, Joshua was on my mind. I surely hoped that Ina would be able to laugh and tell me that someone within the government was playing a horrible trick on Stephen. That he had been lied to. That we all had been lied to, and this all was a joke or a scheme to get back at Stephen. That was my wish, but as I continued to call Ina's and Joshua's cell phones, no one ever answered.

Almost fourteen hours later, I pulled into Ina's driveway, where her car was parked, along with another car. The inside of the house looked rather dark, but as I walked to the door, I could see a light on in the kitchen. I knocked on the door, then rang the doorbell. Minutes later, Ina's boyfriend came to the door. He was tall, kind of handsome, but too thin for my taste. He opened the door, squinting and frowning, as if I had shown up at the wrong time.

"Is Ina here?" I said. "And where is Joshua?"

His brows arched inward; he looked perplexed by my questions. "Ina is in the bedroom. Please come inside."

I walked inside and scanned the living room, my gazing traveling from one wall to the other. It was messy, to say the least, and the smell of funky socks tore into my nostrils. I could see a pair of tennis shoes next to the sofa. Those stinky shoes had to belong to Ina's boyfriend, because Joshua would never wear shoes that smelled like that.

Finally, Ina came into the living room, wearing a silk robe. She tightened the belt around her waist before turning on the light so she could see. I remained by the door and wasted no time asking her about my grandson.

"Where is he, Ina, and why haven't you all been answering your phones?"

"I'll let the two of you talk," her boyfriend said before walking away.

Ina cleared her throat. "Wha . . . what do you mean by where is Joshua? Don't stand there and pretend that you don't know. Where have you been? I can't believe you were that upset with me."

A sharp pain rushed to my heart. "I don't know anything. What am I supposed to know, Ina? And please tell me that what Stephen said isn't true. Somebody lied to him, didn't they?"

Ina moved her head from side to side. Her chest started to heave in and out. Catching me off guard, she rushed up to hold me.

"Stephen didn't lie," she cried. "Joshua is dead. He is no longer here, and it's all my fault. I . . . I thought that you knew and that you missed his funeral because you were upset with me."

I quickly shoved Ina away from me. "Get the hell off of me with that nonsense! I can't believe you've fallen for the bullshit too. How could you believe such a thing? What in the hell is wrong with y'all stupid asses? If these people tell y'all the sky is pink, y'all will believe them! Joshua is not dead, Ina! Trust me, he is not!"

Ina's whole face was scrunched. She charged across the room and snatched a piece of paper off the coffee table. She reached out to hand it to me. I saw that it was Joshua's obituary.

"I don't know what has gotten into you," she said, smacking her tears away. "But I buried my child several days ago. He is not alive, and I'm sorry if you have a problem accepting it."

I snatched the obituary, and sure enough, there it all was, as plain as day. My chest hurt like hell. It felt as if someone was pressing down hard on my shoulders, I wasn't able to stand. I staggered over to a chair and plopped down in it.

"This can't be true. Not my Joshua! There is no way I will ever accept this."

"How do you think I feel?" Ina said. "I don't want to accept it, either, and I would never, ever lie to you about something like this."

"I don't know who is lying, but somebody is. I can feel it. And if Joshua is dead, what in the hell are you doing back there in your room, fucking? Did you see his body? You still haven't said what happened. That's why I don't believe none of this shit!"

"What I do in my house is none of your business. I refused to look at Joshua's body because of the condition it was in. A bomb went off and killed him. I'm sure you wouldn't have wanted to see him like that, either, and in an effort not to go off on you, Teresa, I want you to go. I don't have time for your insults. I'm going through—"

I stood and darted my finger at her. "I don't give a damn what you're going through, and if you're so damn hurt, why are you laying on your back with a low-life, broke nigga's dick in you? That damn well won't lift your spirits. I intend to get to the bottom of all of this, and when I do, you and Stephen are going to pay for lying to me. As for leaving, I'm not leaving until I see my grandson. What in the hell have you done with him?"

I stormed away from Ina to go to Joshua's bedroom. The door was closed, and when I flung it open, he was not there. His room, however, was neater than I had ever seen it. His bed was neatly made, his trophies were on display, the carpet was clean, and his multiple pairs of tennis shoes were lined up against the wall.

"You have lost your damn mind," Ina said, crying even more. "This has been hard for all of us, and I won't allow you to come in here and do this, Teresa. You have to leave. Now!"

I was so taken aback by her disrespect. She should have known better. It was *my* money that had purchased this house, *my* money that helped her pay bills, *my* money that provided everything for Joshua. She had some damn nerve. I snatched that bitch up by her arm, then pushed her against the door.

"How dare you get snippy with me after all I've done for you? I don't know what you've done with my grandson, but you'd better find him quick!"

Just then, Ina's boyfriend came down the hallway, displaying a tight face. He pulled Ina away from me and held her in his arms.

"She told you to leave, so get out. I don't care what you've done for her. You will not speak to her this way and treat her as you wish. Joshua is dead. He is gone, and Ina is not responsible for what happened to him."

I put my hand on my hip, looked at this pathetic fool, who didn't even have good credit. "If she's not responsible, then maybe you are. Things are finally starting to click, and now I get it. When were the two of you going to call for ransom money? Whatever the amount is, just tell me. Let's stop with the games, and tell me how much money I need to give you two idiots to see my grandson again."

Ina released herself from her boyfriend's arms. "I'm going to go call the police. I . . . I can't listen to this anymore. She has lost her damn mind!"

"Yes, baby, please go call them," he said. "I don't want to hurt this woman, but unless you get out of here, I most certainly will."

"Go ahead, you stupid bitch. Call the police," I snarled. "Let them see whose name is on this house, 'cause when they discover who that is, I'm going to have the pleasure of throwing both of y'all out of here."

Ina halted her steps. She knew who had the upper hand. It damn sure wasn't her.

"Teresa, look. These past several days have been the worst days of my life. You, of all people, know how much I loved my son. I don't know why you've come here to hurt me like this. Your behavior makes no sense to me at all," she said.

"And what I've heard doesn't make sense to me, either. Joshua didn't know anything about building bombs. He hadn't become radicalized. He was too damn smart for that, and he would never follow a bunch of damn fools aiming to kill people. I'm so disappointed in you and Stephen, especially you, because you've lived with Joshua all his life. You know what kind of kid he is, and for you to accept this is just . . . just unbelievable to me."

"I have to accept it, because it's true. I failed him, Teresa. I wasn't paying attention like I was supposed to be doing. He got with the wrong people, and they brainwashed him. The last time you were here, you saw how Joshua was. He was different, and the reason why he was always on his computer was that he had connected with a terror organization."

I just shook my head as I listened to this foolishness. "When you take me to his grave, dig it up, and show me his body, I'll believe you. You're the one who is brainwashed, and I am so disgusted with all of you. And if by chance there is any truth to what you said, you are the one I blame for this. You've been a terrible mother. I should have gotten custody of Joshua from the day he was born."

This time, Ina came after me. As she swung wildly to hit me, her boyfriend held her waist to pull her away from me.

"I've had enough of you!" she yelled. She couldn't reach me, so she tried to spit on me and missed. "Go! Now! You can have this damn house! I don't even want to be here anymore! Just go and never bring your evil self back here again!"

Ina's boyfriend backed her up into the kitchen and advised her to stay in there. "Have a seat and don't move. Let me handle this, okay?" He turned to me and sighed. "We will be out of here by tomorrow. Just leave us in peace. Where Joshua was laid to rest is in his obituary. Go see him for yourself. This is no joke. All of us are heartbroken."

"I don't want to see his grave site. I want to see his body," I insisted.

"Unfortunately, Ina will not be digging it up. And no other person has the right to do it, not even your son. Allow Joshua to rest in peace. Please."

"Peace, my ass," I muttered. "You all have not heard the last of this, and in regards to this house, feel free to stay here for as long as you want. I wouldn't let my dead dog stay in here, and if you really want to help Ina, help her clean up in here, get a job, and pay some damn bills around here."

Without saying another word, I walked out. Got in my car and drove to the Hilton, where I spent the night. I couldn't get Joshua off my mind. And while I wanted so badly to believe that he was alive, I also couldn't help but to wonder if, indeed, he wasn't. I was crushed. And, finally, I dropped to my knees, crying hysterically. I had to admit that Ina wasn't the only one who was responsible for this. So was I.

First Lady,

Raynetta Jefferson

While Stephen was away, I kept myself busy with everything from doing interviews on talk shows to feeding the homeless. I did my best to stay calm and not worry so much about Stephen's long trip overseas. I often watched him on TV, and while he was at the Millennials Summit, he seemed happy as ever. He smiled a lot. I guessed that being away from the White House had done him some good. Even while he was with the troops, Stephen looked alive. His words were comforting, and I was extremely proud of my husband.

I regretted that he had been under so much pressure while at home, and there was no doubt that I had contributed to a lot of unnecessary mess. Especially with his mother. I didn't have to go see her, but I did. I couldn't resist seeing the look in her eyes, and knowing that she would be

there for a while made me feel better. I intended
to utilize my time without her around wisely. I
couldn't wait for Stephen to return, and, by then,
hopefully, we'd be able to move on.

Claire and I had just returned from a walk-
athon for women fighting lupus. My body was
sweaty, so I headed to my bedroom to shower
and change. I had made a decision to return Mr.
McNeil's money, so before Claire and I parted
ways, I asked if she would take me to go see
him right after I ate lunch. There was no way
that Alex, my personal Secret Service agent,
would take me there. And for now, I didn't
want Stephen to know about my visit. If I told
him beforehand, he would try to talk me out of
it, especially since he considered Mr. McNeil a
dangerous man. To me, he wasn't dangerous.
He was just a rich, slimy bastard who thought he
owned the world. I was sure he would be happy
to get his money back, and after I returned it, my
hands would be clean. There would be no more
ties; Stephen couldn't be mad about that.

Right after my shower, I went to the dining
room to eat lunch. I had tuna salad, a fruit cup,
and some apple juice. Claire was supposed to
meet me at my office after lunch, but as soon as I
headed there, I saw Alex behind me.

"Do you need to go somewhere else today?"
he asked.

"I do, but you know what? Claire is going to take me, if you don't mind. We'll be gone for only about an hour, and it has been a long time since I've had an opportunity to just go somewhere and chill with a good friend."

"Per the president's order, I am required to take you anywhere you want to go. I don't mind, and I insist."

"Well, I'll call my husband and have him call you. I need some space. A few hours isn't going to hurt, and there are times when I demand my privacy."

"I understand that, but I'm just following orders."

It was a doggone shame that I was going to have to sneak out of here. I hadn't even spoken to Stephen, and even if I called, he would dissuade me from going anywhere without the Secret Service in tow. I entered my office. Claire was already sitting at her desk, waiting for me.

"The briefcase is now in the trunk of my car, and I'm ready to go whenever you are. One question before we go. Did you know that Michelle Peoples was at the Millennials Summit?"

Like always, I shrugged, as if I didn't care. "Nope, but what does that have to do with anything?"

"Nothing, I guess. I just wondered if you knew, that's all."

"I didn't know, but now I do." I quickly changed the subject, even though I felt some kind of way about Michelle being there. "Are you ready to go?"

"I sure am. I'm exhausted from that walk. I hope we'll be able to stop somewhere and get some frozen yogurt."

"Sounds good to me, but we kind of have to sneak out of here. Mr. You Know Who is watching me, so we have to get out of here without him seeing us."

"That's easy. There are plenty of ways to get in and out of the White House without being seen. Just follow me after he moves away from the door."

Almost fifteen minutes later, Alex walked off. Claire and I bolted out the door, and as we cut down a few hallways and made our way to the lower level, we were seen by only a few people, who didn't pay us much attention. When we got to Claire's car, she advised me to get in the trunk and stay there until we passed the security gate.

"Heck no," I said. "What if I just crouch down on the backseat? Don't you have something . . . anything you can throw over me?"

Claire snapped her fingers. "As a matter of fact, I do. Go ahead and get in. I think I may have a parachute that we used for those disabled kids at that circus the other day."

I got in the car, and after Claire covered me with the parachute, we were well on our way. She used her keycard and fingerprint to open the gate and spoke to the guard.

"Have a wonderful day, sir. See you when I get back," she said.

"You too. Drive safely."

She drove off, but I didn't remove myself from the backseat until we were many miles away from the White House.

"That was very uncomfortable," I said, sitting on the front passenger's seat now. "You need to get a new car, because it is very tight back there."

"This car is perfectly fine for little ole me. Now, tell me where to go so I can put the address into my navigation system."

"We're going to Forest Hills North, where the extremely rich live. And no need for navigation, because I know exactly where the house is."

Claire sped off.

On the drive to see Mr. McNeil, I was slightly nervous. I didn't know how he would respond to me returning his money, but this was a start to making things right between me and Stephen.

Besides, who wouldn't be happy to get two million dollars back? I felt as if it was a move in the
right direction, but time would surely tell.

When we arrived at Mr. McNeil's mansion,
Claire parked in the long, curvy driveway. The
house was lit up like it was Christmas, and the
manicured lawn with blooming, colorful flowers
looked beautiful. I turned to Claire, told her to
wait outside for me.

"Are you sure you don't want me to go with
you?" she said.

"No. I shouldn't be long, but if I'm not back in
fifteen or so minutes, call the cops."

We both laughed, but I was serious. I got
out of the car, removed the briefcase from
the trunk, and then made my way to the cas-
tle-like house, which had a double glass door
that offered a view of the inside. The white mar-
ble flooring and arched staircase were breathtaking, as was the immaculate chandelier that
hung above the foyer. I rang the doorbell, and a
few minutes later, a woman who looked to be a
maid appeared at the door. She opened it with
a smile on her face.

"How may I help you?" she said, looking inquisitively at me.

"I'm here to see Mr. McNeil. He's not expect-
ing me, but can you let him know that Raynetta
Jefferson is here to see him?"

"I know very well who you are. You're the first lady. Please come inside. It's a pleasure to meet you."

I smiled, then walked inside. The smell of money and richness hit me, and as my eyes scanned the white-and-black dining room to my left, the maid spoke again.

"I'll tell Mr. McNeil that you're here. I'll be right back," she said.

"Thank you."

I waited in the foyer with the briefcase in my hand. My feet were aching a little in my high heels, and I was glad that I had changed into a pair of comfortable jeans and a blouse. My nervousness had returned, especially when the maid came back and asked me to follow her.

"This way," she said, then led me to the same place I had been before, which was Mr. McNeil's office. She pushed on the tall wooden door and gestured with her hand for me to go inside. I stepped on the plush carpet and immediately saw Mr. McNeil sitting behind his wide wooden desk, an arrogant expression on his face. His beady eyes narrowed, then shifted to the brief-case in my hand.

"I won't be long," I said, moving closer to his desk. "I just wanted to bring this money back to you. It hasn't done me much good at all, and to be honest, I shouldn't have ever taken it."

I laid the briefcase on his desk, and without saying a word, he turned it so that it faced him. He opened it up, glanced at the money, and then closed it.

"It's funny that I used to think you were a smart gal, but I should've known better, because there aren't many smart niggers in this country, period. When I make you a widow, you're going to need that money, so you may as well take it and march your pretty little black ass back out that door and enjoy as much time as you can with that thug at the White House. You people are a fucking joke, and how dare you come to my house without being invited!"

"Your words don't intimidate me one bit, Mr. McNeil, and I'm not going to stoop to your level today," I retorted. "You have your money back, but I want you to be real careful when you talk about doing something to my husband. You don't know what kind of man he really is, and if you keep this up, your wife will be a widow, instead of me."

I turned to walk away, but when I made it to the door and pulled on it, it was locked. I swung around and saw a wide smile on Mr. McNeil's face. He came from around his desk and stood in front of the door.

"I determine when you can leave, and I'm not quite finished with you yet. Before you go, I want you to tell Mr. President that his new executive orders to protect his niggers won't fly. Tell him that any attempt to have me arrested for roughing up his mistress won't work, and that case is on the verge of being dismissed. Let him know that he needs to enjoy the Oval Office while he can, because people in power like me will not allow him to sit his ass in that chair much longer. Also, send him my condolences. What happened to his son was tragic, but he's just one less gang member our society has to worry about."

Showing no fear, I moved within a foot of Mr. McNeil. "I'm not telling Stephen a damn thing, so stop being a coward and go tell him yourself. You won't do that, because you're afraid of my husband. His blackness scares you, and you know who really has the power. You can't even sleep at night, thinking about him. He has you right where he wants you, and I love every bit of it."

Mr. McNeil chuckled and then snatched me up in his arms. For an old man, he was strong. He had a tight grip around my waist, so tight that I couldn't pull away from him.

"The only thing that may keep me up at night is my thoughts of screwing you. I wouldn't mind sticking my dick between those soft, firm breasts of yours, and only God knows what I would do with—"

He covered my mouth with his. I quickly pulled my head back, then spit in that bastard's face and wiped his saliva from my mouth. I then slapped him hard across his face, causing him to release me.

"Don't make me throw up," I yelled with a twisted face. "And don't you ever touch me again! Either you open this door now, or I'm going to scream at the top of my lungs and tear this fancy-ass office up! Now, you pervert, I'm not playing with you!"

Mr. McNeil looked amused, even though he had a red handprint on his face. His bushy brows were raised, and the smirk on his face revealed just how evil he really was. He walked behind his desk, and when he pushed a button, I heard the door click. I cut my eyes at him, then turned on my heels. As I headed to the door this time, I paused when he called out to me.

"Don't be upset with me, sweetheart. You forgot something."

I pivoted to see what it was, and that was when I saw him pick up a blue glass globe and pitch it right at me. I didn't have time to duck. The globe slammed into the side of my face, causing me to stagger. I became dizzy, and just as I was getting ready to fall, Mr. McNeil rushed up to grab me. My vision was blurred, and my head was hurting so badly. I could feel blood trickling down the side of my face, and as he escorted me to the front door, drops of my blood dotted the floor.

"Easy," he said while holding me up and fondling my breasts. "You're going to be *just* fine, especially when you get the hell out of here."

Wobbling, I touched the side of my face, then looked at my bloody hand through blurred vision. I needed help fast, but the only thing I got was shoved on the front porch. Mr. McNeil slammed the door, and since I was not even sure if Claire saw me, I started to crawl my way to the car. What might have been a few minutes later, I heard her voice.

"Oh my God!" she shouted as she helped me off the ground. "What in the hell happened? Did he do this to you?" She helped me into the car and buckled me in on the passenger's side. Claire was in a panic. "Raynetta, speak to me now! Do you need an ambulance?"

I slowly moved my head from side to side. "No," I whispered. "Take me home. I need to get home."

Claire opened her glove compartment and reached for a towel. She pressed it against my face, where there was obviously a deep cut.

"Please," she said. "Let me take you to the hospital. You need stitches. It's the only way the bleeding is going to stop."

I added pressure with the towel, then squeezed my eyes, because the pain was becoming unbearable. But there was no way that I, the first lady, was going to a hospital right now. Everyone would make a big deal about this. I didn't want a scene to be made, so I told Claire to get me to the White House fast. She got in the car and then continuously asked question after question.

"Answer me, please. Did he do this? Are you going to press charges? Are you going to tell the president about this? Are you in pain?"

I ignored Claire, and when we arrived at the White House, she stopped at the security gate. She rushed out of her car and told security that we needed help right away.

"The first lady is hurt," she said, still panicking. "She doesn't want to go to the hospital, but she needs to see a doctor."

I opened the car door and wobbled a little as I tried to stand. The security guard quickly called for help, and within a matter of seconds, several Secret Service agents, including Alex, came rushing toward me. Alex quickly picked me up as they all inquired about what had happened. Before Claire said anything, I hurried to speak.

"A . . . a car jumped in front of us, and when Claire slammed on the brakes, I jerked forward and hit my head. Unfortunately, I wasn't wearing my seat belt."

I was sure that Claire didn't approve of my lie, but I didn't know what else to say. If I told the truth, it wouldn't do any good. Mr. McNeil would lie. I was sure that he would say I went to his house to cause trouble.

"Call her doctor," Alex said before rushing me inside. "And see if someone can get the president on the phone."

I definitely didn't want Stephen to know about this. If I told him what had actually happened, that would send him over the edge. He would lose it, and I would feel horrible for bringing about more drama, especially when he was away, trying to handle business. But right after my doctor stitched up my cut, as I lay in bed, Alex came into the room. A cell phone was in his hand; he extended it to me. I put the phone up to my ear.

"Hello," I said softly.

"What's up?" Stephen replied. "Are you okay?"

It felt so good to hear his voice. "My head hurts a little, but I'm fine."

"That's good to know. I was going to be here for another two days, but I'll cut it short."

"You don't have to do that. I said I was fine. I'll see you when you get here, and just so you know, I missed talking to you."

"We do have a lot to discuss when I get back, but until then, get some rest. I'll see you soon."

Our call ended on that note. I gave the phone back to Alex; he put it in his pocket. As he sat on the bed, he shot me a look that showed much frustration.

"I want to let you know that your little trick from earlier could have gotten me fired. I take my job very seriously, and it was ridiculous for you to pull a stunt like that. You could have been severely injured, you know. From this moment on, you will go nowhere without me."

"I apologize, but you must understand that I need my space sometimes. Claire and I had something very important to do. The last thing I wanted was for you to be tagging along. And as for me not going anywhere without you, whatever. I'll be right here for the next few days, so don't bore yourself by lurking outside of my door."

Alex straightened his glasses, raked his black hair back, and stared at me without saying a word. He was such a nerd, but he was very protective of me, and strong, caring, and . . . cute. He looked as if he wanted to get something off his chest. When I pushed, he said it was nothing.

"Don't hold back. If you want to keep chewing me out, go right ahead and do it. I'm a big girl, and I'm positive that I can take whatever you dish out."

He cut his eyes at me and then stared at me again. "I just don't want you to get hurt, okay? It would really anger me if something happened to you, and just so you know, I think you're a really nice and sweet person."

I smiled and teased him for finally saying something nice to me. "Aw, so you like me now, huh? I thank you for caring, and the last thing I want to do is make you angry. I promise not to leave like that again."

Alex patted my leg, which was underneath the sheet. "Get some rest. And don't watch too much television, because it's not good for you."

I laughed, then asked if he wouldn't mind bringing me some extra pillows so I could prop up my head.

"I'm not your maid," he said while standing at the door. "If you want more pillows, call one of the helpers or go get them yourself."

He shut the door, but in less than five minutes, he came back and threw two fluffy pillows at me.

"There. Don't ask me for anything else until you're ready to play by my rules. I have a feeling that you're not good at keeping promises."

I showed my pearly whites and teased him again. "I'm not, but thanks for the pillows. I did, however, say I was sorry, and I meant it."

Without responding, he closed the door, leaving me at peace. I laid my head on the pillows, hoping that Stephen would come home soon, even though I hadn't requested it.

President of the United States,

Stephen C. Jefferson

My trip to visit the troops was extremely productive. I already knew how brave the men and women who served our country were, but to meet them up close and personal was more than an honor. They were overly excited about my presence at Camp Victory. The entire place was packed, and as I stood at the podium to speak, with a huge American flag waving behind me, I realized how much support I had. Nearly everyone took pictures, and when several soldiers shouted that they loved their president, it damn sure made my day. I signed autographs, took plenty of pictures, and toured as much as I could while I was there.

I had an opportunity to meet with numerous soldiers who had been injured or had lost limbs during combat. It totally impressed me how they had remained so upbeat. After meeting them and seeing how the soldiers lived day by day, I told myself that I would never, ever complain again. I and members of my staff spent several nights in army barracks with the soldiers. We listened to them tell stories about what they had faced during combat, and we also listened to the many concerns they had about being away from their families for too long and about the lack of support they received from the government. The defense budget had been cut over the years, which was another one of those things where I needed Congress to step up.

Due to what had happened with Raynetta, and because I had received a call about my mother leaving the institution, I decided to cut my trip short by one day. There was no telling where my mother was, but I didn't have time to deal with her stupidity. As for Raynetta, I was worried about her. She had sounded as if she was okay, but she was good at putting up a front. After tonight, I figured it would be wise for me to leave, anyway. Things were about to turn real ugly.

But before I left, there was one thing that I had to do. We had received notification from a member of a special forces team who had been on a specific mission for me that it was time to pay a visit. The armed forces team had captured not one, but two of the top leaders of the terrorist organization that had contributed to Joshua's death. One of the leaders was dead, but the other one was still alive, and I couldn't let an opportunity to come face-to-face with him go by.

It was close to midnight when we tackled the rocky dirt roads and made our way to a compound that was surrounded by other houses in an urban setting. The compound stood out because it was approximately 4,500 square feet and four stories tall, it barely had windows, and it was topped with barbed wire. The structure was severely damaged. I could only imagine what the inside looked like.

As soon as we hopped off the jeep, we headed inside. The inside was mostly dark, but a few lit candles here and there, gave off light. I couldn't see everything, but from what I saw, the place was a complete mess. Mattresses were on the floor, newspapers were scattered everywhere, wires drooped above our heads, and the damp, musty smell tore into my nostrils. It was a good thing that I had on camouflage gear and black boots. Puddles of water were on the floor, and we could hear drips every few seconds.

"I . . . I think it would be best if I stood by the door with Levi and the lieutenant," Andrew said in a fearful voice. "You guys look as if you have this under control."

The atmosphere was a bit frightening, so I understood Andrew's concerns. I had never entered a place like this before, either, but I felt safe with Levi, one high-ranking general, and a lieutenant.

"This way, Mr. President," General Stiles said. "Follow me."

General Stiles was an African American woman who was braver than any woman I had ever met. She had earned a lot of respect from the other soldiers; I definitely knew why. I followed her up a tight concrete staircase, and when we reached the third floor, we entered a small room with concrete walls. There was no window, no bed, no nothing. Two candles barely lit the room, but General Stiles's flashlight helped me see. The terrorist leader was on his knees, with his hands tied behind his back. He had been stripped of everything, with the exception of a piece of cloth that was draped around his lower body. His coal-black hair was soaking wet. Beard was scraggly. Skin was sweaty and dirty. Face appeared swollen, and beady eyes showed no fear whatsoever. His eyes grew slightly wide when he saw me enter the room. Apparently, he knew who I was.

I saluted the member from the special forces team, David Burrage, who stood close by the entrance. He saluted me back. He had a flashlight on his belt and a machete in one hand. He shined the bright light directly in the terrorist leader's face, causing him to squint.

"It is my pleasure to introduce you to the president of the United States, Mr. Stephen C. Jefferson. This is our gift to you, Mr. President. We told you that we would eventually catch him," David said.

The terrorist leader spoke with his evil eyes as he glared at me. He licked his dry lips, and even as I removed the machete from David's hand, he did not flinch or attempt to move.

"I've been practicing with one of these things." I looked at the sharp blade, then swung the machete back and forth. I told myself that while I was in America, my hands would always stay clean. This, however, was no America. "Hope I don't fuck up, but if I do, there are other options."

The leader started chanting multiple words that I couldn't understand. He dropped his head back to look up. That was when I swung the machete like a bat, using all my strength to take that muthafucka's head off, like I had witnessed him do in plenty of top secret videos I had watched. Unfortunately for me, though, his head did not detach from his body. It was hanging off, and that was when General Stiles lifted her boot and placed it on his chest. She removed the machete from my hand, lifted it high. In one clean chop, the job was finished.

"That's how you do it, Mr. President. After a little more practice, you should be fine."

"It was the blade," I said. "And I do want my trophy."

I saluted both soldiers before getting the hell out of there. And on my journey back to the barracks to join the troops, who were already celebrating, I couldn't help but to think that this world would never be the same. All credit would go to David Burrage. It would be reported that he was the one who had captured and killed two terrorist leaders. Without a doubt, we were proud.

President of the United States,

Stephen C. Jefferson

I returned to the White House the following day. The American people were celebrating the news, and for the time being, more good things were being said about me. World leaders had been reaching out to me, and everyone was trying to get an interview with David Burrage, who had done such a courageous thing. I even boasted about his accomplishment during a brief speech.

After the speech, I headed to my bedroom, where I was told Raynetta had been resting. I entered the bedroom, feeling slightly exhausted but very pleased about how my entire week had gone. I had to admit that I had missed Raynetta. When I saw her sitting up in bed, reading a book, it felt good to be home. While I was still uneasy about what she had done, I had somewhat forgiven her. She immediately laid the book down, then rushed out of bed to greet me. She threw her arms around me; I wrapped my arms around her.

"I'm so glad you're home," she said, squeezing me tight. "I missed you, and congrats on what you did. I'm so proud of you. I know you had some tough decisions to make."

If only she knew. I surely would never tell— many people had no idea how many secrets presidents kept. Not even the first ladies knew everything, but it had to be that way.

I backed away from Raynetta to examine the cut on her face. It was an ugly wound, but in time it would heal. I kissed the wound and then directed my lips toward hers. As we kissed intensely, there was a light knock on the door. I backed away from Raynetta to go see who it was. It was Levi.

"Sorry to interrupt you, but Andrew needs to see you. He mentioned something about an important phone call that you probably wouldn't want to miss," Levi announced.

I turned to Raynetta, who sighed. "I'll be right here when you get back," she said.

"I shouldn't be long. And pack your bags, because we're going to Camp David tomorrow. We need a break from all of this."

Raynetta seemed happy about the news. I was sure she would pack right away. I followed Levi to Andrew's office, and when we arrived, he informed me that the Pope had been waiting to speak to me. I felt some kind of way about it, considering what I had done. But in no way would I refuse to take his call. I took the call and listened to him condemn violence, all violence, he said, and then he prayed with me. He wished me well, but I had a gut feeling that he knew about everything that had happened behind the scenes. It was kind of scary, but maybe it was just me and my imagination.

The next day, Raynetta and I left for Camp David, a presidential retreat where since 1942 most presidents had vacationed. It was in a highly wooded area, and so it offered Raynetta and me the real privacy we needed. The four-bedroom cabin-like house was not as exquisite as some may have assumed. But the land at Camp David was breathtaking. It was very peaceful, and there was no way to get bored. From heated swimming pools to tennis courts to golf courses to bike riding trails, from horseback riding to skiing to ice skating . . . Camp David had it all. Several of our staff members, along with Secret

Service agents, joined us, but they stayed in other cabins. We completely tuned them out.

As Raynetta rested her head on my lap while on a swing that evening, we enjoyed the scenery from the upper terrace in back of the cabin.

"This is what peace feels like," she said, with her eyes closed, as the swing swayed. "I thought we would never see this day, and I hope that we are allowed just one or two days without something tragic happening."

"I hope so too, but don't be surprised if you don't get your wish."

Raynetta opened her eyes to look at me. She placed her hand on the side of my face and rubbed it. "I almost hate to ask this, but have you heard anything from your mother? It's as if she just disappeared. I know you're worried about her."

"I am, but I'm sure she's okay. She's very upset with me right now, and chasing after her is what she wants me to do. I do have someone looking into her whereabouts for me."

"I figured that much. Hope they find her before she finds you."

Raynetta laughed, but I didn't want to discuss my mother. I leaned forward to give her a special kiss, one that she seemed to enjoy thoroughly.

"Where did that come from?" She licked her moist lips. "You dug deep into the closet for that one, didn't you?"

"I wouldn't say all of that. It was just a kiss."

"A very stimulating kiss that included more of your tongue. I guess it shouldn't have surprised me, because you've been on cloud nine since you got back," she said. "I saw you during the summit, and I was surprised by how engaged and happy you looked. Your demeanor didn't have anything to do with Michelle Peoples, did it? She was there too, wasn't she?"

I had predicted that this was coming, and I was prepared to answer Raynetta. "Yes, she was there, but her presence had very little to do with my mood."

"Did the two of you talk?"

"Of course."

"Did you do more than talk?"

"If you want to know if we had sex, no, we didn't. That's the truth, so eliminate those thoughts from your head. And since you want to question me, I have some questions for you. My first question is, how did you really get that wound on your face?"

I could feel Raynetta's body get tense. She had no idea that I was already ten steps ahead of her on this. I couldn't believe it when she looked me in the eyes and stuck with her lie.

"It happened so fast," she said, describing how Claire had quickly slammed on the brakes. "Next thing I knew, my whole body went forward. My head almost went through the windshield."

I looked down at Raynetta, her head still on my lap. I moved her long, beautiful hair away from her face, then touched the edge of the wound.

"I need to tell you something," I said, slightly irritated. "Claire's car was inspected, and there was no blood on the windshield. I at least expected for it to be cracked, but it wasn't. I asked Andrew to investigate your story a little bit more, and his investigation led him to Claire. I won't tell you what she said happened, but I am going to ask you what happened to your face again. Before I do, let me say this. I take serious issue with a woman who constantly lies to me, for any reason. And if you continue to lie, you need to know that you are gifting me to women who are more than willing to do right by me."

Raynetta quickly sat up to face me. She had no choice but to come clean, but thanks to Andrew, I already knew that Mr. McNeil was responsible for the cut on my wife's face.

"I'm sorry, but I just didn't want to tell you, because I know how you are, Stephen. I didn't want any trouble, and all this craziness keeps pulling us down."

"Regardless, you should have told me. You shouldn't have even gone there. Why can't you stay away from him?"

"Please. Don't make it seem like he's irresistible. I just wanted to return his money so that we wouldn't have any ties to him whatsoever. I wanted us to have a fresh start, and now we will."

"A fresh start is exactly what we need. And as my final warning, no more lies. None whatsoever, all right?"

She smiled. "I promise. No more lies. But why aren't you mad? I thought that if you knew the truth about what Mr. McNeil did, you would throw a fit. Do you not love me anymore?"

I cupped Raynetta's face in my hands while searching her eyes. "I will always love you, and yes, I am very angry about what happened. But for now, my thoughts are about holding you, touching you, being inside of you, and making love to you until my dick hurts. I also want a child, Raynetta. I want you to take your time and give it some serious thought. Can you do that for me?"

She slowly nodded, and within a matter of seconds, we started to remove each other's clothes. We made our way inside the cabin, and right in front of the fireplace was where our naked bodies landed. I lay behind Raynetta, massaging her breasts, squeezing her hard nipples, and stirring her pussy fluids with two fingers. She moaned and groaned from my touch, and when I rested on my back, I positioned her on top of me. She faced the other direction, providing me an opportunity to see her meaty cheeks shake, rattle, and roll. My steel had reached new heights, and as she plunged down on it, it tapped a hot spot that prompted both of us to grunt.

"Tap into it," she said, grinding harder and faster. "Hit it and see how much more you'll get."

Raynetta was already so wet that I didn't think she could offer much more. Fortunately, I was wrong. I was gifted more of her honey dew when I flipped her on her back, separated her legs, and parted her slippery slit wide with my ferocious tongue. It traveled deep, causing her to rake my back with her nails and tremble all over. Her stimulated clitoris begged for attention, and as I flicked it with great speed, she went wild. Her fist pounded the floor; a high arch grew in her back.

"I fucking love you," she cried out, barely able to catch her breath. "See . . . see what you made me do!"

She sprayed me with the sweetest perfume, and after wiping my mouth and the tip of my nose, I was in no mood to make love. I was too hyped for that—there were times when I was in the mood to get downright nasty, freaky, and dirty with my wife. It might have had a little to do with my thoughts of Michelle, but without a doubt, this was where I wanted to be. Right here, watching Raynetta in a doggy-style position, throwing it back and taking me all in. With each lengthy stroke, she painted my muscle with more of her heavy cream. In return, I rewarded her very well.

My eyes closed as my warm milk swam inside of her. I hoped that it would do her body good. I was in deep thought about the feel of my wife's gushy insides when I opened my eyes and noticed someone watching us from afar. I squinted, only to see Claire staring back at me as she stood on the terrace of the cabin across from ours. She stood there for a while, watching as I held Raynetta's cheeks open and sank my super-hard muscle into her tight folds, unable to break my rhythm. Finally, Claire left her terrace and went inside her cabin. I didn't make much of it, and if she wanted to watch again, so be it.

I eased out of Raynetta, and as she lay on her stomach, my tongue traveled down her spine. I kissed her mountain-sized cheeks, which were as soft as cotton, while I lightly ran my finger through her crack. My touch tickled her and made her laugh.

"You earned a gold medal tonight," she said. "I don't know why you're so energized like this, but I surely hope I can look forward to more."

"You, baby," I said, making my way on top of her. "You have me energized. Let's see if I can earn more than just one gold medal tonight."

Raynetta opened the door for me to shoot for another gold. But in the midst of striving to attain my medal, I couldn't help but think about what else had me feeling so exuberant. I closed my eyes, wondering if all was going well at Mr. McNeil's birthday celebration.

Christopher J. McNeil

I was never one to make a big fuss about my birthday, but my wife had been determined to throw me a celebration. Most of our family was at the house, and as we all sat around the rectangular dinner table, which stretched from one end of the dining room to the other, I stood to give a toast before dinner was served. Everyone raised their flutes, and many smiles could be seen around the room. That was because my family loved me. It was because of my good fortune that they were more than just financially stable. They were filthy fucking rich.

"I want to thank you fine people for coming. Family means a lot to me, and I'm grateful to have such a beautiful, gifted family, who wouldn't be here if it wasn't for me."

They all chuckled, thinking that I was kidding around. I wasn't.

I went on. "It saddens me that there is an empty chair here this year. I miss Tyler, but I know that he's in the Almighty's heaven, at peace, and proud of his wife and children for carrying on. I don't know how much longer God will allow me to be here with my folks, but I thank him for the years I've accumulated thus far. I may be getting older, but I feel good and ready as ever to tackle whatever challenges are put forth. With that, happy birthday to me. And, doggone Betsie Ann, I'm ready to eat."

Everyone laughed and agreed. The servers then brought in the food, and while the various side dishes were being served, I stood again to slice the prime rib, one of my favorite dishes. One of the servers placed a silver-plated domed platter in front of me, and with a wide smile on my face, I lifted the top. In an instant, my smile vanished. Shouts and screams rang out throughout the room, and everyone raced away from the table and scattered, many falling on their asses.

"Grandpa!" my sweet granddaughter cried out. "No!"

"Oh my Lord!" said my wife. "Move away from it!"

"I'm getting the hell out of here! Go get your coat, sweetheart! Let's go," my brother said.

The server had fallen to the floor and fainted.

I covered my mouth, gagging, and damn near puked all over myself. Instead of prime rib, there was a man's decapitated head on the platter. I could barely look at it, and I hurried to leave the room so I didn't have to. I was moving so fast that I damn near tripped over my own feet. I was anxious to call the police, but before I did that, I ordered everyone out of my house. I told my wife to go lock herself in our bedroom, and then I stormed into my office to make a call. Just as I closed the door, I bumped into something or someone who felt as solid as a rock. When I flicked on the lights, I saw the president's pit bull, Levi. He startled the fuck out of me, and with a smirk on his face and a long knife in his hand, I knew this wasn't going to be good.

"The president would like to wish you a happy birthday. And as payback for what you did to the first lady, I can't let you live. Sleep tight, muthafucka."

Levi jabbed the knife into my stomach, then turned it in a slow circle. My eyes were wide, and so was my mouth.

"If . . . if you finish me off," I struggled to say, "the president will never, ever see his son again. I know where he is."

In so much pain, I dropped to one knee. Levi grabbed the back of my head, pulled it up so I could look at him. He then yanked the knife out of my stomach.

"What in the fuck do you know about the president's son? Are you telling me that he's alive?"

I slowly nodded while holding my stomach, which was dripping with blood. Levi released my head and quickly reached for the cell phone in his pocket. I figured that he was making a call to the president. That bastard had better order Levi to make the right move, or else.

President of the United States,

Stephen C. Jefferson

We had just finished making love at Camp David, and Raynetta was in the shower. I had joined her but had gotten out because the cabin was frigid and I wanted to add some more logs to the fire so the living room would stay warm. Just as I finished placing the last log on the fire, I heard my cell phone ring. I hoped it was Levi, because I had told him to call and confirm after the job was finished. I answered the phone and immediately heard Levi's voice on the other end.

"I need you to make the call on this," he said. "This asshole just told me your son is *alive*. I don't know if he's fucking with me or not, but he says that he knows where Joshua is."

I froze from what he'd said, but I didn't want to mess this up. Mr. McNeil had to pay for what he'd done to Raynetta; he had definitely crossed the line. She was off-limits, and I couldn't believe that he was stupid enough to think that I wouldn't retaliate this time. He was probably saying that shit about Joshua to save his own life.

"Kill his ass," I said. "Do not let him live another day, and don't fall for the bullshit."

"Your call, my move. See you within the hour."

Levi ended the call, and I sat there for a moment, trying to let what he'd said sink in. I couldn't help but think about my mother's reaction when I told her about what had happened to Joshua. She hadn't believed me. Had said I had been tricked. Had claimed that I was out of my mind for believing such a thing. As I sat there thinking, my mind started to change course. I knew how powerful Mr. McNeil was, but was he really so powerful that he could pull off some shit like that? Hell, money could buy anything, especially people and lies. I thought about who had broken the news to me about Joshua. That person was Andrew. But then, there was something about Claire—the way she had boldly watched me make love to my wife tonight, the way she always looked at me, and how she was always in our business—that couldn't be ignored.

I rushed out of the cabin, a towel still wrapped around my waist, and hurried to the cabin across from ours. I called Levi on my cell phone to see if Mr. McNeil had said anything else, but he didn't answer his phone. My heart was racing fast as I climbed the stairs in front of the cabin. After I pounded on the door, Claire opened it, displaying nothing but her white skin. Her firm breasts stood at attention, and her hand touched the trimmed hairs on her coochie.

"Please come in." Seduction was in her eyes. "I figured you would come. And I want you, Mr. President, to do to me exactly what you did to Raynetta."

This chick was crazy. Didn't she notice the twisted look on my face? In no way was I there to have sex with her, and I made that very clear when I reached out and grabbed her arm.

"Get your goddamned mind right and tell me if my son is still alive. Is he?" I shouted.

"What?" she shouted back. "I . . . I don't know anything about your son. Now, let my arm go! You're hurting me."

I could sense that Claire was lying to me. I didn't let her arm go, and to inflict more pain, I yanked her hair from the back, pulling it so hard that her head fell back.

"I swear, I'm going to snap your fucking neck if you don't tell me the truth! Where in the hell is my son!"

Tears seeped from the corners of Claire's eyes. She hesitated to speak, but when she did, it was not what I wanted to hear.

"Fuck me and I will tell you. I will tell you exactly where to find him. Just . . . just do as I wish and touch me all over."

Her wish was my command. I pulled her ass into the living room, and after shoving her on the floor, my fist tightened. I wanted to hit her, but choking the answer out of her would work just fine. I grabbed her neck, and as I tightened my grip on her neck, she squirmed around. But before she spoke, I heard a voice that sounded very familiar.

"I told you not to trust these money-hungry crackers, didn't I?" My mother had the meanest look I had ever seen on her face. "I don't know if I should blow your fucking brains out first or hers. But since you're my son . . ." She paused, and her eyes homed in on Claire. That was when I saw the gun in my mother's hand. She squeezed the trigger several times, and as bullets whistled through the air, Claire and I both sprinted to avoid being shot. It wasn't long before Claire was shot and collapsed, and that caused me to turn around and face my mother. The evilness in her eyes was still there. I held up my hands, tried to reason with her.

"Put the gun down." Drops of sweat rolled down my body. "Don't you forget who I am to you. Your *only* son, and if you hurt me—"

"Shut your dumb ass up. I know who you are, and you damn well better start recognizing and respecting who I am."

She tossed the gun aside, causing it to skid across the floor. After that, she rolled her eyes at me and walked out.

I looked at Claire, sighed from relief and gratitude that I wasn't in her condition. She was still breathing, so I kept shaking her and asking, "Where in the hell is my son?"

President of the United States,

Stephen C. Jefferson

Unfortunately, I had become one big liar, but as president of the United States, not many people questioned me. Some were skeptical, but they didn't dare call me out on anything. Not even Andrew, who knew my story about Claire's death didn't add up. It made no sense that a white man with a scruffy beard would sneak onto the grounds of Camp David and shoot Claire. To shoot me made more sense, but killing Claire was a far stretch. According to my own words, I *supposedly* saw the killer enter Claire's cabin while I stood on the balcony of mine, waiting for Raynetta to finish her shower. I *supposedly* heard Claire scream, and that was when I rushed to her cabin to find out what was going on. By then, she had been shot and the killer had run into the woods and evaded being caught. That was my story; I was sticking to it.

I had even gone to the extreme of making it look like the killer was a man Claire had been involved with. Pictures of the unknown man had been found at her apartment, as had letters that stressed how obsessed he was with her. I had to do what was necessary to keep my mother out of this. She was already in a heap of trouble for attacking a nurse at the mental institution. That could easily be a case of self-defense, but yet again, it all entailed lies, lies, and more lies.

With Claire dead and Mr. McNeil in critical condition, I had no way to find out more about my son. Levi had been unable to wipe Mr. McNeil off the face of this earth because the police had arrived shortly after Levi and I spoke. He had to get the hell out of Mr. McNeil's house before he was caught. We weren't sure if Mr. McNeil would tell what had happened to him, but we were prepared to *lie*, if necessary.

The one person whom I intended to tell the truth about all of this was Raynetta. She was devastated. She and Claire were extremely close, and Raynetta didn't understand how or why someone would want to hurt her. She just didn't get it, but after the funeral was over, she would learn that Claire wasn't really the person she had pretended to be. For now, though, finding out if my son was alive took priority over everything. And if he was alive, where in the hell was he?

I sat at my desk in the Oval Office, waiting for a call from Ina. I was eager to speak to her, but I was also a little uneasy because I wasn't sure how she was going to respond to my request. The only way to find out if Joshua was dead or alive was to dig up his grave and open the casket. No question this would be very painful for Ina, but we had to start somewhere. I assumed she would want to know the truth too, or, at least I hoped she would want to know.

"Mr. President," my secretary, Lynda, said through the speakerphone, "the call you've been waiting for is on line one."

I thanked Lynda, then picked up the receiver and placed it on my ear. "Ina?" I said as I heard her conversing with someone in the background.

"Yes," she replied in a dry tone. "What do you want, Stephen?"

"I'm not exactly sure yet, but you sound like you're upset with me about something."

"I just want you and your mother to leave me alone. We have nothing else to say to each other, and I already apologized to you for not—" Ina's voice cracked, so she stopped talking. I could sense that she was still in a great deal of pain.

"I'm not trying to upset you, Ina. I only wanted to speak to you about something concerning Joshua."

"There's not much else for us to talk about, and I refuse to listen to any more attacks from you or Teresa. She said a mouthful when she came here, and that woman will never be welcome into my home again."

I hadn't a clue what she was talking about, but it was obvious that my mother and Ina had fallen out.

"Listen. I haven't spoken to my mother in quite some time, so I don't know what happened between the two of you. I do know, however, that there is a possibility that Joshua is still alive. I want your permission to dig up his grave and see if his body is in the casket."

I was surprised by Ina's response. Her screaming caused me to cock my head back and move the receiver away from my ear.

"Hell fucking no, Stephen! No one is going to dig up his grave, no one! I . . . I wish you all would stop with this nonsense about him being alive. Do you have any idea what I'm going through over here? Obviously not! And shame on you and Teresa for putting me through this!"

Ina started to cry hard. While waiting for her to calm down, I rubbed the hair on my chin, thinking hard about this. I then started to unbutton my shirt, and after a few buttons were undone, I spoke up again.

"Apparently, something is going on between you and my mother that I don't know about. But whatever it is, it has nothing to do with why I believe Joshua is still alive." I proceeded to tell Ina about everything that had transpired in the past several days. I had to get through to her, but unfortunately for me, she wasn't trying to hear it.

"That is the most ridiculous mess I've ever heard," she snapped. "I don't care what anyone says. Joshua is not alive. If you look at the bigger picture, it would've taken an enormous amount of planning, scheming, plotting, and illegal crap to make it appear that Joshua was killed in his friend's garage. You're forgetting that his friend's mother saw the boys. She was there, Stephen, and she told me what she saw. I also saw what was on Joshua's computer. I read letters that he wrote, letters expressing his hatred for this country. I witnessed the change in his behavior, and that's why all of this hurts so much. I failed to take action, and now I have to live with this."

I didn't reply until she was calm. "I understand everything you're saying, but please hear me out on this, okay? As president, I can tell you for a fact that when people have an ulterior motive, they can and will plan, scheme, plot, conspire, and do whatever they must to accomplish their

mission. I have a lot of enemies, Ina. They will
do whatever to go after the ones I love. That
includes Joshua. All I want is to be sure about
this. Out of respect, I'm asking for you to work
with me on this. If you don't wish to, I'm sorry,
but I will take action on my own."

There was a sharp silence before Ina responded.
"I said no. No! No! No! No, you will not dig up his
grave, and I will fight you to the end on this. Let my
baby rest in peace, please. I beg you to leave me
alone and let him be!"

The call ended with her hanging up on me.
Regardless of how she felt, I had to do what was
necessary to find out about my son. Before the
weekend was over, I would definitely have some
answers.

Just as I was getting ready to leave the Oval
Office to go see if Raynetta had returned from
the funeral, Lynda buzzed me again. This time,
my mother was on the phone. I needed to speak
to her, so I hurried to pick up the receiver.

"Not on this phone," I rushed to say. "Call my
private line, because I'm about to leave."

That wasn't the reason I wanted her to call my
private line, but a few minutes later she called. I
sat on the edge of the sofa, listening to her speak
to me with a bad attitude.

"Now that the wicked witch is dead, what are you going to do about Joshua? I hope you now know that he is still alive. The second I saw that heifer Claire with Mr. McNeil, I knew something wasn't right. Raynetta got something up her sleeve too, and you need—"

"Don't go there with Raynetta, all right? She had nothing to do with this. I can promise you that. I do believe that Joshua is alive, and I just spoke to Ina about digging up his grave. She's against it, but I must find out the truth before I make my next move."

"You're darn right you do, and if you don't start digging, I will do it myself," she asserted. "All Ina cares about is that low-life nigga she's living with. She don't have time to deal with this, but what kind of mother wouldn't want to know the truth?"

"One who is hurting real bad, Mama. This has to be hard for her and—"

"Yeah, yeah, yeah, whatever," she said, interrupting me. "You need to stop defending these no-good women and start seeing them for who they really are. The only question I have for you is, when are we going to St. Louis?"

"I'll decide, and just so you know, I don't need your help. Besides, you have a bigger fish to fry. The police want to question you about what happened at that institution. The nurse is pressing charges. From what I've been told, she wants a million dollars for her injuries."

"A million dollars!" she shouted. "Please. She'd better go sit her tail down somewhere. If I have to pay a million dollars, she'd better have more than a bump on her head. Besides, she was the one who came after me. I was only defending myself."

"I'm sure you were, Mother, like always. I'll see what I can do about this, but in the meantime, why don't you disappear for a while? Go on vacation and stay out of the way. It's been tough spinning this thing with Claire. You didn't have to go that far."

"For the sake of Joshua, I did what was necessary. You need to be thankful that you're not the one seeing darkness right now. I haven't forgotten about what you did to me. I'm just trying to figure out how I'm going to make you pay for that. I'll think of something, so don't you think for one minute that these little conversations between us have calmed me in any way."

"I'm shaking all over. If you believe your threats move me, I promise you they don't. You need to be thankful that you're not in jail, and after all my efforts to keep you out of there, you'd better think about forgiving and forgetting. It's in your best interest to do so."

"Forgiving and forgetting is the name of *your* game, not mine. And if you keep playing that game, Raynetta is going to turn your world upside down and make you wish you had listened to me. Don't say that I didn't warn you."

She hung up, causing me to shake my head. I looked forward to the day when my mother and Raynetta were able to put aside their differences and get along with each other. Unfortunately for me, I couldn't envision that day coming.

I spoke briefly by phone with Lynda, then left the Oval Office and headed to Raynetta's office, which was where Lynda had told me she was. Lynda had said Raynetta had recently returned from Claire's funeral. I was sure Raynetta had a difficult time there. I'd wanted to attend the funeral with her, but the situation with Claire had left a bad taste in my mouth. Other matters at the White House had taken priority too. I had to meet with the secretary of Health and Human Services earlier, settle certain matters about Claire's death with the FBI, and speak to Ina about Joshua. Raynetta deserved to know the truth about Claire, the woman she'd considered a friend, and I intended to tell her. But just as I got ready to enter her office, I heard her speaking to someone and halted in my tracks. I stood outside the door, which was ajar, and peeked through the crack while listening in.

"It's a shame. I don't know what I'm going to do without her," Raynetta said to Alex as he stood beside her in a tailored black suit. She was sitting at her desk, wiping her tears.

"I'm sure you'll find someone to replace her soon," he said. "It's no fun losing someone you care about, and the good thing is, the person responsible will be caught."

"I hope so. I truly hope so, because she didn't deserve this."

As Raynetta cried, Alex opened his jacket, then squatted to her level. He turned her chair to face him, then lifted her chin. "No, she didn't deserve this, but I don't want to see you so torn. I want to help you take your mind off this tragedy, so if you want to get out of here and go somewhere to relax, just let me know. I'll take you wherever you want to go, and that includes shopping. You're limited to one store, though."

Raynetta cracked a tiny smile. "You hate it when I shop, so stop trying to be nice to me. But all shopping is going to do is make me think about Claire. We shopped together a lot. You, of all people, know that she was more than just my assistant."

"I'm well aware of that, but keep in mind that I'm here for you too. Think about what I said, and if you want to go somewhere, get some fresh air, or go get a bite to eat, just let me know."

Raynetta slowly nodded. That was when I saw Alex gazing into her eyes as if he did more than just care for her. He moved her long, straight hair away from her eye and tucked it behind her ear. His fingers brushed away her tears, and he squeezed her hand with his other hand.

"I am a little hungry," she said. "And you already know what I'm craving."

He laughed. "For God's sake, no more of that gooey butter cake from Alison's Bakery. I'm sick of going to that place. You should be too."

"Never in a million years. I love that place, and before we do anything, you have to take me there so I can get a small piece."

Gooey butter cake? Her favorite? Since when? This was something new to me, and in no way did I appreciate another man knowing more about my wife than I did. I had seen and heard enough, so I knocked hard on the door before entering. Alex quickly stood, then closed his suit jacket. He wiped across his spiked hair, then moved back when Raynetta walked around him as she made her way to me with open arms.

"Hi, sweetheart," she said, wrapping her arms around my waist. I pulled her close to me, and while holding her in my arms, I looked directly at Alex. He stood stone-faced.

"I need to speak to my wife in private," I said. "Please exit."

"Will do, sir. No problem."

He hurried to leave the room and closed the door behind him. Raynetta unwrapped her arms from around my waist, but before we parted, she planted a soft kiss on my lips.

"I'm disappointed that you couldn't make it to the funeral with me, but I hope you were able to get some things done around here," she said.

"I was, but there is always more to do. I don't want to bore you with what's left on my agenda for the day, but before I get back to work, I need to make you aware of certain things pertaining to Claire. When I tell you this, Raynetta, it has to stay between us. It's going to sting a little too, especially when I tell you that Claire wasn't exactly the person you thought she was."

Raynetta stepped away from me with a perplexed look on her face. I began to tell her everything I knew about Claire and Mr. McNeil's involvement. I also mentioned the possibility of Joshua being alive. In closing, I made Raynetta aware of Claire's advances toward me that day. Then I informed her that it was actually my mother who had shot and killed Claire, not an angry companion who was obsessed with her. Raynetta stood with her mouth wide open, touching her chest at the same time.

"Oh my God, Stephen. I don't know where to start. Are you saying that Joshua may not be dead, and that Claire and Mr. McNeil were hiding him? I'm speechless. I can't believe . . ." Raynetta paused, appearing to be in deep thought. "So, your mother killed Claire? I'm so confused right now. Let me go sit down. Please explain all of this to me again."

I sat next to Raynetta on the sofa and broke it all down for her again. I confessed to my ongoing lies to protect my mother and addressed Claire's betrayal. Raynetta looked to be in a daze. She shook her head and let me know how angry she was.

"Just who can we trust around here?" she questioned. "This is so ridiculous, and I feel so stupid for not realizing what Claire had been up to. She was always in my business, but I didn't think much of it. I'm glad Teresa intervened when she did, but what about Joshua? How are you going to find out the truth?"

"I'm working on that now, but let me answer your question about whom we can trust. No one around here can be trusted. Not one single person, especially Alex, who seems as if he has a little crush on you. I hadn't noticed the two of you getting so close."

Raynetta threw her hand back and slightly rolled her eyes. "Alex doesn't have a crush on me. He's just really nice, and that's surprising, because I've always been so mean to him. If you're talking about what he said before you entered the room, he was only looking out for me. That's what he's paid to do, and from what he has shared with me, this job means a great deal to him."

I shrugged. In no way did Raynetta and I share the same views about Alex. "I hope he's doing only what he's paid to do. If he attempts to cross the line in any way, I want you to tell me. I don't appreciate the look I saw in his eyes. It didn't come across as concern to me."

Raynetta reached over to touch my hand. "It was concern. I'm not the best judge of character, but I do know when a man is interested in me or if he simply cares about me. Alex cares. You, however, are interested."

"Very interested," I noted. "So interested that I would love to lean you back on this sofa right now and make love to you. But before I do that, I have to meet with Andrew about Joshua. I need to get to the bottom of this soon."

"You go ahead and do that. Meanwhile, I'm going to let Alex take me a few places so I can clear my head. I hope you'll beat me to the bedroom tonight. That way, we both can share our major interest in each other."

We leaned in at the same time to indulge in a fiery kiss. I hated to back away from it, but the mission to find Joshua weighed heavily on my mind.

First Lady,

Raynetta Jefferson

After Stephen left my office, I went upstairs to change clothes. If I had known what Claire had been up to, I never would have attended her funeral. I couldn't believe how naive I had been when it came to her. The only thing I could think about was her fake reaction when Mr. McNeil caused me harm that day. Claire had pretended to care, but I would put some money on the fact that she knew what was going to happen. I had entrusted her with so much personal information, and I was sure she'd shared it all with Mr. McNeil. And then to ask Stephen to have sex with her? How conniving was that?

Teresa had definitely done me a favor, but I couldn't help but think about the big secret I now had on her. If she ever got out of hand again, I would pull out the killer card and have her sent away for a very long time. Sure, Stephen would

be upset with me, but he just didn't understand what a pain in the ass his mother had
been. Nonetheless, all of this left me speechless.
The next person who worked for me would be
properly screened. Claire had come highly rec-
ommended by Andrew. I was sure that Stephen
had already chewed him out for recommending
her. It was so scary living in the White House.
And just like Stephen had said, we couldn't trust
anyone.

That, of course, included Alex. I had a tiny
feeling that he had a crush on me, but admitting
that to Stephen would only have caused him
to replace Alex. I didn't want that to happen,
simply because I was starting to feel very safe
with Alex. I also needed someone like him to
communicate with. He understood me, and
every woman wanted a man around who could
protect her like no other. Stephen was capable of
doing that too, but he'd been so busy. This thing
with Joshua had him in a different zone.

I was shocked to learn that there was a possibility Joshua was still alive. I figured Stephen
would find out soon enough, but the truth was, I
wanted Stephen all to myself. No kids, no baby-
mama drama, no nothing. Just me and him,
along with our little family, whenever I made
a decision to finally give him a child. The good
thing was, I was almost to that point.

I put on a pair of jeans, a black ribbed tur-
tleneck sweater, and ankle boots. My hair was
parted down the middle, with straight hair
flowing down on both sides. As the first lady, I
had been warned not to go anywhere near a
mall, but today was a day when I felt like being
free. I shielded my eyes with dark sunglasses,
hoping that maybe, just maybe, people wouldn't
recognize me. But in no way was that the case.
The second Alex opened the door for me to enter
the mall, nearly everybody started turning their
heads and whispering.

"Is that the first lady?" one lady said, loud
enough for others to hear.

"That's not her," another said. "The first lady
isn't that cute."

I wanted to give her a piece of my mind, but I
kept on walking, with Alex by my side.

"One store, and then we're out of here," he
said. "When I mentioned shopping, I didn't
think you would want to browse a packed mall."

"We're here, so stop complaining, okay? All I
want to do is stop by two stores, and then we can
go grab a bite to eat," I replied.

Alex strolled around with a serious frown on
his face. He didn't appreciate all the attention,
and as the crowd started to thicken, more people
began to notice me. People waved; I waved back.

One lady rushed up to me but was quickly halted by Alex's hand when he lifted it.

"Not too close," he barked. "Back away."

"I'm sorry, but may I have your autograph, Mrs. Jefferson?" she asked. "It's not every day that I come to the mall and get a chance to see our first lady."

The woman already had a pen in her hand. She held up the shopping bag that she was carrying, wanting me to sign it. I did so with a smile on my face.

"There you go. Have a great day and all the best to you," I told her after I signed the shopping bag.

"You too!" she shouted, with excitement in her voice. "Thank you!"

After she walked away, more people tried to approach me. Alex couldn't handle everyone; he made that clear when he attempted to shove them away. "Move. Back away, or else."

Many people ignored Alex. The scene was starting to get chaotic, and questions were coming at me from every direction.

"Mrs. Jefferson, what did you come here to get?"

"Can I have your autograph too?"

"Are you really the first lady or an imposter?"

"Is the president with you?"

When a man reached out to grab my arm, that was when Alex had enough. He pushed the man away so hard that he fell back and skidded on the floor.

"Back up!" Alex shouted and pointed at the man. "And you, sir, will be arrested if you touch her again."

"Damn," the man said with a frown on his face. "She fine, but she ain't no Beyoncé. I was just saying hello."

I cut my eyes behind the sunglasses, feeling insulted by his words. Many others had backed away, and so Alex was able to pull me in another direction.

"One store. That's it," he demanded. "And make it quick."

I went to Neiman Marcus to purchase a purse and a pair of shoes for myself and a shirt for Stephen. The atmosphere was lively there as well—and chaotic. Everyone wanted to take pictures, including the staff. I didn't mind, but I could tell that Alex was highly upset. The second we returned to the car and climbed in, he shifted in his seat and had a few choice words for me.

"For some reason, you have a deep desire for attention. I don't appreciate you putting me in a dangerous situation like that, and just so you know, we both could've gotten injured in there."

"Breaking news. We didn't. So chill out and stop being so uptight. All people wanted to do was speak to me and take pictures. And the only desire I have is to get out and live freely sometimes. If you can't handle the pressure, then maybe I need another agent, one who understands that."

That surely changed his tune. On our way to get something to eat, he didn't say one word to me. I didn't say anything to him, either, until he drove to the drive-through at McDonald's.

"Are you kidding me?" I asked. "Why are we here? I assume it's to get you something to eat or drink."

"We're here because I'm not driving you any-where else. I'm exhausted by your behavior, and I can't tolerate a woman who doesn't listen to me. If we're in this car, at least I know we're safe."

I crossed my arms while listening to his non-sense. "First of all, you're the one who suggested that I leave the White House to relax, have some fun, and go get a bite to eat. Those were your exact words, so please tell me how going through the drive-through at McDonald's is fun. Maybe I'm missing something."

Yet again, Alex ignored me. He lowered the window to place an order. "I'll have a fish combo and one of those chicken salads with dressing—"

"Fish combo?" I said, interrupting him. "What is a fish combo? You need to be specific when you ask for a chicken salad. Grilled or fried. And please tell her what kind of dressing you would like."

"The salad is for you, so you tell her—"

"Excuse me, sir," the McDonald's worker said, interrupting us. "Can you repeat that again? I didn't hear what you said."

I spoke up for Alex. "He said he wanted a fish combo, but that probably means he wants a Filet-O-Fish Meal. But you can cancel that, along with the salad. We're not eating here, so thank you very much for your time."

"Yes, we are eating here," Alex said. He kept looking around. I could tell he was checking out our surroundings. "I . . . I would like twenty-seven Happy Meals for the school bus of kids coming inside and ice cream for everyone. As a matter of fact, I want to pay for everyone's meal inside. I'll also take a Sprite soda." He turned his head to look at me. "Do you want something or not?"

"Sir," the lady said through the intercom, "there are numerous people waiting behind you to order. We are a very busy establishment. If you're not going to place an order, please drive off."

"I just placed an order. Did you not hear me?"

"I did, but if you're serious, you need to come inside."

"That may be wise," Alex said.

Alex drove off to park the car. I didn't budge once he turned off the engine.

"This is ridiculous, Mr. Big Spender." I displayed an attitude. "I'm not going inside, and I'm ordering you to take me back to the White House. I'll have one of the chefs cook something for me instead."

"You said you wanted to have some fun, didn't you? So let's go have some fun."

Alex got out of the car and then opened the door for me. The last thing I wanted to do was go inside, but since he obviously wasn't going to take me to the White House, I surrendered and went into the McDonald's. It didn't take long for everyone to recognize who I was.

"That's the first lady," several of the kids said in unison, pointing to me.

"Oh my God. It's really her!"

"Were you the one in the drive-through?"

"Can we please take your picture?"

As I posed for pictures and conversed with everyone, Alex went to the counter to pay for all the food. Cheers erupted, and as I greeted more of the people inside the restaurant and played with the kids, I found myself having fun. Many of the kids asked me to autograph their Happy Meal boxes. I took pictures with all of them, as well as with the staff who had brought them there. It wasn't long before the media showed up, and when the restaurant got too crowded, the manager was forced to lock the doors. I sat at one of the tables, eating fries, while one of the cutest little girls I had ever seen sat on my lap. She, along with everyone else, wanted to know why the president wasn't at McDonald's with me.

"Well, the president is very busy," I said. "But he is going to be so upset that he missed you all. I can't wait to tell him how much fun I had."

I was hit with one question after the next. Some were quite interesting, especially one posed by a little boy, who asked me how much money the president made.

"I'm just asking because I want to be president one day. But I want to be sure that the money can pay for my car. I want a Lamborghini," he explained.

Everyone laughed. I encouraged him to pursue his dreams; he promised me he would. I smiled, and when I looked up, I saw Alex gazing at me with a blank expression on his face. I wondered what he was thinking, especially when he delivered a nod. His eyes traveled around the room. He was carefully watching everyone's moves. I diverted my attention to another little girl who wanted to share her fries with me.

"Thank you," I said. "Sharing is a very nice thing to do."

The kids agreed, and before I announced my departure, I gave nearly every kid there a squeezing hug.

"Thank you for the Happy Meal," the kids said in unison.

I waved good-bye, and after one last group photo with the staff, Alex and I left. On the ride back to the White House, he was silent yet again. I spoke up, just to thank him for suggesting McDonald's.

"I really enjoyed myself, and I apologize for putting up such a fuss."

"No need to apologize. I'm glad you had an enjoyable time with the children."

That was all he said, but when we got back to the White House, I forced him into a conversation after he turned off the car.

"I'm curious about something," I said. "Why do you always look at me as if you're looking right through me? I often wonder what your thoughts are, and quite frankly, I don't know if they're good or bad."

He was blunt. "My thoughts are no one's business but my own. Besides, it would be wrong of me to ask what your thoughts are when you look at me."

"Excuse me for asking, and just so you know, I don't mind sharing my thoughts. Here they are. You're a nerd, and you would look so much better without those glasses on. Two, I think about why you're so serious all the time. I wonder what kind of cologne you wear, as it smells really good, *and* I think about how miserable your wife and kids must be, because you're never at home. And finally, I wonder why you chose a job that puts your life at risk."

Before responding, Alex removed his glasses, revealing his piercing, mysterious olive green eyes, which reminded me of Daniel Craig's, the sexiest Agent 007. Alex put his glasses in the glove compartment and removed a bottle of cologne from it at the same time.

"It's called Jack Black," he said, tossing the cologne to me. "The next time you go on one of your adventures to the mall, why don't you buy the president some? It costs only around seventy-five bucks."

I removed the cap to sniff the nozzle. "Maybe I will. Thanks for the recommendation."

"As for my wife and kids, I don't have either. I chose this job because I love to take risks, and it takes a serious person to do what I do. Trust me when I say that you wouldn't want me to be any other way."

"Probably not, so thank you for being so serious. I appreciate you for tackling my thoughts, but you still haven't shared your thoughts."

Alex tapped his fingers on the steering wheel while looking straight ahead. "My thought is we'd better go inside before it gets too late and the president starts looking for you. Other than that, there is nothing else on my mind."

I didn't bother to push, even though I was curious. Instead, I exited the vehicle with Alex, and we both went inside. He followed me to the second level, and right at the Yellow Oval Room was where we parted ways.

"You know how to reach me if you need me," he said. "Until then, rest well."

He walked off, and I headed to the bedroom, hoping that Stephen was there. Unfortunately, he wasn't. My gut told me that it was going to be another long and lonely night. I definitely wasn't looking forward to that.

President's Mother,

Teresa Jefferson

See, I wasn't playing with Stephen or Ina when it came to my grandson. I was already back in St. Louis, waiting for Stephen to come to the cemetery. He and Ina had been arguing all week long, and now it was time to take action. I had a shovel in my hand, just in case there was more stalling. And sure enough, there was. Ina and Stephen arrived at the cemetery within minutes of each other. Stephen was with a crew of men ready to dig, and Ina was there with an attorney who was supposed to stop all of this from going down.

"I don't care who you are," her attorney threatened while standing in front of Stephen. "You need my client's permission, or you will be sued."

"Sue me," Stephen said and walked off. Ina ran in front of him, halting his steps.

"I can't believe you're going to go through with this. What are you thinking, Stephen? Why are you doing this?"

As he stood there, trying to explain, I marched over to Joshua's grave site with the shovel in my hand. I wore a sweat suit and my old tennis shoes, so I did not care if my clothes got messed up. With anger and pain in my heart, I stood on top of the muddy section of earth where Joshua was supposed to be laid to rest and started to dig.

"Mama!" I heard Stephen shout. "What in the hell are you doing?"

"What did you think I was going to do with this shovel?" I shouted back. "Dig for gold?"

"She is crazy. I want everyone out here arrested!" Ina yelled as she rushed up to me, then attempted to snatch the shovel out of my hand. This time, I threatened her.

"Back up before I use this shovel to knock some sense into you! This is serious business, fool. You need to stop all that crying and think about Joshua right now. What if his body is not in that casket? Don't you want to know?"

"It is in there," she said through gritted teeth. "Stop trying to convince me otherwise. You need to get the hell out of here with that shovel."

Stephen agreed and told me to put it away. He asked the diggers to come forward, and it wasn't long before a Bobcat digging truck came revving through the cemetery.

Ina's attorney pulled out his cell phone. "I'm calling the police, unless I see some kind of legal paperwork that gives you the authority to do this," he warned. "This is not right, and if you're talking about abuse of power, this would be it."

Ina's attorney was a clown. Not only that, but he was useless. We all ignored him, because at the end of the day, not one police officer in this city would come here and arrest the president. A lead detective from the FBI was there, as well as Levi. All Ina could do was shut her fat mouth and allow the digging to begin.

"How long is this going to take?" I asked Stephen. His face was scrunched up as he watched the Bobcat dig up several scoops of mud.

"Thirty minutes or so. Back up and please don't get in the way."

I moseyed several feet away from Joshua's grave site, hoping and praying that the casket was empty. Ina had finally shut her mouth, and as the digging proceeded, more tears fell from her eyes. Her body trembled; it seemed difficult for her to catch her breath. Stephen moved in her direction, then tried to console her by wrapping his arms around her.

"I know this is hard, and I never would have done this if I was a hundred percent sure Joshua was dead. If he is, please forgive me. If he's not, then all of this will be worth it."

Ina didn't respond. She was so distraught, and when Joshua's casket was lifted from the ground, she couldn't take much more. She turned her back, while clutching her chest. Unable to stand on her own, her attorney held her up. Stephen moved closer to the casket, with a look of worry, confusion, fear, and pain trapped in his eyes. As for me, I sucked in a deep breath and held it. My eyes filled with tears; legs were weaker than they had ever been. The last thing I wanted to see was my grandson's body in that casket. I couldn't bear to look, but when Stephen said, "Open it," in no way could I turn away. The casket top was flipped upward, and everyone gasped. More confusion appeared on all our faces, as it appeared that *someone* was in there. But when Stephen lifted an effigy with a noose around the neck, my whole body felt as if it had deflated. A white sheet around the effigy's head read ONE LESS NIGGA. HA. HA. HA.

We were all stunned, but no one more than Ina. Her eyes were wide; mouth was wide open.

"Who . . . ? What in the hell is going on?" she cried out as she rushed up to Stephen. "Tell me what is happening! Where is my child?"

Ina's whole face shook. Much anger was visible—I had never seen her look so irate. Stephen, however, remained calm. He released a deep breath while looking at the effigy, shaking his head.

"I can't explain this, Ina, but I will find out where Joshua is." His eyes shifted to Levi and the FBI agent, who stood stunned. "Please, do whatever—"

Ina interrupted. She wouldn't allow Stephen to speak. "You darn well better find out. None of this would've happened if it wasn't for you! We were doing just fine without you, *Mr. President*. What are you doing in that White House, and why are so many people out to get you? Why is Joshua in the middle of this? I want him home with me right now!"

This bitch was getting totally out of hand, yelling at my son like she had lost her mind. What in the hell did she think he was trying to do? I refused to sit back and let her attack him like that. I marched right back over to where they stood to give her a piece of my mind.

"You need to shut the hell up and let Stephen handle this. How dare you stand there and blame him for this mess? It wouldn't have ever happened if you had told him about his son to begin with. Instead, you chose money, remember? My money. Instead of doing what was right for Joshua."

Ina pouted and rolled her eyes. "Whatever, Teresa. You're not going to put all of this on me. You had your hands in all of this—"

"We all have dirty hands," Stephen said, interrupting her this time. "And if the two of you want to stand out here and keep pointing fingers at each other, go right ahead. Meanwhile, I have other important matters to tend to."

He walked away, talking to Levi and the FBI agent as he went. I stood next to Ina, who continued to display a tight face. I honestly did not think that I could despise a person as much as I did Raynetta. But this trick here was slowly but surely crawling to the top of my list. Without saying anything else to her, I walked away to find out what we were going to do next to locate Joshua. When I was a few feet away from Stephen, my cell phone rang. I was shocked to see Raynetta's phone number flashing on the screen. I assumed she couldn't reach Stephen; she knew he was with me.

"What do you want?" I said in a nasty tone.

"Hello to you too, Teresa. I was trying to reach Stephen, but he's not answering his phone. I've been waiting to hear the news about Joshua. I'm sure everyone must know something by now."

"What nerve do you have calling me, especially after our last encounter? If you were that concerned, you would've been out here digging up dirt with me. Since you wasn't, I'm not telling you anything. If Stephen wants you to know, he will call you."

"You are such an evil and ugly woman. But if I were in your shoes, I'd be real careful. You wouldn't want anyone to find out what really happened to Claire, would you? I wouldn't, either, and as long as you play nice, your secret is safe with me. Until then, if you happen to see my husband, please tell him to call me."

"Wait on it," I said, then ended the call.

Stephen talked too much. Why in the hell would he tell her the truth about what had happened to Claire? Didn't he know she would use something like that to her advantage? I didn't know what in the hell my son was thinking. My patience was running real thin with him.

Putting aside for a moment what Raynetta had just said to me, I pulled Stephen away from the men he was talking to and inquired about his next move.

"I will call you later, I promise," he said. "And for the last time, I don't need you getting involved in this."

"I'm already involved. And when you get time, the two of us need to have a long talk. I had thought that what happened with Claire was between us. Not between you, me, and Raynetta. She's been calling me and making threats. I don't appreciate that one bit."

"Making threats about what, Mama?"

"About going to the police and telling them what I did. I haven't said one word to her. Been trying to avoid her, but every time I look up, there she is, trying to stir up trouble. Even while I was at that crazy place you put me in, she brought her tail there, making threats. You always want to blame me for everything, but when are you going to tell her to back off?"

The frown on Stephen's face told me that he didn't approve of Raynetta's actions. That, indeed, was a good thing.

"I'll handle Raynetta, and I'm going to find Joshua soon too. You and I will have a lengthy discussion whenever I can squeeze in some time. For now, I have to get back to Washington. There's a lot going on, and in addition to all of this, I still have a country that needs me."

I didn't want to hold him up much longer, so I gave him a hug and kept my mouth shut. I looked at Ina, who seemed to be engaged in a heated conversation with her attorney. Instead of going off on her again, I got in my car to go do my own investigation regarding Joshua's disappearance. I expected to find him before anyone else did.

President of the United States,

Stephen C. Jefferson

As of now, there was only one person who could tell me where Joshua was: Mr. McNeil. But according to a source who had been keeping an eye on things, Mr. McNeil was unconscious and still in recovery. I would be notified whenever his condition changed. Meanwhile, I had numerous people working on this for me. Phones were being tapped, certain people related to Mr. McNeil were being watched, and there were plenty of eyes and ears open. I predicted that Joshua would be found soon. It was such a relief to know that he was possibly out there somewhere, still alive.

In addition to all that had been going on, VP Bass had been trying to meet with me, and we finally scheduled a time for that. Things needed to get done. She was upset with me for taking matters into my own hands and not communicating with her. She certainly knew why that was the case, and according to her, this was her last effort to try to make things right. As always during our meetings, Andrew was there to lend support and to offer his advice.

"All I want you to do is to consider a fresh start," VP Bass said as we made our way down the West Colonnade. "We've all gotten off to a rough start, but it's time to mend some fences and get things done for the American people. Let's focus on legislation that most of us agree on. Like green energy jobs for the American people, infrastructure projects that are long overdue. I'm even willing to see if I can persuade some Republicans to push for more restrictions against the big banks. They are squeezing the pockets of the middle class, and it's time to loosen the grip."

"I'm glad you feel that way. I'm in agreement with you too, and I'm all for a fresh start."

"Great. Because if you are, I would love for you to join me for a surprise visit on Capitol Hill today. It's time for you to reach out to congressional leaders again and let them know you're willing to work with them. You won't be able to get through to everyone, but maybe your visit will prompt some individuals to join with us."

Andrew quickly chimed in. "I think this is a great idea, but let's keep in mind that the president currently has a sixty-two percent approval rating. Congress's approval rating is below fifteen percent. They are the ones who need to do more reaching out than he does, but in no way will this initiative on the president's behalf do him any harm. If anything, it will improve his status."

"It will improve mine too," VP Bass said. "But either way, something like this could benefit us all."

I was skeptical, but I also knew that I couldn't sit in the Oval Office for the rest of my term, dishing out executive orders.

"Count me in," I said to VP Bass. "All I need to do is return a few phone calls, and then we can make our way to Capitol Hill."

With a smile on her face, VP Bass entered the Oval Office with me and Andrew. "Thank you," she said. "I'll meet you on the lower level within the hour."

That was the plan. And after VP Bass left, Andrew stayed to inform me that he would have Sam reach out to the media.

"I would like for the press to join you on Capitol Hill too," he said. "It's good for your image, and you can also take questions. As a matter of fact, why don't you and Raynetta sit down for an interview this evening? The two of you have been getting along rather well, and the American people always like to see and hear what the first family has been up to. You can discuss your visit to Capitol Hill, share some of your future plans, and help remove some of the fear regarding our shaky economy. What do you think about that?"

I nodded, feeling as if an interview would do no harm. "That's fine with me. I'll let Raynetta know before I leave. She's been busy this week, but I'm sure she won't mind."

"Sounds good. I'll tell Sam to prepare his statements for the press briefing today. We'll request that Chris Potters from CNN do the interview. He's a well-respected guy in the media, and his show has millions of viewers. In reference to the first lady, we need to discuss a replacement for Claire. I apologize again for recommending her. I had no idea that she would turn out to be such a disgrace."

"I'll speak to Raynetta about filling that position, but leave it as is for now. I'm more concerned about finding my son, and I don't want anyone to know that he may still be alive. I have no idea how I'm making it through all of this right now, but knowing that there is a chance for us to be face-to-face with each other is giving me hope."

"As long as you're president, your strength will continue to be tested," Andrew noted. "There is a reason why you're here, and the timing couldn't be more right. Try to enjoy yourself on Capitol Hill. I'll see you when you return."

Andrew exited my office. Before I went to Capitol Hill, I called Ina to give her an update. She didn't answer her phone. I then returned a phone call from the director of National Intelligence, and after speaking to him for fifteen minutes, I contacted Raynetta to let her know about the interview. She was with Alex, at a luncheon for survivors of breast cancer.

"We have an interview this evening," I said. "Just wanted to prepare you for it, and tell you that I love you."

"I love you too, but you know how I feel about interviews. I just hope someone with good sense will be conducting it."

"Chris Potters will be the man. Are you good with him or not?"

"I like him. He's reasonable. What do you think?" she said.

"He's okay to me. And as long as he doesn't step on my toes, I won't step on his."

Raynetta laughed. I let her get back to the luncheon and then prepared myself to make an appearance on Capitol Hill.

***

Hours later, I returned from Capitol Hill, feeling pretty good. Things had gone better than expected. So much so that the VP and I found ourselves locked in a pleasant conversation while on the Truman Balcony.

"I told you it wouldn't be that bad, didn't I?" she said. "I think we're on the right track, and we must take advantage of what happened today."

"I couldn't agree with you more, but to be honest, we both know why some of our congressional leaders are eager to make some moves. Midterm elections are not far away, and nobody wants to be booted out by their constituents."

"I'm sure that is the case too, but I see it all as progress. I'll follow up with you later this week. Enjoy your interview tonight. I'll be watching. And for the sake of God, please be on your best behavior."

We both laughed before VP Bass departed. It was my intention to be on my best behavior tonight. Before I did anything else, I went to my bedroom to change clothes. I put on a dark blue blazer with a light blue shirt underneath. My black slacks matched my leather shoes. I avoided a tie altogether. I brushed my waves, which were sharply lined, and then dabbed aftershave on my cleanly shaven face. Just as I was getting ready to tighten my belt, Raynetta entered the bedroom.

"I'm not late, am I?" She hurried to her closet.

"No, but you only have about thirty minutes to get dressed. You can wear what you have on. In my opinion, you look just fine."

Raynetta turned and stood in the doorway. The white and tan dress she wore fit her body like a glove. Not one strand of her hair was out of place, and the high heels she wore made her look real sexy. I repeated that I had no complaints.

"Are you sure this is okay? I really don't have time to change, and you know it takes a while for me to decide on something else."

I walked up to her, eased my arms around her waist. "I said you look fine. And if we had just a few extra minutes right now, I would show you how much I mean what I say."

She placed her arms on my shoulders while looking into my eyes. "Maybe we should let Mr. Potters wait. I've been thinking about you all day, and there is something about the cologne you're wearing that just turns me on."

"I was hoping that it takes more than my cologne to turn you on. Tell me about something else, and then I may consider pushing the interview back about an hour, maybe two."

Raynetta liked my suggestion. She told me and showed me something else when she unzipped my pants and carefully held my heavy meat in her hands.

"In addition to the cologne, this right here really gets me riled up. I love the way it feels, and just between the two of us, the taste of it is very satisfying too."

"Since your taste is much sweeter than mine, why don't we start there?"

I unzipped the back of Raynetta's dress, and after she wiggled it over her hips, it hit the floor. She stood there in a sexy pink bra and sheer panties that revealed her precious goods. I couldn't wait to serve myself, so I moved her onto the bed, where she lay back and opened her legs. I maneuvered myself in between them, and as she unhooked the front of her bra, I removed her panties, then tossed them over my shoulder. My hands latched on to her firm breasts; my mouth found her sweetness. She moaned loudly and squirmed on the bed as her body caught fire from my touch. Her nipples were rock hard as I massaged her breasts, and her pink pearl stiffened more with every delicate lick. Her sugary taste was every bit of what I expected it to be; it was a crime for something to taste this good. I savored every bit of her—my wife, the love of my life.

"Y-you are always so good to me," she said, trying to calm herself by taking deep breaths. "And as much as you do this to me, it always feels like this is the first time."

Raynetta lightly rubbed the back of my head, and as her legs began to quiver, she lifted them up in a wide V. Her juices rained on my tongue, and as I slurped her fluids into my mouth, she secured her legs around my head. Her grip left me unable to breathe, and when she loosened it, I was eager to get out of my clothes and resume from another position. I positioned my steel between her healthy cheeks, then carefully separated her slippery folds from the back. The feel was so on point that we both moaned simultaneously. I expressed how much I loved moments like this, and in return, Raynetta communicated her love by delivering an orgasm that soaked us both. I couldn't do anything else but return the favor. My semen poured into her, and with each rhythmic stroke, the sound of our fluids mixing together echoed in the room.

Raynetta screamed loudly while laying her head on the pillow. "Without a doubt," she said, "I'm the luckiest woman in the world! How do you make my body react to you like that? I don't know how you manage to get all of that out of me."

I eased out of her to see the wetness covering me. "Don't give me so much credit. Needless to say, we do work well together."

I lifted Raynetta off the bed, and as she straddled the front of me, I carried her into the bathroom so we could shower. It took longer than expected, and by the time we were finished, it was an hour or so after our scheduled interview time. I called Andrew to let him know that we would join Mr. Potters shortly. We hurried to change into casual clothes, and with glee in our eyes, holding hands, we made our way to the Blue Room, where the interview was expected to take place. As soon as we opened the door, we found Mr. Potters waiting with his crew.

"Sorry we're late." I extended my hand to him, then shook his hand. "Something came up at the last minute."

"No problem," he said with a smile on his face. "Whenever an opportunity comes along like this, I don't mind waiting. I thank you and Sam for reaching out to me. It truly makes me feel important."

That was what they all said, but either way, Raynetta and I were ready to do this. We both seemed to have a lot of energy, but no one needed to know why.

"I have to say this," Mr. Potters said as the interview got under way. "The two of you make a lovely couple. The first lady is simply beautiful, and in person, you have such a warm and likable spirit. I'm not excluding you, Mr. President. You're very likable in person too. But why do you think that so many Americans misjudge you?"

"First of all, I'm not attacking the media, but some of the things you all say and do are out-rageous," I replied. "I am who I am, no doubt, but the media will play snippets of things I say and do without revealing the whole picture. In defense of the media, I think every person can be misjudged, if you haven't had an opportunity to meet that person. The American people I've met seem to understand me better than the ones I have not. Hopefully, during my term, I'll have an opportunity to meet as many people as I can."

Mr. Potters nodded. "That would be great. It was also a good thing that you visited Capitol Hill today. Many of the senators referred to your visit as a huge step in the right direction. Some even went as far as to call it a success. Then there were others, like Senator Peterson, who said you were wasting your time. He said that working with you on your agenda would destroy our country and that he would never contribute to any legislation that is in line with your vision for the American people. What do you say to Senator Peterson or to any senator like him who feels that way?"

"I refuse to say what I want to say on television, but I will share my thoughts with Senator Peterson and any other senators who share his views. What I feel is sorry for them. They will lose big in the midterm elections, as I am confident that the American people have had enough. If you don't believe me, just examine the polls."

"I have, and they tell us that there are plenty of Republican incumbents who are in trouble ahead of the midterm elections," Mr. Potters noted. "You, however, have not only the Democratic Party on your side, but there are a substantial number of Independents who support you too. Do you believe that by this time next year, you'll be able to hold on to that support or grow it? After the honeymoon stage is over, most presidents sink in the polls. Why wouldn't that be the case with you?"

"My honeymoon stage has been over for a while, but that could very well be the case with me," I answered. "My question to you is, who cares? I certainly don't make decisions based on the polls, and it would be foolish of me to think that I will remain a popular president throughout my entire term. That's not how it works."

"No, it doesn't, and it seems as if you're catching on quickly." Mr. Potters chuckled, then lifted a newspaper that featured pictures of Raynetta during her visit to McDonald's. He smiled as he looked at her. "The other day, these photos were on the front of almost every major newspaper. It looks as if you were having a great deal of fun. But why McDonald's? We've never seen a first lady at McDonald's. Is that one of your favorite restaurants?"

This time, Raynetta laughed. I thought it was a stupid-ass question, and from the look in his eyes and the smirk on his face, I could sense that Mr. Potters was leading up to something. What, I didn't know.

"No, it's not my favorite," Raynetta said politely. I wondered if she could sense the bullshit coming too. "But even though it's not, plenty of people love McDonald's. We were in a rush that day, and that's where we wound up going. People were surprised to see me, and needless to say, I had an amazing time. As for the other first ladies, we are all different. They did their thing, and I will continue to do mine, make my mark and be me."

Mr. Potters ignored her last statement. "I'm sure those kids will remember that day for the rest of their lives. And to be honest, I don't think

I've met anyone who has ever said anything harsh about you. There are, however, rumors that you and your mother-in-law despise each other. Are those rumors true, and what would make anyone not like you?"

I really didn't want Raynetta to answer those questions, but she went for it.

"My mother-in-law and I get along okay. She's just very protective of the president, her son, and I totally understand that. I step on her toes sometimes, but when all is said and done, we're family. We love each other, and nothing will ever change that."

If only that were the truth, I thought while waiting for Mr. Potters's next question. We delved into some of the executive orders I'd put in place, then touched on national security, the lack of support for our veterans, and immigration. We even talked about race, and I didn't hold back on discussing the divisions within our country. We were just about ready to wrap it up when Mr. Potters started traveling down a path that I didn't approve of.

"I think that history will recognize you as being a fairly decent president who kept many secrets. Many presidents kept secrets that their wives weren't aware of until their husbands were completely out of office, and maybe you fit in

that category. I started this interview by saying
what a lovely couple the two of you make. You
inspire many couples, but what kind of message
are you sending, Mrs. Jefferson, if you allow
your husband to have his cake and eat it too? I
mean, he has admitted to being unfaithful to you
before, and we all have seen photos that indicate
to us that infidelity issues exist. I just wonder
why a woman of your stature stays committed
to him. Some people may say you're naive, but
what do you say to the hundreds and thousands
of women, especially African American women,
who have cheating husbands? Do you encourage
them to stay in their marriages?"

I was so shocked by this fool's comment that
for a moment, all I could do was sit there, speechless. Raynetta had been holding my hand, and I
felt her get real tense. She also appeared shocked,
but as soon as she opened her mouth, I spoke up.

"I simply do not understand why you muthafuckas always have to pull a rabbit out of the hat.
This is crazy, and every opportunity that you are
given to belittle the black man, you assholes take
that shit and run with it. Then you try to make
it seem like the white man can do no wrong.
But we both know better, don't we, Mr. Potters?
This interview is done, and if those cameras are

not off in five seconds, the American people will witness me get up from this chair and beat your ass."

In an instant the cameras were shut off. Mr. Potters sat there with a surprised look on his face. He spoke as if he hadn't done or said anything wrong.

"I . . . I asked a legitimate question that I thought some people would want to know the answer to. A lot of first ladies have faced questions like this, and I only wanted an explanation for these pictures."

"What pictures?" Raynetta said, looking at what was in his hands.

"These pictures. They were taken a few weeks or so ago, I guess. I'm not sure," Mr. Potters explained.

I wasn't sure who or what was in the photos until he handed them over to Raynetta. She looked at them one by one. All I could do was shake my head and release a deep breath. The photos showed intimate moments between me and Michelle. Not only during dinner, but inside her hotel room as well. I could tell that someone had taken the pictures from across the way, and it wasn't a pretty sight for Raynetta to see me lying naked in between Michelle's legs.

Raynetta straightened the photos, stood, and then gave them back to Mr. Potters. "I hope and pray that you weren't about to share those photos on live TV. And if you were, shame on you. To answer your question about why I stay, I'll tell you what stupid people like you think and what you all want to hear. It is because the president has a big penis and his mouth works wonders. I am guaranteed multiple orgasms during sex, and nobody screws me like he does. Quote just that on your show, especially if you believe it to be factual. Or you can quote the truth, which has to do with so much more than love. The truth, which I wouldn't waste my time sharing with a person like you. But I am positive that there are plenty of women, from all races, who can share with you their own personal reasons for staying. Have a good evening, Mr. Potters. Thanks for being just another clown."

Raynetta walked off. I followed, deciding not to waste my time with Mr. Potters. When I called out to her, she didn't answer. And when I got to the bedroom, she was sitting on the bed, removing her shoes.

"You lied to me," she said with fury in her eyes. "You told me that you didn't have sex with Michelle, and I believed you."

"I told you the truth. I didn't have sex with her, but we came very close to that happening."

"You must think I'm an idiot. I just saw, with my own eyes, photos of you and her *naked* in bed. Not only that, but you and her *naked* as you carried her across the room. You *naked* between her legs. I guess there's a new way of having sex that I don't know about. I thought it all started with people's clothes coming off."

I stood in front of Raynetta, trying to calm her. This conversation was moving in the wrong direction; I wanted to prevent us from going down this path again.

"Listen to me, okay? I know how this looks, but I did not have sex with her. And even though I was upset with you that day, I realized that having sex with Michelle wasn't going to do our marriage any good. I'm sorry that you had to see those pictures, but just like everything else, you have to realize that there are so many people out there trying to destroy me—destroy us, for that matter—and I ask that you trust me and recognize when I am telling you the truth. I haven't lied to you before about my past indiscretions. Why do you think I would lie to you now?"

"Maybe because you knew this would be the last straw. I can't and won't continue to be humiliated like this. And why do you always

run to another woman when we have problems? You don't waste any time, and it pisses
me off that all you think about is sex when
you're upset."

"That's not true, and for the last time, I did
not have sex with her. Either you believe me or
you don't. I'm not going to stand here all night,
trying to convince you that I didn't do it."

Raynetta cut her eyes at me; I could tell this
was going to be a long night. "You don't have
to stand there all night. I'm sure you have other
things to do. Besides, all I'm going to do is piss
you off and give you a reason to go pay your
lover a visit. It's only nine o'clock, but I'm sure
her legs stay open for you twenty-four-seven,
don't they?"

"This crazy talk is silly. Just like it was silly for
you to visit my mother at that institution and
silly for you to call and threaten her."

Yes, I was trying to change the subject, but
maybe that wasn't a good idea. Raynetta's
demeanor changed—her whole face was twisted.
Bringing up my mother had only made matters
worse.

"You know what?" she said, pointing her finger
at me. "Fuck your mother and screw you too.
I'm tired of her, just like I'm sick and tired of
you. Please don't say anything else to me tonight.
Just . . . just go somewhere and get away from

me, before I say something I'm going to regret."

Raynetta knew that I wasn't about to listen to her orders. I expected her to be upset, but her harsh words would get us nowhere. I remained calm about the situation, and in my last attempt to get her to calm down, I sat next to her on the bed.

"Only a real man is willing to admit when he is wrong. I was wrong for having dinner with Michelle and for going to her room. But I'm not leaving this room until we talk this out," I told her. "We've been getting along very well, and I hate for something like this to come between us. I didn't expect for you to jump for joy after seeing those pictures, but I do expect for you to believe me when I say that nothing happened. If you can just trust me on that, we'll be okay."

She looked me straight in the eyes and rejected what I'd said. "We won't be okay, because I don't believe you. The eyes do not lie. And how dare you feed me this crap about having a wake-up call? The truth is, you never should have been in her room to begin with. You never should've taken off your clothes, and there shouldn't have been a cozy little dinner going on. I have put up with so much from you, Stephen, and I'm finally starting to realize how much this has affected me. I sat there tonight, during that interview, feeling like an idiot. I do want to inspire women, but in no way do I want them to put up with as much as I have."

I wasn't getting through to Raynetta, and when I released a deep sigh, she caught me off guard and slapped the shit out of me. My head jerked to the side; the stinging blow caused my eyes to water.

"Huff and puff all you want!" she shouted. "What I'm telling you is real! This hurts, and you will never understand unless you're in my shoes!"

After that smack, it was time for me to go. She didn't have to go there, but since she had, this conversation was over. I got off the bed, made my way to the door.

"Have fun tonight, and feel free to make some babies with your mistress. I refuse to have a child with a man who doesn't respect me. Maybe she's a bigger fool than me," she raged.

Those words deserved a response. "Keep talking like that and I will make some babies elsewhere. I will also do what you're blaming me for, so hurry up and get your mind right. You get a pass tonight for putting your hands on me, but if you're brave enough to go there again tomorrow, keep in mind that I do to others exactly what they do to me."

Raynetta mumbled something under her breath, but I kept it moving. I made my way to the Oval Office and locked the door behind me. The first thing I did was call Levi to see if he had any news about Mr. McNeil's status.

"He was taken back to surgery this morning," Levi said. "Old man got more problems than a stab wound to his stomach. I really don't see much change in his condition any time soon."

"That's not what I needed to hear. I need to hurry up and find my son. Any word from the others about incoming and outgoing phone calls?"

"Not yet, but we're on it," he assured me. "And trust me when I say we're going to find Joshua. I'm going to pay Mr. McNeil's brother a visit tomorrow. If I can get anything out of him, I'll let you know. I know it's hard, but be patient. At least we know he's alive."

"Thanks for being optimistic. At least we know he wasn't in that casket. We also know that someone from that racist-ass family was involved. I can't believe the funeral home had no idea that that effigy was put in there. You may want to speak to them again. Somebody had to see something."

"I'll fly to St. Louis later this week to see what else I can find out. And while I'm gone, I'm going to ask Lenny to keep an eye on things at the White House. He's the only one who has earned my trust. The rest of them muthafuckas ain't shit."

"We haven't had any problems lately, but in your spare time, I want you to keep an eye on Alex. He's been getting real close to Raynetta. I don't want any surprises, if you know what I mean."

"I do, but Alex is cool. He would never overstep his boundaries."

"For his sake, I hope you're right."

Levi got back to business, and I got comfortable on the sofa, where I would stay for the rest of the night. The TV was on in the background. All I could hear was Mr. Potters preparing himself to *quote* Raynetta's words from earlier.

"If there are any children in the room, you may want to have them leave. I was shocked by the first lady's response, but these were her own words, not mine," he said.

A typed version of what Raynetta had said was plastered on the screen. Specific words had asterisks next to them. He bleeped out several words when he read her comment. I shut my eyes, thinking about what I had gotten my family into and wondering if all of this was worth it.

First Lady,

Raynetta Jefferson

I couldn't get those pictures out of my head for nothing. Nor could I explain why this time seemed so different from all the others. Maybe because my fears had come true. That was, Michelle had a hold on Stephen that he wasn't willing to let go of. For him to still be involved with her confirmed one thing. He liked her a lot, and for me, that was troubling. Confronting her would be a waste of time. Just as arguing with him was. Stephen knew darn well that he'd had sex with her. He was just trying to spare my feelings and make me believe that he had been putting forth every effort to save our marriage.

Those pictures proved that that was in no way the case. Whether he was upset with me or not, that was the wrong thing to do. And this time, there would be consequences for his actions, because I was tired of being the good wife. I had to do something that would hurt him to the same degree that he had hurt me. For years, and throughout our entire marriage, I had never been unfaithful to him. Not once had I ever sought revenge, but this time would be different. This time, I intended to pursue what I wanted, and not surprisingly, that was one night, just one, with Alex.

After being ignored by Stephen for two days and avoiding him, I put a plan in motion to be alone with Alex. Three days later I told him that I needed to be driven to several events that afternoon. He had no idea what I had been up to, and when the afternoon rolled around, we set off. After he had driven me from one event to the next, I informed him that I was ready to return to the White House.

"But before we go there," I said from the back-seat, "I want to stop at the Omni Hotel to see a friend of mine who just arrived. I promise you that I won't be long, okay?"

"No problem. And by the way, I enjoyed listening to your speech today. Your message was powerful, and I'm seeing a lot of positive changes in you as the first lady."

Now, why did he have to go there? I wondered if he would feel the same way after this evening. "Thank you for saying that. I appreciate your compliments. They really mean a lot to me."

I sat back and enjoyed the ride. When we reached the Omni Hotel, Alex parked in a valet spot and was given clearance to escort me inside. The lobby area was nearly empty, and without being seen, we made our way to the elevator.

"What floor is your friend on?" he asked when we got in the elevator.

I told him where to go, and Alex led the way to the suite while observing our surroundings. He was so good at his job, and after we reached the suite, he knocked on the door.

"What's your friend's name?"

"Uh, Tracy. Tracy Buchanan."

Alex hadn't a clue what I was up to. He waited for Tracy to open the door, but I knew that she would never come.

"Did you tell her you were coming?" he asked.

"I did, but she told me to just go inside if she wasn't here when I stopped by."

I removed the key card from my purse. The card had been delivered to me yesterday at the White House, and the suite was already paid for in full. I stuck the key card in the slot, and when the green light flashed, I opened the door. The first thing that I saw was an ice bucket with wine in the center of a table. On one side of the room was a spacious sitting area decorated with yellow, white, and gold accessories. The old-fashioned cherrywood furniture resembled much of what was in the White House, and all the furniture was polished to perfection. Silk drapes covered the windows, and thick crown molding went from wall to wall. A double-sided fireplace lit up the sitting area, as well as the bedroom area, which was open. Plenty of velvety pillows were on the bed, and dimly lit lamps sat on the nightstands. A lounging chair was in a corner of the bedroom, and a small desk was on the other side. Alex took a seat in the sitting area, then reached for the remote to turn on the TV.

"Nice room," he said, unbuttoning his suit jacket and propping his feet on the ottoman. "I hope your friend comes soon. If she doesn't, I'm afraid I may fall asleep."

I certainly didn't want him to do that, but when he yawned, I predicted that I didn't have much time.

"If she's not here in ten or fifteen minutes, I'll call her. Meanwhile, I need to use the bathroom. Yell loudly if she comes."

Alex turned his head sideways and looked at me as I entered the bathroom. I shut the door, then gazed at the huge mirror. I started to feel nervous about this. This was the first time I would ever ask a man, with the exception of Stephen, to make love to me. There was also a part of me that felt guilty. I wondered how Stephen made this seem like an easy thing to do. I bit my nail, but when thoughts of those pictures flashed before me, I decided to push forward. I unzipped my fitted skirt, watched it fall to the floor. My silk blouse was next, and then I removed my heels.

Underneath it all I wore a sheer black negligee with silk thong panties. My breasts were clearly visible, and when I turned around, so were my meaty cheeks. My hair was full of long curls today, but in an effort to look sexier, I had clipped part of my hair up in the back. Several strands dangled along the sides of my face. To wet my lips even more, I had painted them with a shimmery nude gloss. I examined myself in the mirror, thinking about the last time I got dolled up for Stephen. It had been a while—he was always too busy. Nonetheless, he would probably kill me if he knew what I was up to. I didn't think Alex would tell, and even if he did, I would do as Stephen had done and would not confess.

Finally, it was showtime. I sprayed myself with several dashes of perfume, then looked in the mirror at my nipples, which had already hardened. I opened the door to the bathroom, and from a short distance I saw Alex, with his head leaning slightly to the side. He was snoring lightly, with the remote still in his hand. His chest heaved in and out, and as I stood in front of him, I looked at his coal-black hair, which was trimmed on the sides and spiked more on top. His thin body was fit and displayed much strength. I smiled as I thought about him doing away with his glasses, per my request. He hadn't worn them since our discussion that day. That proved to me that he cared about what I thought of him.

Ready to wake Alex, I straddled his legs, which were still propped on the ottoman. I bent over until I was face-to-face with him. My lips barely touched his before he jerked his head back and squinted. His eyelids fluttered; eyes grew wider and wider.

"Who . . . What are you doing?"

Alex appeared out of it—maybe a bit confused. That was until I stood up straight, allowing him to see all of me. He quickly removed his legs from the ottoman, then adjusted himself in the chair. After several blinks, his eyes traveled from my breasts to the tiny gap between my legs. The tip of his tongue quickly rolled across his lips before he cleared his throat. His eyes shifted back to mine.

"Why are you dressed like that?" he asked. "Are you waiting for the president or for your friend?"

I moved my head from side to side. "No, I'm not waiting for the president, nor am I waiting for a friend. The only thing I'm waiting for is for you to remove yourself from that chair, take off your clothes, and have sex with me. I know you want to, Alex. I can see it in your eyes."

Alex swallowed a lump in his throat, then sat up straight. He grabbed at his hair before wiping across his sweaty forehead.

"Just so you know, I don't appreciate jokes. This is not funny, Raynetta. Why would you do something like this?"

"Do you really think this is a joke? I whole-heartedly confirm that it is not, and I'm willing to do whatever to prove it."

Kicking things up a notch, I reached for the string on my thong, lowered it past my hips. Alex glanced at my goodies, then lowered his head into his hands, refusing to look.

"Stop this, Raynetta. Please stop this. I don't want to see you like this, and I wish you . . . you would go put on your clothes so we can leave."

I tossed the thong in his lap, hoping that he got a whiff of my sweet scent. "You don't want to leave, Alex. Neither do I. What you really want to do is take off your clothes and touch me all over. I'm granting you permission to do that, so what are you waiting for?"

Alex wiped down his face, then looked at me again. He tried not to look at my private parts, but he couldn't help himself.

"I'm leaving," he said in a stern tone. "You can stay here if you want, but—"

He couldn't find the right words to say. And without any further ado, he stood to leave. As he stepped away from me, I grabbed his hand and made him face me.

"I'm not going to beg you to do this, but here's the truth. I'm tired of being nice. I'm sick of playing by Stephen's rules. I don't want to keep being his doormat. You, of all people, know what he has done to me. The only other man I'm interested in is you. The only other man I've thought about is you. You're the one who makes me laugh when I want to cry. You understand me, and you are so kind and sweet to me. Allow this to happen, even if it's just once. It will be our secret, and I will never, ever tell one single person. You have my word."

Alex appeared to be defeated, but he also looked as if he wanted to run. "I . . . I don't know how to respond to what you just said to me, but the one thing I will say is there is no way in hell that I'm having sex with you. I'm not interested in you, and I'm sorry that the president is making you feel this way. You need to speak to him about your concerns, Raynetta. Talk to him, because all of this . . . this is wrong."

His rejection didn't feel good. Maybe I was wrong, but then again, maybe I wasn't. "I don't believe that you're not interested in me. Your eyes tell me that you are. I see the way you look at me."

"I look at you that way because it's my job to pay attention to you. And while you're a very beautiful woman, I . . . Again, I'm not interested."

Feeling desperate for an explanation, I pushed, with frustration in my voice. "Why not? What is wrong with you? Am I not good enough?"

Alex reached out and held my shoulders. He searched my eyes before taking a deep breath. "You are more than good enough. I . . . I'm just not into women. I'm gay, okay? I prefer men."

It felt as if someone had punched me right in the gut. I couldn't even repeat what he'd said, and I was so embarrassed that all I could do was slowly back away from him and apologize. My eyes watered; this was one very disappointing moment. Alex couldn't bear to look at me, and when he headed for the door to leave, I rushed into the bathroom to gather myself. I quickly wiped my face with a wet towel, then removed the clip from my hair. As I raked the strands with my fingers, thoughts of what had just happened made me feel sick.

I was too ashamed to leave the room and go meet Alex in the car. Of course he would wait for me, but I just didn't want to face him right now. More than anything, I was ashamed of myself. This wasn't me, and as beautiful and intelligent as I was, my insecurities had gotten the best of me. I was so pleased that Alex had the courage to stop this. I wasn't sure if he had told the truth about being gay or not, but if I had to put some money on it, I would say that he wasn't. He had just made the right decision for both of us. And if he hadn't done so, I would be living with many regrets.

Feeling slightly better, I splashed my face with water. I patted it with a towel, then laid the towel on the counter. I had to call the front desk, ask them to find Alex parked outside, and tell him to leave. I didn't want him to stay the night, and this was the perfect opportunity for me to relax and reflect. I opened the bathroom door, and to my surprise, Alex stood on the other side, naked. I swallowed hard, then quickly glanced below his tight abs. His chest heaved in and out, and without saying a word, he grabbed my waist, pulled me to him.

"I don't know why I can't walk away," he said. "But I wish like hell that I could. You very well may be the death of me, Raynetta, but I've waited many months to do this."

Alex's lips touched mine, but I backed my head away from him.

"No, I'm sorry, but you were right," I said. "We can't do this. We shouldn't be doing this, and I apologize for bringing you here. Please forgive me."

He ignored everything I'd said, and as he pulled me toward the bed, I was surprised by his aggressiveness.

"No, we should be doing this," he said. "I've always wanted to do this, and you don't owe me an apology for anything."

It wasn't until Alex pushed me back on the bed that I realized how serious this was. He lay on top of me while holding my hands over my head and roughly sucking my neck. I kept turning my head from side to side, trying to make him stop.

"Alex, please," I said, attempting to get through to him. "I don't want this. You don't, either, so let's just go and—"

"No," he replied, then released my hands. "You can't tell me what I want. I know what I want, Raynetta, and that would be you."

Alex expressed just that sentiment when he yanked the sheer fabric aside to expose one of my breasts. His whole mouth covered it, and as I squirmed and tried to push him away, his body seemed to get heavier. I rejected his touch over and over again. Did my best to convince him not to go further, but Alex would not listen.

"You're going to regret this." I squeezed his hand to prevent him from touching me. "I said I don't want this, and you must listen to me before this goes too far."

"I *am* listening. I'm listening to your body, which says you do want this. You need this, and you can't just walk away from what we're feeling now."

I tried to walk away, but to no avail. Alex was one strong man. He held me down, and within a matter of seconds, he entered me, using much force. I felt so responsible for this; I shouldn't have ever brought him to this hotel room. I was the one who had seduced him, so was it fair for me then to say no? Hell yes, it was, but saying no had come too late. I lay there like a bump on a log, numb. And seeing how uncooperative I was, Alex opened his eyes, which were previously tightly closed.

"What is wrong with you?" he said, halting his strokes. "You just can't do this, Raynetta. Don't you understand that I have feelings too?"

I slowly nodded my head. "I do, but please get off of me. Now, Alex, right now."

He released a deep sigh before easing out and backing away from me. Disgust was written all over his face, and after he went into the bathroom, he slammed the door. I remained on the bed, numb as ever. What a huge mistake this was, and unfortunately for me, I had a feeling that I had unleashed a monster.

President of the United States,

Stephen C. Jefferson

My mother had been missing in action; so had Raynetta. I had reached out to both of them within the hour, but neither one had answered their phone. I left messages before I went into a three-hour-long meeting in the Roosevelt Room, where we discussed the new strategy for dealing with terrorism. Many terrorist organizations had been making threats about bombing some of our football stadiums, and the Olympics were a target as well. Several unfortunate incidents had been happening around the world, but no one could deny that there had been a decline in terrorist activities. That was due to our highly skilled soldiers, who had always put forth their best efforts to keep us safe. The United States was always expected to lead, not follow. We were doing just that, and with two other world leaders on a conference call with me, we all listened in as the Secretary of Defense reminded us that another high-ranking terrorist leader had been killed.

"You are well aware that we are making progress, Mr. President, and many of these organizations are on the move. They are lacking the necessary funds to keep going, and there is no question that many of them have been crippled."

"That's very good news, but it's not time for anyone to celebrate," I replied. "Stay on our new mission, and with a collaborative effort from other countries as well, I expect things to keep turning for the better."

The other leaders, along with the Secretary of Defense and VP Bass, agreed. We finally wrapped up the conference call. That was when Andrew turned his swivel chair toward mine.

"Looks like this is a new playing field, huh? I never thought we would get to this point. Now the only thing we have to worry about is homegrown terrorism."

"Don't get ahead of yourself," VP Bass advised. "We always have to worry about what is happening around the world, but I agree that homegrown terrorism needs to be dealt with. It requires a very different strategy, and it also requires a little more assistance from individuals in Silicon Valley. They are the leading hub for high-tech innovation.

We desperately need them to work more with government, even though many people prefer not to."

I surely knew why people preferred not to work with the government. There were a lot of problems within the system. "That doesn't surprise me, but tackling terrorism requires an all-hands-on-deck approach," I asserted. "Let's talk about creating a new team to join with the individuals in Silicon Valley. We must somehow convince them that this isn't about interfering with people's privacy. It's more about keeping the American people safe."

VP Bass nodded, then stood to gather her notes. Andrew was ready to move out too, but after VP Bass left, he hung around to ask me some questions.

"I don't know if it's just me or not, but do you want me to submit my resignation? Things seem a little awkward between us lately. I don't know if you're still upset with me about recommending Claire as Raynetta's assistant or if you think I had something to do with Mr. Potters's ridiculous interview. I asked him to conduct the interview based on the way he presents himself on TV. It's not like I knew the guy on a personal level."

"If I wanted your resignation, I would ask for it," I told him. "I'm not happy about your recommendations, but you're my senior adviser. I listen to what you recommend, and then I make my own decisions. I can't be that upset with you if things don't always work out according to plan. With that being said, if you don't wish to be here any longer, you are free to walk. No hard feelings, and trust me when I say I'll understand."

"I'm perfectly fine with working for you. I just want you to trust me . . . my judgment, and I don't want you to assume that because I'm white or I haven't known you for a long time, like Levi has, I can't be trusted. We are a team, and I hope you recognize that."

"I have no problem with you Andrew, but a man who continues to yell, 'Trust me,' simply can't be trusted. It took years for Levi to earn my trust, and as much as you think those years don't matter, to me, they do. At the end of the day, we are a team. I appreciate you more than you will probably ever know."

"I'm not going to comment on you and your friend, but I assume that many of the changes I see in you have a lot to do with your son," he replied.

"Frankly, they do. I can't stop thinking about him. I feel as if I'm not doing enough to find him, but the truth is, everyone is working their asses off to find out where he is. It's almost like he just vanished."

"With all the equipment we have to find out where someone is, I think you may have to accept that there is a possibility Joshua is no longer in the United States. I thought about it last night, because it doesn't make sense that we all are coming up empty. That's just my take on it, and until Mr. McNeil is able to wake up and say something, our hands are pretty much tied."

I nodded. "I hate to admit it, but that may be true. Levi tried to pump his brother for information, but it was pretty clear that he didn't know anything. He's in St. Louis, meeting with the owner of the funeral home. I hope he'll have some luck with him."

Andrew stood, then patted me on the back. "I hope so too. Try to get some rest. And if I hear anything, I'll let you know."

He left the room, I returned to the Oval Office, and almost fifteen minutes later, as I was reading through some important papers on my desk, Levi called.

"I have good news and bad news," he said. "I'll start with the good news first. The funeral home owner was paid off by someone he said he didn't know. According to him, he was offered a lot of

money to keep quiet about Joshua not being in
that casket. He was also asked not to let anyone
open it, and he claimed that he didn't know what
was inside. I was able to watch videos of people
coming and leaving the funeral home that whole
week. I saw the person who put the effigy in the
casket, but I couldn't make out his face. I can tell
you this, though. He was black."

"That doesn't exclude Mr. McNeil, does it? He
could have paid a black man to do it, couldn't
he?"

"Yeah, but I'm starting to get a funny feeling
about this. When I asked the owner how much
he was paid, he said twenty-five Gs. Mr. McNeil
offers millions to get what he wants. Twenty-five
Gs seems kind of low for him. . . . I'm just saying.
He was the one, however, who claimed to know
where Joshua was."

"Right. And that means he knows he's alive.
Now, if all of that is the good news, what's the
bad news?"

Levi paused before saying anything. He then
cleared his throat and spoke up. "Alex had sex
with Raynetta. It happened yesterday at a hotel.
Lenny wasn't able to get any photos, but he said
they were in the room for several hours. I know
that's not what you wanted to hear, and I'm
surprised that Alex made a decision to go there."

Was this a total shock to me? No. Every time we argued, Raynetta made threats about doing something like this. She was determined to make me pay for what I had done, and now she had gotten her wish. The news, however, broke my heart. I couldn't even stay on the phone with Levi, and after ending the call, I laid my arms and head on the desk. Yes, I had done Raynetta wrong. I'd failed her as a husband. I had taken her for granted, but I had also tried to change course and focus more on improving our marriage. She was no saint, either, and a lot of her own actions drove me to do some of the things I had done. We both were equally responsible for this madness, but in no way would I accept this. The shoe on the other foot didn't fit. I couldn't wear it as well as she had, and the thought of her giving herself to another man made me sick to my stomach. I slowly got up from my desk, then made my way to the door. Lynda was sitting at her desk when I asked if Raynetta had returned my call.

"No, she hasn't. Would you like for me to reach out to the Secret Service? Alex probably knows where she is. Most likely, he's with her."

Without a doubt, he was. Probably somewhere knocking her damn back out. "Yeah, uh, call Alex. Tell him I need to see him right away.

Don't bother to ask him about Raynetta. Just tell him that I need to see him."

"Will do, sir. But are you okay? Do you need some water or something else to drink? You don't look well."

"A pitcher of ice-cold water will be fine. Please, if you don't mind."

I staggered away from the door and then plopped on the sofa. With my head tilted back, I couldn't help but to think about my damn mother again. I hated that she was always right about certain things. I wanted her to be so wrong about Raynetta. Of all people, why couldn't my mother be wrong about her? I kept telling myself that it was only sex, but thoughts of Alex and Raynetta having sex had me feeling down and out. I didn't even know how to handle this, and I couldn't even say that I was mad. Disappointed? Absolutely. Jealous? Of course. Mad? Nope. But mad as hell? Yes. Yes. Yes.

Lynda came into my office with a pitcher of water. She put it on the table in front of me, then smiled.

"Alex said that he and the first lady were on their way back to the White House. She attended some kind of rally today, and Alex said it took longer than expected. I told him you wanted to see him. He'll be here soon."

"Thank you, Lynda. Send him right in when he gets here, and then you can leave for the day."

"Thank you. I will. See you tomorrow."

I did my best to gather myself before Alex arrived, and even though I did a little, it all went back down the drain the second he entered my office. It was as if I could see Raynetta with her legs wrapped around him. And when he opened his mouth, I expected the sweet scent of her pussy to slap me in the face.

"You wanted to see me?" he said, then moved closer to where I was on the sofa. He appeared to be just fine; there was no fear in his eyes whatsoever. I was sure he knew the reason why I wanted to see him.

"Have a seat," I said as my eyes shifted to the gun I had already placed on the table. "We need to talk."

Displaying braveness, Alex sat across from me and crossed one of his legs over the other. He scratched his head, then raked the front of his hair with his fingers.

"I just wanted to commend you for doing such a great job protecting the first lady. I told you a while back that she could be quite difficult at times, but it looks as if you've been able to handle her."

He slowly nodded as his eyes shifted to the gun as well. "Yes, sir, I have been able to handle her. Quite well, I must say, and in no way is she difficult to me."

"I figured you would say that, so let me not beat around the bush. I assume you're talking about the way you were able to handle her in the hotel room last night."

He shrugged his shoulders. "No, she actually handled me. Handled me so well that I wouldn't mind taking another risk."

I was surprised by how blunt he was. "So, in other words, you're willing to die for a piece of my wife? That's crazy talk, and I can't believe you're that stupid. I have to ask what your motive is."

"No motive. I just did something that I have longed for so very much."

I had vowed never to hurt anyone on American soil, but Alex was pushing me to change my mind. I couldn't have sympathy for a man who was willing to die for sex, and in the Oval Office or not, he had to be dealt with.

"You got guts, Alex, but you chose the wrong woman. We all have feelings that we can't control sometimes, but it seems to me that you are unapologetic for your actions."

I carefully reached for the 9 millimeter, eased it my way, and placed it on my lap. Alex shifted in his seat, his nervousness starting to show.

"Just so you know, the first lady pursued me," he insisted. "I don't wish to go into details about why it was difficult for me to reject her, but it was very difficult. My feelings were uncontrollable. But before you decide whether or not to splatter my blood all over the presidential seal, I want to cut a deal with you. The deal is if you allow me to walk out that door for good, I will never touch your wife again. I will put you on a path to finding your son, but you have to promise me that you won't hurt Raynetta and you won't come after me once I'm gone. I don't have anything against you, Mr. President. I just fell hard for your wife. I often dreamed of having sex with her, and if you want to kill me for exploring my feelings, I can't do much to stop you."

It was interesting that whenever killing was on the table, everybody had information about Joshua. I refused to travel down this road with Alex; he was about to be dreaming for a very long time. I tilted the gun sideways on my lap, then aimed it at the center of Alex's chest. I couldn't believe that he didn't attempt to run, and thinking more about the braveness he displayed, I asked him another question.

"Three words. Where is he?"

"I can't tell you specifically where Joshua is, but the one thing I am sure of is your ex-girlfriend, Ina, knows. The reason why I know this is that I saw her speaking to a close confidant of Mr. McNeil's right after the funeral. He gave her an envelope, and she smiled as if she had just won the lottery. She didn't appear to be a grieving mother, and her demeanor was quite different from what it had been inside the church. I'm very observant, Mr. President. My suggestion to you is to follow her. The only reason I hadn't said anything sooner was that I predicted that you and I would find ourselves in this situation. I held on to this information, hoping that it would spare my life when necessary."

Just that fast, Alex had my mind spinning. I couldn't even imagine Ina being behind any of this. Was she capable of putting on an act like this and lying? Of course she was. She'd been lying for years. And why? Because of the almighty dollar.

"Alex, I'm going to take that deal and let you walk out of here a free man. But I suggest that you move quickly, because I am known for abruptly changing my mind."

Alex stood and made his way to the door. Before opening it, he turned to address me. "I

trust that you and Raynetta will work through
your differences, sir. She's an amazing woman,
and deep down, she really does love you. I hope
you know how lucky you really are."

"You're the one who is lucky. And it would
be wise for you to get the fuck out of my office,
instead of offering me some last-minute advice."

Alex left without saying another word. I quickly
got on the phone to call Levi.

"Ina," I said to him. "Go to her house. See if
you can find her. Talk to her about Joshua, and
see what kind of vibes you get. If you can, keep
an eye on her for a few days. Somebody just told
me something that points in her direction. I'm
feeling it. We're on to something."

"Ina?" he questioned. "I'm shocked to hear
this, but you know I'll see what's up. Maybe
we are on to something, and no stone must go
unturned."

I ended the call, laid the receiver down, and
then left the Oval Office to go deal with my
darling wife.

First Lady,

Raynetta Jefferson

Alex had taken me to an event earlier, but our conversation had been kept to a minimal. He'd apologized, and the only thing I'd advised was for us to move on and put the incident behind us. He hadn't said much after that, but what he didn't know was that he would soon be replaced. I no longer wanted him around: even though I might have stirred up his feelings, it was best that he was as far away from me as possible. I felt horrible about all of this. Even felt terrible for him. But this was what it had come to, and I had to someway or somehow deal with one of the biggest mistakes I'd made thus far.

I had just finished my shower, so I turned off the water, then reached for a towel to wrap around myself. I combed my wet hair back, and after brushing it into a sleek ponytail, I went into the bedroom. Catching me off guard, Stephen stood by the window with his hand in his pocket. He was gazing outside. When he heard me, he turned his head to look at me.

"How was your day?" he said.

"It was fine. I plan to turn in early for bed. I'm a little tired."

"Yeah, you made that quite clear. You're tired of me, tired of my mother, tired of everything, including this marriage. The questions is, are you tired of having sex with Alex yet?"

In an instant, my heart dropped somewhere below my stomach. Now, I always knew that news around the White House traveled fast. But how in the hell did Stephen know about me and Alex? Did Alex mention it to Stephen? I couldn't tell him what had *really* happened, and there was no way for me to explain why I had invited Alex to the hotel to begin with. In that moment, I had to deny everything.

"I don't know where you're getting your information from, but that would be very incorrect."

Stephen snickered as he moved away from the window. His movement caused me to move in another direction. I eased over to the bed and stood by the post. The towel started to slide off my body, so I pulled it up with one hand. Stephen squinted at me from a distance before moving closer to me.

"Incorrect? Okay." He reached out to touch my neck, causing me to jump. "No worries. I'm not going to hurt you, so stop flinching. But, uh, what's that on your neck?"

His calmness made me fearful. I moved his hand away from my neck, unaware of what he was talking about. Then it hit me—the red marks and bruises I had seen on my body while showering. I had resisted Alex even more when he sucked my neck and breasts and just wouldn't stop.

"I don't know what you're referring to. I had a minor altercation with someone at the event earlier. There was pushing and shoving. I was in the middle."

Stephen shot me a look that killed me a thousand times. I was just not prepared to go there with him right now and explain my actions. But as I attempted to move away from him again, he yanked the towel away from my body, then pushed me back on the bed. I sat up on my elbows and saw something in his eyes that told me to stay calm.

"Don't move and don't say one word, or else I will slap the shit out of you, just like you did to me the other day." His eyes scanned my body from head to toe. "You have no shame, do you? You feel safe to come in here with suck marks on your neck . . . on your breasts. . . ." He grabbed my leg, pulled it until it was straight. "And there's a bruise on your thigh. What did you let him do, Raynetta? Beat your ass? Whatever he did, I'm sure you enjoyed yourself." He pushed my leg away from him, causing it to hit the bedpost. I didn't know what he was going to do to me, but maybe I could tell him something . . . anything that was some kind of justification for what I had done.

"My only objective was for you to feel my pain. You—"

Stephen silenced me when he reached forward and grabbed my face. His fingers were pressed into my cheeks, while his hand covered my mouth.

"Mission accomplished, because I feel your fucking pain! I told you that I didn't have sex with her, but whether I did or not, you would've fucked him, anyway! If you think this was the best way to get my attention and seek revenge, you are sadly mistaken. You don't mean shit to me anymore, Raynetta. Nothing. And I hope you're real proud of yourself for scoring another point against me."

He released my face; my mouth was stiff, and my cheeks were sore. His words stung, and I hoped that mine did too.

"You can't keep running over me and expect for me to sit back and do nothing. Maybe this wasn't the right thing to do, but what's done is done. It's *done*, and I'm sorry if you can't handle what I have endured for many years."

I could sense that Stephen wanted to hit me; that was something he had never done. The tight look on his face said it all—I was in major trouble. His eyes shifted to the suck marks on my breasts again. He clenched his fists, and with a heightened level of anger, he yanked me off the bed, causing me to fall on the floor, hard on my ass. He kneeled over me, then grabbed the back of my head. His face was close to mine, forcing me to look into his eyes.

"Alex is no more. You are no more. This marriage is no more. And if I ever hear you boast about what he did to you, I will kill you, Raynetta. I swear to God that I could kill you right now, and I'm fighting real hard not to snap your fucking neck."

I blinked the tears from my eyes, remaining real silent. He appeared very unstable. I was so worried about what he would do or what he had already done. What did he mean by "Alex is no more"? Had he done something to him? That would be so messed up, but for now, I was more concerned about Stephen's behavior and about

my safety. Since I hadn't responded, he released
his tight hold on me. He stepped over me, and
then he went into the bathroom. I heard the
water come on, and after I got off the floor and
sat on the edge of the bed, he left the bathroom.

Without saying another word, he opened the
door to our bedroom, walked out, and slammed
the door behind him. I felt relieved that he had
left without really hurting me. My forehead
ached, and as I massaged my temple, I reached
for my cell phone on the nightstand. I dialed
Alex's number just to express my regrets.He
didn't pick up, so I left a message.

"Forgive me for putting you in the middle of
this mess. I don't want any trouble, and I regret
all of this. Stephen knows what happened, and
I don't think it would be wise for you to come
back here ever again. Stay away, Alex, and if you
appreciate your life, you will."

I turned my head to place the phone back on
the nightstand. That was when I felt my ponytail
being pulled backward. Stephen had a tight grip
on me, and I didn't realize how powerful it was
until I was pulled across the bed and my body
hit the floor hard. Apparently, calling Alex was
a bad idea.

"You couldn't wait for me to leave, could you?"
he said. He unbuckled his leather belt, removed

it from around his waist. I couldn't believe that
he was about to strike me with it, but when he
wrapped part of it around his hand, this shit had
gotten real.

"Nooo!" I shouted to get through to him. He
was gone. The rage in his eyes said so. The sweat
rolling down his forehead showed how heated
he was, and the vein popping out of his neck
displayed that as well. "Stop and listen, okay?
I didn't want it. I swear to you, I made a big
mistake! Don't do this, Stephen, because if you
do, we will never recover from this!"

"I don't give a damn about a recovery, and
you're absolutely right you made a mistake!" He
raised his hand, and when it came down, the belt
slapped the floor right next to me. I rolled over,
hoping to avoid being hit.

"Please don't do this! Don't hurt me. . . . I
know you don't want to hurt me!" I uttered
quaveringly.

This was so unbelievable to me, I started to
cry. What had I done to my husband, *to us*?
Where in the hell was he? He dropped the belt,
but as he clenched his fist, I covered my face
with my hands. Stephen fell over me, and right
beside my head, I could hear his fist pound the
floor.

"Why, Raynetta?" he shouted. "I have all this shit going on, and all you can do is keep on bringing me your fucking drama! Time and time again, you just keep on trying to break me! You haven't said one damn thing about my son. You haven't asked how you can help alleviate some of the pressure I'm under. You . . ." Breathing heavily, he paused, then dropped his sweaty forehead on my heaving chest. And after a long moment of silence, he spoke in a soft tone.

"You are so selfish, and you are exactly the woman my mother said you would be. I had faith in you, but you have disappointed me in so many ways. Damn, Raynetta. Why have you failed me, especially at a time when I need you to stand with me?"

It did me no good to explain myself to Stephen right now. He wasn't in the right frame of mind to listen. I had never thought that my being with another man would bring him to this, and no matter how much I tried to justify what I had done, this was bad. Real bad. And the guilt I felt was unlike anything I had ever felt before. I lifted Stephen's head from my chest, held it with my hands. He closed his eyes so I wouldn't see his emotions.

"I regret all of this, but something tells me that no matter what I say, you will never forgive me,"

I told him. "And no matter how many times that I've forgiven you, none of that will matter. If you want me to go, I will go. We can't continue to destroy each other like this and then think that the love we have for each other will save us."

Stephen swallowed the lump in his throat before opening his watery eyes. He wiped his hand down his face, and after he got off of me, he calmly walked out of the room. I honestly did not know what to do, but it was evident that we needed some space. I couldn't live up to my role as the first lady—not like this. I couldn't be the woman I knew I could be if hurting him was my objective. The battles, even the ones he faced as president, could be won only if we had each other's back. We didn't, and this was a result of that.

No, we weren't perfect, but I had to admit that this was messy. I wasn't pleased that we had been gifted with an opportunity to show the world that being messy wasn't always a way of life, especially with African American couples, and then we had failed miserably to make our case. Shame on us. . . . Shame on me. And now I had to go back to the drawing board and examine my mistakes. Unfortunately, that meant leaving the White House and focusing not so much on Stephen but on myself.

President of the United States,

Stephen C. Jefferson

With me occupying the highest office in the land, I didn't have much time to deal with personal problems. World issues refused to wait, and the very next day after my gut-wrenching evening with Raynetta, several other things were on the horizon. Three African American men, armed and dangerous, had gone into a beauty salon in an affluent neighborhood in California and blasted eight Caucasian women and one child. The men were still on the loose, and the media was going crazy. The White House was pretty active too, and every time I put my phone down, it rang again.

If that crime wasn't enough to get everyone riled up, a major hurricane that had hit the East Coast surely was. Many lives had been lost, and it had been reported that the United States hadn't seen a storm quite like this one before.

The governor in North Carolina had declared a
state of emergency. I had to sign off on allocating
millions of dollars to help the state clean up and
rebuild. In the midst of it all, there was no word
on Joshua. All the people I had looking into this
matter had come up empty, even Levi, who had
confirmed that Ina was in no way involved in
Joshua's disappearance. I was back to square
one.

"I don't know what Alex was talking about,"
Levi said when we finally spoke at length about
the matter by telephone. "But he was barking
up the wrong tree. I spoke to Ina. She seems
more upset about this than anyone. She's particularly mad at you. Stressed how she never wants
to see you again."

"I have no problem with that, but what did she
say about Joshua? Is she investigating where he
may be at all? Did she give you the impression
that she was looking for him?"

"She mentioned that she had some people on
her end trying to find Joshua. I followed her
around for a few days, but I didn't see anything
out of the ordinary. I suggest that when things
calm down, you reach out to her. Let her know
that you're on her side, and try to work together
on finding out where Joshua is. The more people
involved, the better."

Maybe Levi was right. I would reach out to Ina in a few more days, just to see if we could put our issues to rest and put together a collaborative effort to find Joshua.

"I'll call her in due time. But when are you coming back to Washington?" I said.

"Sometime early next week. I've been visiting a few family members in St. Louis. Promised my cousin that I would stay for her birthday party this weekend. If you need me to come back sooner, let me know. I'm sure it's hectic around there, and it's a damn shame what those men did. Stuff like that makes it harder for us. The language I've heard referencing those men on the news and on the radio isn't good. That kind of hatred only angers more people."

It wasn't often that Levi and I disagreed. I told him I'd see him next week and asked him to keep me posted on any news.

For the next several hours, Andrew, Sam, the VP, and I sat in VP Bass's office, waiting to hear if the men who had murdered those women and a child had been captured. We all feared that more people would be injured, so there was a huge effort by law enforcement and the FBI to shut this down quickly. As of yet, we weren't sure what the motive for the crime was, but there were plenty of people speculating about it.

Even VP Bass. She didn't hold back on what she was feeling inside.

"This is why you can't pick and choose sides, Mr. President," she asserted. "These idiots come in all shapes, sizes, and colors, and I have a hunch that those women were targeted because they were wealthy white women. You can deny that all you want, but it is what it clearly is."

I wasn't looking for an argument with VP Bass, but obviously, she was looking for one with me. "I haven't said much to you at all, and I will keep my opinion to myself until we have all the facts," I said.

She snapped back. "You should weigh in. There are eight women dead, along with a child. It doesn't matter what color they are, and as president, you should be willing to say that the killers were wrong! Wrong! Wrong! Wrong! There is no other way to put it!"

I wasn't sure what kind of reaction she wanted from me, but I remained calm. "It was wrong. Very wrong. And whenever those men are caught, they will face consequences for their actions."

She crossed her arms and pouted. "Saying it's wrong isn't enough. Why aren't you running to the podium to deliver one of your speeches about racism in America? If it was the other way around, you would be pandering to African

Americans, shouting black power, and making promises to them about finding the killers. I've watched you, Mr. President. I know whose side you're on. It damn sure isn't the side of white women."

Andrew interjected a remark before I did. "Wait a minute. You're being very unfair. The president cares deeply for everyone in this country. He wouldn't be here if he didn't."

"She's just making that claim because she's upset," Sam added. "We all are, but your comments are a bit of a stretch."

"No, they're not." VP Bass kept it going by defending her words. "Any other time, the president would be walking around here, shouting, pointing fingers, and ordering people around. Today, however, he's calmer than I have ever seen him. It's as if nothing has happened and there are no freaking Negroes on the loose."

I guessed she'd made her point, because I had enough of her foolishness. "Right now, the only white woman whose side I am not on is yours. If you want me to show my ass, I will do so, per your request."

I grabbed her by the arm and escorted her to the door. She snatched her arm away from me, then straightened her jacket.

"I don't know how many times I have to warn you, Mr. President, but this is the last straw. Keep your dirty, filthy hands off of me, or else you will be faced with—"

I grabbed her arm again, this time holding it much tighter. "Yeah, I know. You'll sue, and I'll win, because I have witnesses who are sick and tired of you making everything about whites and niggers. Niggers like me, with filthy hands. Go wash off the residue from my touch, and while you're at it, use some soap to clean your dirty-ass, slick mouth, which I have seriously had enough of."

I shoved her out of her own office, then slammed the door and locked it before I walked away. She pounded on the door.

"Open this door right now! This is my office! You can't shut me out of my own office, sir!"

"Face reality," I shouted from the inside. "You were just shut out, and you will not come back in!"

I heard her using vulgar language as she marched away from the door. The truth was, I didn't have time for her insults today. There was too much on my mind. It wasn't that I didn't care about those women. I did care. I was just saddened that it had come to this in our country. We had seen it brewing many years ago, but little effort was made to unite us. That was the sad part. So sad. There were days when I wanted to walk away from it all. This was one of those days, but I had to tough it out. I simply had to, because the fight was in me to make things better, especially in the area of race relations.

Nearly five hours later, thankfully, the men were caught. But as they surrendered by lowering their weapons and holding their hands up in the air, the officers unloaded their weapons, killing the men dead in the street. The video of this played over and over again on television. Everyone who had something to say found a way to say it. The TV reporter talked to a number of people on the street to get their opinions.

"The officers didn't have a choice. One of the men looked as if he was moving forward."

"If you look closely at the video, you can see that the one on the left had a knife in his hand."

"Those men surrendered! They deserved to have a trial, just like everyone else in this country."

"How can anyone defend what we all witnessed with our own eyes? Those officers are no better than the men who killed those women."

"They were thugs. What's the big deal?"

Everybody weighed in. In an effort to calm a nation that was overwhelmingly divided on

many issues, I went to the podium in the press
briefing room to speak. Feeling the way I felt, I
wasn't sure if the message I attempted to convey
about peace, responsibility, and accountability
was received well or not. But in the moment,
it was all I could do. I was exhausted—everyone
could tell. Even Michelle. This was apparent
to me when I glanced at her before stepping
away from the podium. I was midway down the
corridor when Sam rushed after me and told me
that Michelle wanted to speak to me. I refused
without providing an explanation.

I went to the bedroom, where there seemed to
be a little peace and quietness. Raynetta wasn't
there, and this time, some of her clothes had
been removed from the closet. With my suit still
on, I climbed in bed, placed my hands behind
my head, and stared at the ceiling. I struggled to
close my eyes and go to sleep, and I was lucky to
get at least three hours in.

Later that week, things started to simmer
down. I left Washington to go survey the hurricane damage on the East Coast. To say it was
one big mess was putting it mildly. Many people
shared stories with me about how horrific the
storm was, and so many others were just thank-

ful to be alive. I offered my support by making a promise to the people that their government would not leave them hanging.

"Thank you so much for coming," the governor from North Carolina said when she greeted me at the Red Cross. She was a woman who definitely had her hands full. Everyone was counting on her to utilize the state's emergency funds appropriately, and with money pouring in from all around the country, I was optimistic about things getting back to normal soon.

"No need to thank me," I said to the governor as we sat down to get a bite to eat. "I'm just glad I'm in a position to help."

As the governor and I ate, people took pictures with us and commended me on doing a great job. Some even offered me advice, but as I said before, no one really knew what it was like to work in the Oval Office every day. When the governor and I were in the middle of a conversation with a lady who had just lost everything, my phone kept vibrating, so I excused myself and stepped away to answer it. It was my mother. I hadn't heard from her in several weeks. After we dug Joshua's grave, I'd told her to take a vacation, not to disappear completely.

"Where have you been?" I whispered into the phone.

"I've been busy. I told you that the two of us needed to talk, and I hope you're prepared for what I need to say to you."

"I'm always ready. I'm sure it won't be anything different."

"It will be, and before I go any further, what's up with you and Raynetta?" she quizzed. "The media is reporting that she may have left the White House. Some speculate that she's been with Alex. The media lies so much, but is any of that true?"

In no way would I tell my mother what was going on between Raynetta and me. "I don't know why you would ask me anything about what the media says. Raynetta decided to take some time away from the White House to deal with Claire's death. She took it real hard. She knows what you did, and that makes it even harder."

"I guess you didn't share why I did what I did. If she knew, maybe she'd be singing a new tune. Then again, we are talking about Raynetta. She's always looking for something to whine about. I wish she would grow the hell up, and I hate that you're married to such a weak, whining b—"

"Mama, I have to go," I said, interrupting her. "If you have something that you need to speak to me about in person, you know where to find me."

"I do, but before you go, have you heard any-thing about that crazy woman who said she wants to sue me for a million dollars?"

"That's been settled, thanks to me. Now, I have to go. I'm in North Carolina, looking at all the damage from the storm. It's horrific. Pray for these people, all right?"

"You know I will. I'm going to pray for you too, because you are heading toward a storm too."

My mother left it at that. What she didn't know was my storm had been brewing for a long time. I was surprised that she hadn't mentioned Joshua—that was, indeed, strange.

By six o'clock that evening, I was on my way back to Washington. I had been getting updates from Andrew throughout the day, and when he told me Michelle had been trying to reach me, I asked him if he knew why.

"I didn't inquire. She spoke to Sam, told him that it was urgent. If you would like for me to have him call you, I will."

"That won't be necessary. But do me a favor, please."

I told Andrew what it was; he said he would get on it right away. When I returned to the White House, he was in the Oval Office waiting for me.

"The children left with the grandmother," he said in reference to my favor. "And Lenny will take you there whenever you're ready. As for the other thing you requested, I'm not sure of Alex's location. That may take more time for me to investigate. The first lady, however, has been at a nearby hotel."

I wasn't sure if that was a good thing or a bad thing. I thanked Andrew and encouraged him to continue his investigation.

"Before you go," I said, "I don't want any of the facts leaked to the media. People are only speculating about Raynetta, but please continue to say that she has had a hard time with Claire's death and is taking time for herself."

"I will keep everything on lock. But tell me this. Are you and the first lady on the verge of a divorce? That wouldn't be good, Mr. President, especially if it has anything to do with Alex."

"I can't answer that right now. That's all I can say, and I don't wish to elaborate on Alex," I replied.

"Okay. Have a good night, sir, and be safe."

Andrew left the Oval Office, and within the hour, so did I. It was almost one in the morning when Lenny drove me to Michelle's place. On the drive there, my thoughts were deep. I knew that if Raynetta and I were serious about correcting our marriage, we had been going about things the wrong way. And the truth was, both of us had been unhappy with each other for a long time. She wasn't willing to let go of certain things about me, and to some extent, I was still holding on to certain things pertaining to the past too. I hated that this was what it had come to, and after so many attempts to straighten up our acts, I had lost all faith that we could do it. Especially after what she had done with Alex. I couldn't even imagine a day or time when I would be able to let that go. Then again, who knows? I was speaking for today. And today I wanted to be in the presence of a woman who made me feel as if I mattered.

Lenny and I stood outside of Michelle's door, but neither one of us knocked.

"Open it," I said to him.

He used a small instrument in his hand to maneuver the lock. When the door squeaked open, he backed away.

"I don't need you to stay," I said. "I'll call you when I'm ready."

Without hesitation, Lenny walked away. I went inside, then locked the door behind me. The first thing I saw was the TV on in the living room area. An empty wineglass was on the cof-fee table, and next to it was Michelle's cell phone,

a book, and several notebooks. I walked over to
the coffee table, then picked up one of her notebooks. Written inside it was a list of names and
phone numbers. Most of the names belonged
to men; only three were women's names. I laid
the notebook on the table, then picked up her
cell phone. Keeping in mind the names I had
just read in the notebook, I searched through
the names and numbers on her phone. I paused
when I reached the tenth person, but before I got
busted, I laid the phone down.

I took my time as I made my way down the
hallway, making every effort to be quiet, but
my leather shoes made the hardwood floors
squeak. I didn't know if Michelle was awake or
not, but when I entered her bedroom, I heard
light snoring. The recessed lighting was dim, so
I could see her lying in bed. She rested mostly
on her stomach, with her leg lying on a pillow.
The silk gown she wore clung to her sexy frame.
Right next to her were several magazines and a
newspaper. The front-page headline read FIRST
LADY HAS LEFT THE WHITE HOUSE. I had already
read the article; it had pissed me off, even though
it was partially true. I figured Michelle probably
hoped all of it was true, but I doubted that she
would mention it.

I moved closer to the bed, then put the magazines and the newspaper on the floor. I looked at Michelle again, wondering why a woman this beautiful, sexy, and smart was sleeping all alone. I regretted that the only option she probably thought she had was me, especially when she was capable of having so much more. I had already informed her that I could never give her what she deserved. That was still the case, and after tonight I doubted that would change.

Making the next move, I began to remove my clothes. I slipped on a condom, and as soon as I got on the bed, I lay over her backside. My hand crept around to her mouth, only because I knew she would scream when she woke up. That she did, but the sound was muffled.

"Shhh," I said, whispering in her ear. "It's me. Calm down. It's only me."

She silenced herself; I felt her tense body relax. That was when I removed my hand from her mouth.

"You . . . you scared the hell out of me, Stephen. How did you get in here?"

"You left the door unlocked."

"No I didn't." She was still a bit startled, and she kept taking deep breaths to calm herself. "Feel how fast my heart is racing. You just don't know how scared I was. Don't ever do that again."

"I didn't mean to scare you. Sorry, okay? But just so you know, I didn't come here to feel your racing heart. I came to feel something else."

I inched her gown above her hips, then lowered my hand to her inner thighs. I massaged them for a few seconds, and then I lightly pinched her shaven, damp folds. My fingers separated her slit, which was also being toyed with by the top of my head. It was right at the entrance, throbbing and ready to break right in. I placed delicate kisses on the nape of her neck, then whispered in her ear. "What was so urgent? Tell me what you wanted."

She lowered her hand to show me. She grabbed my steel, then forced it inside of her. "It was urgent for me to feel this. I wanted you, all of you and every inch of this."

I removed my fingers so I could push my lengthy muscle farther into Michelle's tight pocket. She gasped, and as I slow-stroked her from behind, she moved her hips to a tranquilizing rhythm, working with me. The smooth pace continued for a while.

"Mmm, I . . . I want to tell you something," she said, changing positions.

She rolled on her back, and that was when I was able to remove her nightgown, which was in the way. I pressed my naked body against hers, and after going back in, I satisfied my hunger even more by sucking her firm breasts. Her legs and arms were wrapped around my back; she rubbed it so well with the tips of her fingers. I appreciated the feeling, and I dug deeper and reached her G-spot. She cried out for me to look at her, so I backed away from her breasts to do just that. I searched her eyes, which were filled with nothing but love for me. She didn't have to say it; I could see it.

"I don't know what is going on with you," she said softly. "But I've been watching you on TV, and I've heard about some of your troubles. I want you to know that I am here for you. Not just for this, but for whatever you need from me. I'm not ashamed or afraid to say that I love you. Even if it doesn't matter, at least you know."

For the first time tonight, we kissed. We kissed passionately. We had sex for what seemed like hours. We thoroughly enjoyed ourselves, and I was willing to admit to Michelle one thing, simply because I knew I had other options.

"I'm not solely here for convenience," I said as she straddled the top of me. "And this could very well be a different ball game if the facts weren't what they are. I don't want to spell them out right now. I would rather you just keep on doing what you're doing and send me to sleep with a smile on my face."

Michelle honored my wishes. And what seemed like many hours later, I woke up, squinted, and looked around the room. The curtains were closed, but a sliver of light came in from the outside. My clothes were lying neatly on a chair; the spot next to me was empty. I removed the thick blanket that covered me, and after putting on my slacks and shoes and tossing my shirt over my shoulder, I went to look for Michelle. She was in the kitchen, cooking breakfast. I smelled the maple syrup and could see her scrambling eggs. Two plates were on the marble-topped kitchen island, which stood in the center of the floor, with several stools surrounding it. Michelle's back faced me. She was wearing a short silk robe, revealing her legs, which looked like they had been dipped in creamy milk chocolate. I crept up from behind and wrapped my arms around her waist. Yet again, she was startled.

"You really shouldn't do that, but I forgive you," she told me. "Only because I'm standing here feeling so lucky that the president broke into my home and made love to me. And now I have the pleasure of cooking you breakfast. What a morning, and a good one at that."

With the front of Michelle's robe being open, I could feel her nakedness. I turned her around to face me, then wrapped my arms around her again. She placed her arms on my shoulders.

"I don't think I'll have time for breakfast, but thanks for being so kind. Sometimes, even kind people want something in return. I really want to know what that is, because I know there will come a time when you will refuse to go on like this," I said.

Before responding, Michelle leaned in to deliver a passionate kiss. She wiped her wetness from my lips and then gave me her answer.

"Like it or not, I'm going to be real honest with you. I want you to get a divorce. Not necessarily for me, but more so for yourself. You are a gifted man, Stephen, and you have an opportunity to go on and do many great things. But something or someone is holding you back. I don't know if that's Raynetta, but you know better than I do. I just want the best for you, and just so you know, I don't have any fantasies about moving myself and my children into the White House. That's not my goal, nor is it my ambition to hurt your wife. I just happened to be in the right place at the right time. I needed you just as much as you needed me. For as long as you do, I'm here, loving you from a distance, until you decide what is truly best for you."

I responded with a tight hug and a lengthy kiss that left her speechless. Then again, so did my next words.

"I appreciate a woman who is honest, and I love the way you just put all of that into perspective. But if you really want to be honest, I want you to think long and hard about what I'm going to ask you. I'm sure you won't be able to answer this right away, but give me a call later, once you've had time to think about it. Okay?"

Michelle nodded while displaying a smile on her face.

"I want to know why you've spoken to my mother on numerous occasions. Why is her name and home address written in your notebook? What are the two of you up to, and why in hell would you get involved with anything relating to her?"

Michelle stood stock-still, as if cement had been poured over her. I removed her arms from my shoulders before backing away from her. She opened her mouth, but no words came out.

I placed my finger over my lips. "Shhh. Think before you speak, because saying the wrong thing could hurt you more than it will hurt me. Call me when you're ready to, as you say, be honest."

I walked around Michelle and smacked her ass hard before exiting. I couldn't help but think about what I'd told Raynetta about not trusting anyone. Not one single person. I could only hope that she had been paying attention like I had.

President's Mother,

Teresa Jefferson

Shit was about to hit the fan. I meant what I'd said about not wasting time and finding my grandson. And what I'd discovered over the past few weeks had led me straight to Mexico. I had disguised myself a little; therefore, Ina, her boyfriend, and, to my surprise, Levi hadn't known who I was. I had watched them celebrating as if someone had gotten married. Drinking margaritas, sipping wine, and dancing the night away. This had all been a total shock to me, but after Joshua's grave was dug, many things about Ina had been disturbing me.

First of all, I wondered where she'd gotten the money to pay an attorney. I also thought about how much she had fought Stephen not to open the casket. Her crocodile tears and dramafied reaction had been a bit too much for me that day, and when that heifer had pulled up in a brand-new Mercedes, I'd had to ask myself what in the hell was going on. I had then watched her for several days. She and her boyfriend had shopped at some of the finest stores in St. Louis, had gone to exquisite restaurants, and had even gone house hunting. Not in St. Louis, but while in Mexico.

And guess who had gone house hunting with them? Joshua. He probably had no idea what had been going on. Obviously, Ina had sent him here before everything had gone down. I didn't even have to question her motive. Just like all the others, Ina had been paid big money to do this. The fact that she was willing to destroy Joshua's life and reputation made me angry. But knowing what she had done to Stephen, this bitch was going to pay. It mattered not that she was Joshua's mother.

Just when I thought I had mostly everything figured out, Levi showed up to join the party. I couldn't believe what my eyes were witnessing. Stephen was going to be devastated by this news, and I wanted to get all the facts before breaking it down to him. Levi was probably the only person Stephen trusted; they had grown up together and everything. What a doggone shame—some friends weren't worth a damn. Levi would regret his involvement. I would make sure of that.

Since Ina's boyfriend, Theo, was the weakest link, I decided to go after him first. I had seen him flirting with several Mexican women while Ina wasn't looking, so I used a woman I'd met last week, Sofia, to lure him to where I wanted him to be. That was to my room, where I intended to pump him for information. I had to know more details about this little plan of theirs, and I was sure that fool would talk.

With my sundress on, a sombrero on my head, and dark sunglasses, I was getting ready to leave my room. I wanted to see how well things were progressing with Sofia and Theo. But the ringing of my cell phone stopped me. I snatched the phone from the table and saw that the number was Michelle's. I had other things to deal with right now, so whatever she wanted to discuss had to be put off for another day.

"Hello," I said in a sharp tone.

"He knows, Teresa," she said softly. "He saw your number on my cell phone and your address in my notebook."

Awww, what a shame, I thought. I hated stupid tricks who couldn't follow through with the plan because they were supposedly in love. All I wanted her to do was make sure Stephen divorced Raynetta. Apparently, her snatch couldn't seal the deal. How dare she call me with

this nonsense about a notebook and her cell
phone?

"Who is this? I'm not sure what you're talking
about. You obviously have the wrong number."

I hit the END button on my phone and moved
on to what was really important.

I left my room and headed to the beach. There
were hundreds of people relaxing on the beach.
The blue water was a beautiful sight, and I had
never seen so many palm trees. Since my trip
was all-inclusive, I grabbed a coconut drink
before sitting on a comfortable lounging chair
beneath a large thatched umbrella. Ina, Theo,
Levi, and another woman, whom I assumed
was his girlfriend, were several feet away from
me. I could see what they were up to. I wasn't
sure where Joshua was; I assumed he was still
in Ina's room. He stayed in the room quite often.
That was a good thing, especially since I needed
him to be alone when we made our getaway.

Dressed in a two-piece bikini, Ina ran into
the water and splashed it all over herself. Theo
followed, and as they playfully splashed water
on each other, they laughed. I was sick to my
stomach because my son was in the Oval Office,
trying to figure all of this out and catching hell
from everywhere. If I could've pulled out my gun
and blown all of them away, I certainly would

have done it. The best thing I could do was let Stephen handle them—this time. He would want to do so; I didn't want to steal that opportunity away from him.

As Ina and Theo played around like kids who didn't have a care in the world, Levi sat on a lounging chair, looking like a big, fat black whale that had washed up on the beach. There were too many sexy bodies traveling up and down on the beach; he should have known better than to let himself loose like that. Miss Ina thought she had it going on too; she had definitely taken enough pictures of herself. Unquestionably, she had a nice figure, but that sure didn't stop Theo from turning his head to glance at other women. He'd been engaging in small talk with Sofia whenever the coast was clear, and the second he saw her standing by a bar area that was surrounded by many people, he left Ina in the water and eased his way over to Sofia.

Ina started talking with the other chick in their group. From the corner of my eye, I witnessed Sofia work her magic. Along with her sexy Spanish accent, she used her body to talk to Theo. I saw her slip the room key to him, and then I knew I was in business. A few minutes later, Sofia made eye contact with me and winked. I finished my drink before going back to the hotel to meet her in my room.

"He said he was going to slip away," Sofia said with a smile when I met up with her in my room. "In about ten . . . fifteen minutes, he should be here."

We stepped into the bathroom so that Theo would not see us when he entered the room. She held out her hand. That was when I gave her three hundred dollars. She looked at the money, then at me.

"You said five hundred. I would like five hundred," she insisted.

"I don't have the other two on me right now. And after the deal is done, you will get the rest of your money, okay?"

I didn't believe in paying people in full until the work was finished. That was why Michelle wouldn't get another dime from me until Stephen divorced Raynetta. I couldn't believe she had gone and messed things up. Now I had something else to fight with him about when I returned to Washington.

While we were in the bathroom, Sofia and I heard Theo enter the room. He called out to her.

"Sofia, where are you? Are you in here?"

I looked at her, then nodded.

"Yes, sweetheart, I am," she responded. "I'm in the bathroom, getting ready for you. Why don't you take your clothes off and relax on the bed? I'm coming."

Sofia smiled; so did I. Her smile, however, vanished when I reached between two towels to retrieve a gun. She put up her hands as she backed away from me.

"You're fine," I whispered. "You've done a good job. This is not for you."

She looked relieved but was in a hurry to exit the bathroom. We both walked out at the same time, and right to our left, Theo was lying naked on the bed. His pearly whites were on display, until he saw the gun in my hand, which was now aimed at him.

"Thanks again, Sofia. You may go," I said.

She took one glance at Theo's package. I knew exactly what she was thinking.

"I know," I said, shaking my head. "It's a good thing you didn't waste your time with nothing that little. What a shame, especially for a man out there vigorously promoting it."

Sofia snickered, then hurried to the door. She turned before exiting. "Don't forget about the rest of my money. I want it, okay?"

This bitch was working my nerves over two hundred dollars. "Why don't you go somewhere and prepare some damn tacos, nachos, or something? I said I would catch up with you later, didn't I? Damn."

She cut her eyes at me before leaving. I turned my attention back to Theo, who kept eyeing the gun, as if he was about to jump up and try to take it from me.

"You really need to get those thoughts of taking this gun away from me out of your head. That's not going to happen, and one move, Theo, just one tiny move, will end your life. If you cooperate, you have my word that you will leave here a free man. Got it?"

Theo slowly nodded; his eyes shifted back to me. I began to question him about everything, and as I had predicted, he snitched. The identity of the head honcho in charge came as no surprise to me. It was Mr. Christopher McNeil.

"Someone working for him reached out to Ina, made her an offer she couldn't refuse," he revealed. "The money will set us up for life, and she knows that Joshua won't ever have to worry about anything. You must know how difficult it is to walk away from five million dollars. We were willing to do whatever, and if that meant some people had to suffer a little, hey, whatever."

I shaped my lips like an O. "Oh, five million dollars is a lot of money to walk away from. You are so right, but understand that I don't like to see my son suffer. I don't appreciate people who smile in his face, then stab him in the back. And more than anything, I myself don't like to be made a fool of. This was a real clever plan, but unfortunately, somebody has to pay for all of the damage that's been done. For starters, I think it should be you. And since that thing between your legs is so useless as is, maybe the doctors will be able to repair it and add a few inches."

Theo attempted to dive off the bed, but he was too late. I fired off one bullet, which hit the target I was aiming for. I had never heard a man scream so loudly, and as he rolled on the floor, swaying back and forth, with his hand cuffing his manhood, I grabbed the one bag I had and got the hell out of there. I hurried to Ina's room, hoping and praying that Joshua was still there. After several urgent knocks on the door, he answered, with a frown on his face. When he saw me, he cocked his head back.

"Grandma?" he questioned. I guess he didn't recognize me with the ruby-red lipstick and the dark shades on. "Is that you?"

I was so happy to see him up close. Tears were in my eyes, but this was not the time for me to break down and get emotional. Instead, I spoke in a panic.

"Yes, baby, it's me. Go get your passport and any important documents you need to get out of here. We have to go now. Your mother and them told me to come get you. They're already at the airport, waiting for us."

"Why? What's going on?"

"I'll explain it all to you when we get to the airport. Do as I just told you, before things turn chaotic. Again, we need to go."

Joshua seemed a little reluctant, but at the end of the day, he trusted me. He took several minutes to gather his things, and when he came back to the door, I grabbed his hand and pulled him along until we reached the exit doors. A cab was already waiting to take us to the airport, and on the drive there, Joshua kept questioning me.

"Shhh," I said, eyeing the taxi driver, as if he was somehow involved in what we were running away from. "Not one word. I'll explain soon."

Joshua remained silent, and as soon as we got to the airport, I purchased our plane tickets and we went through customs.

"Where is my mother?" he asked. "Do you see her . . . anyone?"

Looking around, I pretended to be searching for them. "No, I don't, but let me check on something. Go sit down over there and don't move. There is a chance that they may be gone already."

Joshua scratched his head but did as he was told. I quickly ran off to the restroom and found a pawn who would say exactly what I wanted her to say. Money, trust me, could pay for anything.

Slightly out of breath, I plopped down in the seat next to Joshua. I fanned myself with my hand and then pulled out my cell phone, as if I was about to call Ina. "Let me see if I can reach her. Do you have your phone?"

"No," he said. "I left everything at the hotel, because you said we needed to go."

That was good, just in case Ina tried to call him. I didn't know how far behind us they were, but the plane needed to depart, like, now. Unfortunately, we had a layover before arriving in Washington. There weren't any nonstop flights available at this time.

"Doggone it," I said, looking at my phone. "Where is your mother and them at?"

Just then, the Mexican woman I had met in the rest-room came up to us. "Miss Jefferson?" she said with a thick accent.

"Yes, that would be me. Who are you?"

"My name is Anna. Your daughter-in-law told me to let you know that she couldn't wait for you guys and that they had to go. She said that she would see you later in Washington. She also told me to tell you, Joshua . . ." The woman's eyes shifted to Joshua. "You are Joshua, right?"

Joshua nodded. "Yes, ma'am, I am."

"Well, she . . . your mother told me to tell you to go with your grandmother. You're safe with her, and your father . . . no, I mean your mother will see you when you get to Washington."

I quickly spoke up, just in case this stuttering, slow-talking fool messed up again. This was why I never paid people until the job was finished. People always screwed up. Too bad I had already given her the money. "Okay," I said. "Thank you very much. We were wondering if they'd left already."

"Yes. They . . . the mother, Levi, and . . . uh, well, they departed a couple of hours ago."

I shooed that dummy away. "We got it, girl. Thank you."

Joshua sat there with a confused look on his face as she walked away. I was sure that none of this made sense to him. And unfortunately, I made up the biggest lie about Levi getting into a heated argument and killing a member of some Mexican drug cartel. Claimed that they were after us, and it was best for us to get out of there before we got killed. The reason why we were on our way to Washington was that the government wanted to know some vital information that the cartel member had shared with Levi before he was killed. I wasn't sure if Joshua was on board with what I'd said or not, but after all that had been going on, it very well could make sense.

"Things have been so crazy lately," he said. "My mama took me out of school, told me I needed to come here, and then I find out we're moving here. Now we have to go to Washington, D.C. I'm so mad, Grandma, and I don't want to move to Mexico, even though the house she's thinking about purchasing is real nice. But things are moving too fast. My head is spinning, and I don't know what is really going on."

I touched his hand, held it in mine. "I know it's crazy, but soon, Joshua, soon you will understand it all."

President of the United States,

Stephen C. Jefferson

I was in a meeting with several congressional leaders who had come to me earlier, asking what they could do to help turn things around. The only reason they were probably making an attempt to do so was that they were all way behind in the polls in their particular states. I was willing to listen and get as many people on board with me as I could. But as we discussed items on my agenda, we were interrupted by chaos that had erupted outside the Oval Office. Within a matter of seconds, my mother burst through the door and closed it behind her.

"You need to remind Mr. Freckle Face to keep his hands to himself and tell him who I am." She looked around the room at everyone staring at her. I assumed they were thinking what I was, which was that she was simply out of her mind.

"I don't mean to break up the party," she continued, "but I need to speak to my son about something very important. Is there any way that you all can reschedule and come back at another time?"

With a twisted face, I answered for everyone in the room. "No, they will not come back at another time. You need to leave, Mama. Whatever is so important must wait."

She appeared disappointed by my response, and before I knew it, right before my very eyes, my mother threw a tantrum. She lifted her hands in the air and then started pounding everything in her sight—from the tables to my desk to the sofas on which people sat. She marched around, pounding on things, acting a complete fool. In fear, two of the congressional leaders started gathering their things to go. And after she fell to the floor and kicked and screamed loudly, as if someone was killing her, it didn't take long for everyone to jump up from their seats and jet.

"Maybe another time, Mr. President," one senator said. "I think you may need to deal with this."

"Ah," my mother cried out like a possessed demon, while holding her chest. "Ooh, no, ah!"

I had never witnessed anything like this; it was quite a show. Back to the mental institution she would go. I didn't have time for her foolishness, and to say I was embarrassed would be an understatement. I was embarrassed as hell!

After the last senator left, I headed over to my desk to call the Secret Service. Obviously, the agent near my office couldn't handle her, but Lenny would be able to. If Levi was here, I would've called him. This never would have happened on his watch—never.

As I started to press the button on the phone with my finger, my mother jumped to her feet, raked her layered hair, then straightened her clothes. She appeared to be a new person, just like that.

"Put the phone down and listen to me, Stephen." She spoke sternly. "I'm sorry I had to do that, but it was the only way to get them out of here and get your attention."

I put the phone down, only because there was something in her eyes that said this was a serious matter. She began to tell me about Ina, Theo, and Levi's trip to Mexico. I wanted so badly not to believe her, but so much of what she said added up. I was so stunned by the breaking news that I had to drop back in my chair. Anger crept on my face, as enough harm had been done to damage me. I had tried so hard to do right, had tried to give others an opportunity to do the same. This was un-fucking-believable, and the only good thing that I held on to was the fact that Joshua was still alive. I just hoped he would be enough to keep me from going insane and doing things that no man, especially the president, should ever do. Yes, I had already done a lot. But there were many presidents who had done so much more to protect our country, as well as themselves.

As I sat there, stone-faced, plotting my next move, my mother walked to the door and opened it. She was gone for a few minutes, and when she returned, Joshua was behind her. He wore a black hoodie, which covered his head. He was much taller than I had expected, quite thin too. More nervous than I had ever been, I slowly stood, with my eyes locked on him. I almost couldn't catch my breath and was barely able to stand.

"Take your hood off," my mother said to Joshua.

He did so, and as I stared at him, he stared back at me.

"Hel . . . hello, Mr. President. Wow," he said, appearing stunned. "I never imagined that I would have a chance to meet you, and my grand-mother never mentioned that the two of you were close friends. This is one of the best days of my life, I swear. When I tell my friends about this, they're never going to believe me. That is, unless you allow me to take a picture with you. May I please just have one picture?"

I couldn't help it that tears welled in my eyes. All he wanted was a picture, when I wanted to offer him so much more than that. I walked around my desk, ignoring my mother, who had tears rolling down her face. That immediately caused Joshua to direct his attention to her.

"What's wrong, Grandma? Why are you crying? Did I say something wrong?"

"No, baby," she said, wiping her tears. "You said everything right. What I've been trying to tell you is, this . . . this is not only the president. He is also your fa—"

I finished the sentence instead. "I'm your father. Your *real* father. And I'm sorry that no one told you that sooner."

Joshua's whole face was scrunched up. "My father?" he questioned. "This must be some kind of joke." He chuckled as if it was. "Grandma, stop joking with me. You know who my father is. Your son. You told me he was in jail for murder."

My mother walked closer to Joshua; so did I. I didn't want him to be upset with her for lying. After all, it seemed as if she had gone to hell and back to make this right and bring us together.

"I am her son, and thankfully, I wasn't in jail. And now I'm here. We have a lot to discuss, but for now, son, I'm here."

I reached out to hug Joshua—it was a feeling that left me choked up. He seemed reluctant to reciprocate, but it wasn't long before I felt his arms around me. I lowered my head, closing my eyes. This moment gave me so much hope for the future, but when I opened my eyes and saw Andrew rush through the door, I had a feeling that his breaking news wasn't going to be good.

"Mr. President," he shouted. "There has been an explosion! It occurred at the hotel where the first lady is residing. There have been reports that many people were killed. The whole area is a mess, and I . . . I don't know when we'll be able to . . ."

Andrew paused when he saw me slowly back away from Joshua. I wanted just to fall to the floor and die. This couldn't be happening right now, and as my heart rate increased, I felt myself about to lose it. All eyes were on me, but before I reacted to the devastating news, I fixed my eyes on the door. There stood Raynetta, with scratches, bruises, blood, and ashes all over her face and trembling body. Her clothes were ripped; her hair was completely disheveled. Tears poured down her face, and as the entire room fell completely silent, we stared at each other without one single blink.

Thank God she was alive.